NOVELS BY PAMELA CHAIS

Final Cut
Split Ends

FINAL CUT

a novel by
PAMELA CHAIS

SIMON AND SCHUSTER

NEW YORK

This novel is a work of fiction. Names, characters, places and incidents are either the product of the author's imagination or are used fictitiously. Any resemblance to actual events or locales or persons, living or dead, is entirely coincidental.

Designed by Stanley S. Drate
Manufactured in the United States of America

10 9 8 7 6 5 4 3 2 1

Library of Congress Cataloging in Publication Data
Chais, Pamela, date
  Final cut.

  I. Title.
PS3553.H243F5   813'.54   81-2455
                                    AACR2
ISBN 0-671-25196-1

For Stan,
for Mark, Bill, Emily,
and for Diana.

You could drive up and down the streets of Beverly Hills, year in, year out, and you'd never see a garbage can out by the curb or a plastic sack full of trash. It's that kind of a community. On Wednesdays, trucks slip up and down the back alleys gathering the hidden waste of the very wealthy.

Sometimes there might be a fine chair with loosened joints that can be easily repaired. There could be a bridge table with maybe only a cigarette burn wrong with it, or hats, or purses (lots of purses, almost brand-new, with bits of loose tobacco in the bottom). But mostly there's just garbage because the maids grab off the good stuff before it ever gets back to the alley. Just garbage and the branches of expensive trees that the gardeners are too lazy to cart away in their trucks.

It's August and 868 North Bedford Drive has got practically a whole goddamn tree lying across the garbage cans. It's happened here before. Some smart-ass gardener who had to know better. So Floyd stops the garbage truck, blocking the whole alley. He's that sore now because it's the middle of the day and probably a hundred degrees already.

Floyd sits there behind the wheel and Hubie, his partner, takes out his citation book and opens the gate into the backyard. It is another world here, cool and green and shimmering. Hubie walks around the tennis court, its surface too dazzling even to look at in the August sun. He looks resentfully at the Olympic-size swimming pool. He sees a furry new tennis ball lying on the grass and kicks it into the water. It makes him feel only a little better.

He starts to ring the kitchen doorbell when he sees a note that says it's out of order. He knocks five times, but nobody comes to the door. Then he sees a chocolate-brown Mercedes convertible in the driveway, so he walks around the back, across the thick dichondra lawn, until he comes to the sliding glass doors that lead into a large playroom. He cups his hands around his eyes so that he can look inside. His citation book rests against the spotless glass which has been tinted at the top to resist the late afternoon sun.

He thinks the room is empty at first. He thinks now he will have to slip the citation between the sliding glass doors and he is disappointed.

Then he sees something unusual in the far corner of the playroom, something he will never forget as long as he lives. He sees a man sitting erect in a wicker chair, his face olive green. And he also sees a large, business-like knife buried to the hilt between the second and third buttons of the man's Pierre Cardin sport shirt.

1

Bud Bacola entered his apartment, took off the clothes he had worn the night before and forced himself to stand in front of the full-length mirror on the inside of his bedroom closet door.

Five pounds, he thought. I've got to take off five pounds, maybe seven. He stepped away from the mirror and began doing the Canadian Air Force exercises, a frenzied penance for two nights of Italian food, a falafel sandwich and a quarter pound of halvah.

While he was on his seventh push-up, he saw a box of Triscuits under the bed. At the end of the tenth push-up, he rolled over and reached for it. He shook the box, hoping it was empty. It wasn't. Then he hoped the crackers would be stale. They were. He ate two anyway, then threw the box in the wastepaper basket and continued exercising, his back to the mirror.

Anybody else looking at him would think, This is a man who takes care of himself, a man with no weight problem—but he had not stopped thinking of himself as fat for as long as he could remember.

A woman who had lived with him briefly had had a poster printed up for him stating: "A man who is five nine, weighs under 155 pounds and has a thirty-inch waist is not by any rational consideration fat." He read the poster and smiled, and still refused to let her keep Famous Amos cookies in the apartment.

He jogged every day it didn't rain, running along the center divider of Burton Way in front of his apartment, hating every moment of it, praying reverently for a lingering storm front.

Bud believed you never stop being who you were when you were fourteen. If you were fat or funny-looking then, no matter how many years go by or what you turn into, when you close your eyes you still perceive yourself to be that fat, funny-looking person.

But whatever he thought of himself, he could still get all the women he wanted. He didn't know if it was because he was a detective on the Beverly Hills police force or had been Buddy Bacall when he was a kid (not that he went around advertising it) or if it was just that he lived in a town where there were a lot of horny women. But he had no problems in that department.

He sat on the edge of the bed and called Cedars-Sinai Hospital. He asked for Chuck Coleman's room. The phone rang five times, and as Bud was about to hang up he heard a series of noisy clicks and then his partner's faint nasal cursing, which made him smile.

"How's it going?" Bud asked.

"Don't ever get your nose fixed," Chuck whispered, "no matter what."

"That bad, huh?"

"They've got these two huge tampons up my nostrils. I can't breathe."

"So big deal. Tomorrow you'll look like Robert Redford."

"You're telling everyone, I know it," Chuck said in a drugged, accusing voice.

10

"I'm sticking to your story, I swear it. You're having polyps removed."

They had been partners for five years. Chuck was older, in his early forties, an ex-college football star, his still-boyish good looks marred only by a nose flattened and distorted over the years by chance encounters with knees, fists, a steering wheel, and, finally, a runaway surfboard.

Several weeks earlier, Chuck's nose still angry and swollen from the surfboard accident, they had gone to the home of a Beverly Hills plastic surgeon that had been ransacked the night before. While they were going over the house, the surgeon suddenly reached out, took Chuck's chin and turned his face back and forth professionally.

"What exactly do you plan to do about that nose?" the surgeon asked bluntly.

"Breathe through it for another thirty, forty years," Chuck said politely, but Bud could hear the hostile edge in his voice. Chuck's nose had always been a touchy subject.

"You will never breathe adequately through that nose again without a lot of help," the surgeon said, now tilting Chuck's chin up very high. Even from where he stood halfway across the room, Bud could see the enlarged, jutting septum.

A week later, Chuck admitted himself to Cedars-Sinai Hospital. Only his wife, Melba, and Bud knew that he was having his nose rebuilt. Everyone else was told that he was having some benign polyps removed.

Chuck had married Melba right after high school. They gave up trying to have children following a series of late-term miscarriages and began raising Airedales behind their home in Woodland Hills instead.

Bud and Chuck were a good team. They had desks facing each other, but they seldom spoke, seldom had to. Their eyes might lock after a phone call, or one might smile and shrug or push a paper across the desk. They understood each other perfectly: two people still slightly mystified as to what they were doing there in the first place.

Chuck would be in the hospital another day; then he and Melba were driving up to Santa Barbara where they'd rented a condominium for two weeks so that he could recover far away from anyone they knew. They had asked Bud to come up on the weekends, but he said no, he'd rather wait for the formal unveiling.

Bud did not want to admit to himself that he felt even slightly incapacitated by his partner's absence. There were other detectives he could work with, but he always chose to go it alone rather than have to adjust to somebody else's idiosyncrasies, or have anyone else try to adjust to his.

"Anything doing?" Chuck asked, his n's coming out like d's.

"It's pretty quiet here."

"Swear to me on you mother's heart you're not telling everybody." Now the m's were coming out like b's and it was an effort for Bud not to laugh.

"They'll know when you come back, won't they?"

"No, no," Chuck insisted nasally, "they'll just think I parted my hair different."

"Stop talking," Bud said, "you sound ridiculous." He hung up smiling.

Chuck was the only male friend he'd ever had, the only man he had ever permitted himself to trust, to count on. They both knew it, and at times it was a burden for both of them.

Bud had never been the type to go out drinking, horsing around with the boys. If he didn't have a steady woman or a date, he had always preferred staying at home by himself, reading, watching TV. If he got restless, he would go out on the prowl. Alone. But that's who he was and he accepted it, had no problem living with it.

It was a hot summer Wednesday and Bud was planning to take the day off. He had a lot of vacation time coming to him and nowhere he wanted to go, no one he particularly wanted to go with, so he had started taking single days here and there. Sometimes he'd just sleep in. Sometimes he'd go to the beach or drive up the coast.

This day he was going to see his mother. He hadn't been there for maybe a month and she was starting to let little sighs escape over the telephone.

He tried on a pair of Jag jeans that wouldn't zip all the way up, then a pair of Chemin de Fers that did. Barely. The pale-blue sport shirt he'd just bought at the Eric Ross sale pulled across his chest, but then he'd thrown it in the dryer by mistake.

While he was brushing his teeth, he studied his face in the mirror. He had good hair, dark, curly, reliable, his father's hair, and all still there at age twenty-nine.

He knew the face was okay. It hadn't changed that much since the days when people stood in lines just to see that face, that smile. Now the features were stronger, harder. His teeth, when he wasn't smoking, were very white. Good, even Italian teeth. The lips were full, bluish under certain lights. *Petulant*, his last lady friend had described them, but they both knew she was on her way out so he didn't take it too seriously.

His eyes were dark and guarded. They'd seen a lot.

He had been stopped on Rodeo Drive once by a young girl from South Dakota who refused to believe that he wasn't Bobby Blake, and twice by out-of-towners who thought he was Dustin Hoffman. Give or take ten pounds, it was that kind of face.

He was already in his car in the garage when he remembered he had not checked his telephone-answering machine since he had come home that morning. He got out of the car and took the elevator back upstairs and entered his apartment.

He was struck, as he always was when he entered his apartment, by the tastefulness of it, the harmony of the colors, the fabrics, the textures. He had spent over a year making his selections, ignoring the suggestions and advice of the many women he had been involved with while he was decorating. He had used their resale numbers, but had paid little attention to their ideas. He knew exactly what he wanted, and now that he had it he was satisfied. He had made no mistakes. He wished he could say the same about the rest of his life.

He pushed the button on his answering machine and waited. "You rat, you're never home." It was Bonnie's voice, soft and reproachful. He smiled guiltily. "I have this weirdo notion we had a date for tonight, and if you don't call by twelve, I'm starting without you."

She was right, of course. He had said that he'd see her Tuesday night, but he had chosen to believe that it had been left up in the air, that it had not been a firm commitment, because something better had come up.

He had met Bonnie when he came to her home a few months before. She'd had a television set stolen, some jewelry, and a few cameras. And she was a knockout.

He had dropped by later that night, for no particular reason other than that he dug her looks. She was in real estate and ultimately drove him away by her nonstop descriptions of the houses she was showing, a dull litany of the market value of every home in Beverly Hills, street by street, block by block. As if he cared.

He would call her back, but not until later, not until after his lunch at his mother's, not until all other possibilities had been exhausted.

"I am calling in answer to your call." It was a male voice, formal and guarded. "This is Mr. Edwin at Cannell and Chaffin. You say there's a problem with your couch. I'm off till Thursday . . ." The allotted time was over and the rest of the message was lost.

He would call Mr. Edwin back tomorrow. There was not enough down in the goddamn couch cushions. He had told them that when they delivered it, but they as-

14

sured him that any more down would make the couch uncomfortable to lean back on. Well, he'd sacrifice comfort for looks in the living room. In the bedroom it was comfort all the way.

There was one more message. It was from headquarters. He recognized Tom Edwards' voice. "I know it's your day off, pal, but there's a homicide here that might interest you. A Hollywood type. Call if you want info."

Who cares? he thought as he erased the messages. But he felt the curiosity, the excitement start to rise within him.

He walked slowly to the radio by his bed and turned the dial until he found a news broadcast. He knew he could call headquarters and find out who was murdered, but then he knew he'd be hooked, would cancel out his mother, would give up his day off.

He listened impatiently to reports of a fire in Panorama City, an L.A. city official's indictment, and then he heard it, found out what he wanted to know. The victim was not just any man. It was *the* man. It was D. P. Koenig. The only thing that surprised him was that it had taken somebody so long to get around to it.

He would not be going to his mother's now. He would not have a day off after all. He called her and thought for a moment about telling her, then changed his mind. She'd hear soon enough. It was big news.

He took off his jeans and sport shirt and put on a suit. He strapped on his gun, his handcuffs, a bullet clip. He climbed back into his Porsche and drove to headquarters. He parked his car and got into the dark Plymouth sedan assigned to him by the department. He did not have to get any additional information. He knew just where he was going.

He could feel his heart rate quicken, his skin start to shrink along his bones. He thought he had left all that behind so many years before, but he knew then that this tension, this excitement, had only been lying there dor-

15

mant, an old disease waiting to take hold of him once again.

D. P. Koenig. Jesus Christ.

When Bud Bacola arrived at 868 North Bedford Drive, the house had already been sealed off. Across the street and on both sides of the house were crowds of people, some of them obviously neighbors because a few of them were still in their bathrobes.

Three squad cars were parked in front of the large Mediterranean house with the lush tropical vegetation. Bud got out of the Plymouth and walked through the open front door into the tiled entry. He stopped and looked around. He had not been in this house for twenty years. It was known in Beverly Hills as the Joan Fontaine house because she had rented it for a summer twenty-eight years before from a dentist who owned it.

So now Bud Bacola, once Buddy Bacall, was investigating a homicide in the old Joan Fontaine house, now the late D. P. Koenig house, where once he had felt very much at home. He walked through the entry, through the formal living room which was now swarming with patrolmen.

"What time did he go down?" Bud asked.

"Doc says just after midnight."

"Cause of death?"

"Knife wound. Hit a lung or maybe the heart."

"What kind of knife?"

"Kitchen knife," the patrolman said, now checking his notes. "Eight-inch blade, five-inch hilt. The word 'Sabatier' on it. Nasty-looking bastard, too."

Bud jotted down the information, then walked into the playroom. When he knew the house this room had been a screened-in porch. Now it had been enlarged and glassed in with a quarry tile floor and a built-in bar with suede-covered bar stools.

The body had already been removed, and a stunned, nervous young man was standing at the sliding glass door, looking out over the swimming pool and the tennis court.

"That guy says he's the secretary," one of the patrolmen whispered to Bud. "We called the office and he was over like a shot."

His name was Peter Lutz, he was twenty-two years old, and his hands were shaking. He was slightly built and had pale, intelligent eyes. He was wearing an expensive gray three-piece suit, a costly tie. Bud walked over to him and touched his shoulder.

"You want a drink?" Bud asked gently. "Bad morning, huh?"

The two men walked over to the bar. Bud slipped behind and poured a shot glass of Chivas Regal and pushed it across the bar to Peter Lutz.

"How long have you worked for him?" Bud asked.

"Just over a year."

"Know anybody who might have wanted to kill him?" Bud asked. Peter looked up quickly and Bud thought he saw a faint smile on his face, in his eyes, somewhere. Amusement.

"In this business," Peter said lightly, "everyone has a few enemies."

"Just a few?" Bud asked. "I guess things have changed." He poured Peter another shot, which he drank down as quickly as he had the first one, although it was just eleven o'clock on a Wednesday morning in August.

"What did he do last night?" Bud asked. "Who did he see?"

"I have nothing to do with his social life," Peter said quickly.

"Maybe it was a business dinner, a business meeting. You'd know about that, wouldn't you?"

"I just told you, I don't know what he did last night." The voice was impatient—a superior talking to an inferior.

"Look, Mr. Lutz, the guy you work for has been murdered, and you're going to be my best friend until we find out who did it."

"I don't think he did anything last night," Peter said quietly. "He called me at home about eight-thirty to tell me something and he said he was going to bed early."

"What'd he call to tell you?"

"Oh, something." Peter's voice caught for a moment, then he smiled. "Something unimportant."

"I'd like to know what it was that was so unimportant he called you at home at eight-thirty."

"To apologize to me," Peter said, a taut, amused smile on his face.

"Yeah? For what?" Bud studied the young man's face closely. There was no sign of grief or emotion, but there was also no sign of guilt or fear. Bud sensed there was something else, something held back, something he knew he would have to find out.

"He'd been an absolute prick all day yesterday, and I think he was afraid I was going to quit," he said after a look at Bud's eyes, which were capable of reflecting a cop's hard, professional menace.

"And were you?"

"No," Peter said slowly. "I'm far too ambitious."

"But you were plenty sore, right? Plenty hot under the collar?"

"Am I a suspect? Are you holding me, or may I go back to the office now?" There was nothing particularly defiant in the way he asked it, but Bud found himself growing angry, resenting his cool indifference, and also understanding it.

"Do you have an alibi for last night? Any witnesses?"

"I believe so," Peter said uneasily. "May I leave now?"

"Is there anything different here, Mr. Lutz?" Bud asked him. "Do you notice anything out of the ordinary here in the house right now?"

"Yes," Peter said, smiling as he said it. "There are a

lot of working-class people in the house right now, and, believe me, that's different."

"Man, you're really grief-stricken, aren't you?" Bud said.

"Wait until you see me at the grave," Peter said, and he said it with such a straight face that Bud laughed out loud and realized that he liked this cool young man and believed that he was innocent. He also believed that he could be enormously helpful if he were handled properly.

There was a sudden commotion at the door to the playroom. Bud turned around and saw two patrolmen trying to restrain a noisy, excited woman from entering. She had been crying and her face was red and swollen.

"Peter, for Christ's sake," she called out. "Tell them who I am."

"Who's that?" Bud asked, turning to look at her again, realizing that she was younger, prettier than he had first thought.

"Her name is Glenda Deering. She's a client . . . sort of," Peter said.

"What does 'sort of' mean?" Bud asked, studying the woman's legs, which were long and slender, high-fashion legs, more elegant than sexy. But he kept staring at them.

"Let her tell you," Peter said. Bud nodded to the restraining policemen and Glenda pushed through, giving them a filthy look as she passed. She hurried out to Peter, turning away from Bud as if he were not there, as if he did not matter at all. She was upset, probably in a state of mild shock. Bud knew she was hyperventilating because he was watching the rapid rise and fall of her nipples under her Indian gauze blouse.

"What happened?" she asked Peter in a dazed voice. "Does anyone know anything?"

"This is the detective," Peter said, indicating Bud.

19

"You might as well ask him a few questions before he starts in on you."

She turned around and looked squarely at Bud for the first time. She had shrewd green eyes, all the greener now for the tears she had recently shed, for whatever the reason. Bud suspected that it had very little to do with love or grief. She had red hair, thick and wavy and wild, and a full, slightly contemptuous mouth. There was something about her that made Bud suspect she might be a little crazy.

"May I go upstairs?" she asked Bud. She enunciated each word carefully, as if she were addressing the deaf or the foreign-born. "Some of my belongings are upstairs and I'd like to get them."

"You tell me what it is, Miss Deering, and I'll set it aside for you," Bud said politely, enunciating his words as carefully as she had. She looked up at him instantly. She knew she was being put on, and she also knew that she deserved it. He even thought he saw her smile.

"Look," she said, speaking naturally now, "I have to have it now. It's terribly important."

"I'm sorry, I can't let anything be removed from the premises."

Her eyes narrowed, and she turned and walked out of the playroom. Bud watched her walking away, watched her calf muscles flex slightly with each angry step.

"Get her address and phone number, Barney," Bud called out. He did not feel that she was capable of murder, but he believed that she knew a lot more than she would be willing to tell.

"If I were you," Peter said, "I'd let her get her belongings."

"Yeah, why?"

"Because they're hers, and because they don't have anything to do with the murder."

"I've read her name in the columns. Who is she?"

"Just another noble experiment that failed," Peter

20

said quietly. "Am I being held, or may I get back to the office?"

"Mr. Lutz," Bud said to him, "I want you to take a look at this face and remember it, because it's all you're going to see for the next couple of days—maybe even weeks."

"Well, good luck," Peter said, an amused smile on his face.

"I'll see you at the office. Don't go out to lunch until you hear from me."

Peter turned and walked out of the playroom. Bud walked into the living room and watched Peter get into an old Mustang convertible. With nine cops around, he watched the Mustang make an illegal U-turn. Peter leaned out the window of the car and waved to Bud through the living-room window and then sped off down the street.

Christ, Bud thought disgustedly, get into show business for even a year and you think you own the world. He was still standing at the window when he heard footsteps over his head. He turned and ran up the stairs and into the master bedroom.

It was Glenda Deering and all he could see was her rear end sticking out from under the bed, and the rope soles of her shoes.

The bed looked as if someone might have been lying in it, but had not yet slept in it. The sheet and blankets were thrown back, as if someone had gotten out of bed quickly. The electric blanket was still on.

"Hey," Bud said gently, "talk to me, huh?" He saw her body go tense, then she just stayed where she was, her head under the dust ruffle.

"Shit," he heard her say. "Shit, shit, shit."

"Did you at least find it?"

"No." She came out from under the bed and switched into a sitting position. She did not look up.

"It must be very important."

"It isn't," she said, her voice leaden, her head still down. "It has nothing to do with him, with his death, with anything."

"What was he to you?" Bud asked gently. "Lutz said you were a client . . . sort of. What does that mean?"

Suddenly she rose to her feet in one fluid, graceful motion, leaving Bud to conjecture that her thighs were probably as lean and muscular as her calves. She crossed quickly to the dressing room and started to open a wide, mirrored door, but Bud caught up with her and closed the door before either of them had a chance to look inside.

"I can't let you do that, Miss Deering," he said, his hand covering her hand on the crystal doorknob in an effort to keep it closed. "But I can sure cooperate with you if you cooperate with me."

"I could report you for that," she said icily, pulling her hand out from under his, deliberately wiping it against her skirt. She studied his face with contempt, and he realized that she had misunderstood him, had probably thought he wanted a fast, furtive bang right there in the murdered man's bedroom in exchange for letting her walk out with some important evidence.

"Miss Deering," Bud said, enunciating savagely, "it may surprise you to learn that I get more ass than I know what to do with and I don't have to make bargains with a pale, over-the-hill Hollywood groupie." He took her arm and led her out of the bedroom without looking at her. He only realized how angry he was when she asked him to let go of her arm, when she told him that he was hurting her.

Immediately he released his grip on her arm and she walked beside him down the circular staircase, her head thrown back, Marie Antoinette on her way to the guillotine, or, at least Norma Shearer. He found himself admiring her dignity and composure.

"Hey," he said gently, "that was overkill. I'm sorry."

22

"It was lousy, but it was accurate," she said stonily, still not looking at him. When they got to the bottom of the stairs she turned to him. "What happens now? Am I free to go or what?"

"Do you have anything that could resemble an alibi for last night?" he asked her.

"No," she said, almost lightly. "I was alone all night. Pathetic, isn't it, even for a pale, over-the-hill Hollywood lady?"

"I think maybe we're going to have to talk some more," Bud said. "We can do it at headquarters or your place. Take your pick."

"Are you trying to tell me I'm under arrest?"

"No, I'm trying to tell you I want your help, but if I don't get it, I'll break my ass to get out a warrant on you for obstruction or attempted removal of evidence. The charges are endless."

"My house, then," she said finally. "Do I have to go in your car or will you follow me?"

"You be at your house," he said, looking swiftly at his wristwatch, "at, say, three P.M. I'll try to be there as close to three as possible."

"I almost get the feeling you trust me," she said, smiling for the first time.

"I'd like your word that you won't hop a plane to Argentina this afternoon," Bud said.

"I couldn't afford to get to Pasadena," she said quietly, then turned and walked out of the house.

He watched her through the window as she walked down the brick pathway to the street. He was curious to see which car was hers. There were a shabby Pontiac convertible, a recent-model Cadillac and a Mercedes 280SE parked in a row one house down. If she didn't have enough money to get to Pasadena, Bud reasoned, the Pontiac was probably hers, but he was not at all surprised when she opened the door of the metallic-gray Mercedes and climbed inside. He watched her light a cigarette, open all the windows and the sun roof. She made no move to turn on the ignition.

"Get someone on her," Bud said to the nearest patrolman, indicating the gray Mercedes, "and don't let them off her until I say so." Then he went to the telephone and dialed headquarters.

"Hey, Bry, do me a favor. Get me everything you can on a Glenda Deering," he said into the phone. "And I need it by a quarter to three at the latest. And see what you can get on a Peter Lutz at the same time. And if you need me I'll be at the dead man's office."

"Buddy-boy, you're really eating this up, aren't you?" Bryan said. "Lights, camera, action, huh?"

Bud hung up the telephone and walked down the narrow corridor to the butler's pantry and then into the kitchen. He was startled by the drab seediness of it compared to the condition of the rest of the house. All the appliances were old and yellowing, with some of the handles and knobs missing. There was scuffed, buckling linoleum on the floor and the tile on the wall was the color of old toenails. It was definitely the kitchen of someone who didn't do any cooking himself. This was the kitchen of a man who had servants to take care of his appetites.

The countertops were empty except for a heavy glass dome under which was a chocolate cake, dark and rich, with only one slice gone. He felt a quick craving in the pit of his stomach. He had an overwhelming urge to cut himself a piece of this cake. He would even have used the murder weapon to slice it if nothing else was available. That's the kind of trouble I'm in in the eating department, he thought. He turned quickly and walked out of the kitchen as the fingerprint team started to work its way through the large pantry.

When he stepped out into the hot summer air, he saw the gray Mercedes was no longer there. He wondered what it was she had been looking for. He intended to

24

find out; but now he saw one of the patrolmen signaling him to where a crowd had gathered on the sidewalk.

It was the kid who lived next door. He looked to be about twelve, white skin, plump, with no visible neck, no waistline. Glandular, as if in addition to everything else, a testicle hadn't made its way down. His name was Gilbert Ritner and he had spoken to the dead man the night before and he wanted to be taken to headquarters and questioned. A real pain in the ass.

Gilbert had been playing his stereo in his upstairs bedroom, full blast. About 11 P.M. he got a call from next door telling him to turn the goddamn thing down.

"Did he say anything else?" Bud asked the kid, taking out his note book.

"No," Gilbert said, his voice high and nasal. "He just said, 'Turn down the goddamn music, fatso.' He called me fatso."

"Are you sure of the time?" Bud asked, looking at the boy's shapeless body, determined not to eat for the rest of the day, maybe even the week if he could swing it.

"How do you know it was eleven o'clock?"

"Because I looked at my Panasonic clock radio when the phone rang," Gilbert said. "I was expecting a friend to call and he only calls me during station breaks."

"Are you sure it was Mr. Koenig?" Bud asked.

"I know it was him because I know his voice and he also told me it was him before he called me fatso."

Okay. So he was still alive at eleven o'clock. Alive and complaining and abusive. Bud looked at the young mound of a boy standing eagerly before him. He wondered if it were possible a kid that age could have gotten so sore, so outraged, that he hung up the phone and . . . No. It was out of the question. Twelve-year-old boys with soft, doughy bodies don't commit murders.

"Did you see anybody come to the house, hanging around the house, any time after that?"

"No, I was in my room for the rest of the night."

"Did you hear anything?"

"No, I closed my windows and kept playing the music just as loud," Gilbert said, pleased with himself.

"Was anyone else here in the house with you last night?"

"Just the maid," Gilbert said, shrugging, "but she *no habla Inglés.*" The way he said it irritated Bud. A spoiled rotten kid who at twelve was already aware of the limitations of a maid who didn't speak English.

Bud asked for her name, jotted it down and then headed for his car. Gilbert followed closely behind him.

"He always called me fatso," Gilbert said, "but I called him faggot when he called me that." Bud turned quickly and studied the moon face staring up at him.

"Why did you call him that?" Bud asked quietly.

"I don't know," Gilbert said. "Just to make him sore, I guess."

"And did it?"

"Listen, he started calling me fatso first."

"Well, you are fat," Bud said, intentionally trying to needle him in hopes of getting more information out of him. "Was he a . . . faggot?"

"You're not so thin yourself," Gilbert said quickly. It was not so much an insult as a statement of fact, and Bud found himself sucking in his gut. In front of a twelve-year-old kid. Christ.

"Yeah, you're right," Bud said, letting his breath out. "It's no fun, huh?"

"It sucks," Gilbert said. He leaned against the car and smiled at Bud. "Can I come to headquarters with you?"

"Did you have any reason to call him a faggot? Any real reason other than trying to get him sore?"

"No," Gilbert said reluctantly, not anxious to let go of the one piece of information that had gotten him the biggest reaction. "There were good-looking girls here a lot."

"Last night?"

"I didn't see anybody here. I told you already, but if you show me people's pictures, you know, mug shots down at headquarters, I can tell you if they've been here."

Bud smiled at him and gently took his arm and pulled him off the fender of his car. Later on, maybe the next day, he'd call the kid down to headquarters, send a patrol car for him. In his years on the force, Bud had come to realize that lonely, alienated children have an insatiable curiosity about their neighbors and they make good, reliable and generally unshakable witnesses.

"You're not really fat," Gilbert said to Bud as he started to climb into his car, "you're just a little overweight. Maybe a pound or two."

"Fat is fat," Bud said, grinning out at him, "and they don't let you forget it."

"My mom put me on this crappy diet, you know, boiled vegetables. A whole plate full of gray things, but they're in Rome now so I eat what I want," Gilbert said. Then he leaned down and peered in the car window.

"I'll bet Koenig was into dope and heroin and things," Gilbert whispered conspiratorially, his round face framed in the car window. "You can tell me now."

"What makes you say that?" Bud asked quietly.

"Because of you. Because you're always driving by here very slowly, always staring into his house," Gilbert said. "I've seen you maybe a million times."

"This is my beat, kid," Bud said in a voice a lot lighter than he felt. "I drive by all the houses slowly." He turned the key in the ignition and started the engine.

"Maybe, but I'll bet you drive by here more than all the others," Gilbert said, still hanging onto the car door with both hands. "How come?"

It was a good question, Bud thought. Chuck had accused him of the same thing before, too, always going to or from headquarters by way of North Bedford, always going blocks out of their way to do it.

27

"Just a restless Beverly Hills housewife I like to keep tabs on," Bud had lied years before, and Chuck had believed him, had only grumbled minimally from then on when they hung an unnecessary left or right on Bedford on their way to somewhere else.

So his partner was aware of his interest in the Bedford Drive house, and now the kid next door. Before he knew it, Bud thought dryly, he might end up as the prime murder suspect himself.

"The guy who found the body," Gilbert called out over the sound of the idling engine. "Don't believe everything he says."

"You mean Hubie?"

"Yeah, I think he's kind of crazy."

"Are you just trying to make yourself invaluable to me or do you really know what you're talking about?"

"Take me down to headquarters and you'll find out for yourself." Gilbert gave him a quick wave and ran back to his house. Bud watched him run, watched the short, jerky motions, saw his ass move up and down.

I'm going to jog two miles from now on, Bud said to himself. Maybe three.

The D. P. Koenig Agency was on a street south of Wilshire Boulevard in Beverly Hills. It was a corner building with a used-brick facade and glossy black shutters. A lush Boston fern stood in a terra cotta pot on either side of a highly lacquered double door.

Bud pulled into the parking lot across the street. He saw a reporter and a photographer from the Los Angeles *Times* interviewing the parking-lot attendant. The man was old and black and Bud could tell by the look on his face that nothing this exciting had ever happened to him before.

The photographer nodded to Bud as he passed—the impersonal look of people who see each other only over corpses and disasters. Bud heard the attendant measuring his words, trying to make his involvement in the murdered man's life appear larger than it could possibly have been.

The receptionist was young and sun-tanned with long, chocolate-colored fingernails. In the overhead light, Bud could see the hint of a bleached mustache on her upper lip.

She was talking on the telephone and staring impersonally through him. He asked her where he could find Peter Lutz, but she continued talking on the phone, continued staring through him. When he finally turned, annoyed, and headed for the elevator, she hung up the phone quickly and called after him. "Can I help you?"

"I'm looking for Peter Lutz."

"Do you have an appointment?" she asked, now rising to her feet.

"I'm with the Beverly Hills Police Department," Bud said. "What office is he in?"

"I'll take you up," she said and stood next to him at the elevator. She was taller than he was, and thin, and had dark, downy hair on her arms.

"This place has been a madhouse all morning," she said in a soft, chatty voice, as if the murder were only a minor irritant like the phones going out.

"Do you have any idea who did it?" she asked as they stepped into the elevator.

"Funny, I was about to ask you the same question," Bud said. "Got any suspicions, clues, notions you'd care to discuss?"

The elevator door opened and she led him down a thickly carpeted hallway. At the end of the hallway was a small flight of stairs. She led him up the stairs, looking back to make sure he was following her because no footsteps could be heard on the costly, lush carpeting.

He could hear Peter Lutz's voice. The receptionist gave a quick knock on the door and then opened it. She stepped aside and then nodded toward the desk, where Peter was shuffling papers and talking on the telephone, one shoulder raised grotesquely to his chin to hold the phone in place. The Hunchback of Beverly Hills.

"No, don't come here," Peter was saying, his voice professionally soothing. "Please, I beg of you. It won't do any good." He looked up for a moment, acknowledged Bud's presence minimally, then returned his attention to the file propped on his lap and continued to flip through the papers.

Bud walked around Peter's office touching things, pulling manuscripts out without reading the titles, but when he started to open the door to Koenig's private office, Peter hung up quickly and stood in front of the door.

"I'll take you in there myself," Peter said. He was smiling, but it was a professional smile, a learned smile, that only in a small way masked the annoyance below.

"I'm investigating a murder, friend," Bud said, "and I don't want to wait while you're involved in earning your ten percent."

"I'm straight salary," Peter said, still guarding the door, "and goddamn low at that."

"You know I'm getting in there with or without you, Lutz, so why don't you make it easy on both of us?"

"Hang on," Peter said, a genuine smile on his face now. "I want to show you something first." Bud nodded and Peter crossed quickly to his desk, shuffled through a pile of papers, picked up an eight-by-ten glossy print and then handed it to Bud. "Recognize him?"

"Yeah, I recognize him," Bud said, looking down at the face of little Buddy Bacall with the baseball cap turned backward, with the striped T-shirt hanging off the thin young body, and the bright, confident eyes. "So what?"

"So you're running a check on me, I'm running a check on you," Peter said lightly. "You can keep the picture, by the way."

"Are you going to open the door now?" Bud asked, still studying the photograph, trying to remember what it was like to be someone who had eight-by-ten glossy photos of himself in an important man's filing cabinet. "Whatever happened to you?" Peter asked. It could have been a snotty, put-down question, but there was something else, a mixture of compassion and curiosity in his voice that made Bud look up quickly and then look down again. The old pain. The old bewilderment. They could still get to him without even half trying.

"Let's find out what happened to D. P. Koenig first, okay?"

Peter opened the door and stepped aside, allowing Bud to enter first.

It was a large, sterile office with floor-to-ceiling windows on two walls. There was no desk, just a rectangular slab of thick plate glass resting on a spotless chrome base. Except for a beige telephone, the surface of the glass was bare; no blotter, no pencil holder, no smudges, no dust. There were several expensive-looking leather chairs, a wall of built-in bookcases, most of them empty, and a Lucite wastepaper basket. It was also empty. It was the office of a man who kept his life uncluttered, or at least kept his clutter very well hidden.

"Not exactly cozy, is it?" Bud said, looking around.

"Whatever you might want, whatever could help you will be in my office, not in here," Peter said. "He hated papers and letters and scripts and memos, any kind of mess, so everything came back to me after he looked at it."

"What about Glenda Deering?" Bud said, walking to a closet door. He tried to open it, but it was locked. "Have you got the key?"

"Forget about her," Peter said, unlocking the door. "She's a poor, pathetic lady and she has nothing to do with any of this."

"What was she looking for back there?" Bud asked, as he stepped into the closet. There were several unopened bottles of Perrier and a strange spongy platform on the floor.

"What's that?" Bud asked, pointing to it with his toe.

"It's an indoor jogger," Peter said. "He went nine minutes every day with no sweat, no strain, no hard breathing. It was spooky at his age."

"How old was he?" Bud asked. "High fifties somewhere?"

"He would have been fifty-nine this October."

Bud stopped for a moment to calculate how old Koenig was when Buddy Bacall had posed for the eight-by-ten glossy in the other office. The agent would have been in his mid-thirties, at that time still a young man, but to Buddy, age five, he seemed ancient, over the hill, one foot surely in the grave.

"What was Glenda Deering looking for?" Bud asked again. He did not want to think about the dead agent as a young man, did not think he could handle it—for a while anyway.

"Forget her," Peter said. "She's nobody. I will work hand in hand with you on this, I swear it, but when I tell you something isn't relevant, that it's not going to have anything to do with the murder, I think it would be cool if you'd believe me."

Suddenly they heard a commotion in Peter's office. Both men got there at the same time. The receptionist was arguing with a girl who appeared to be somewhere in her early twenties. Bud studied the girl as she sailed imperially past the receptionist, an unmistakable fool-suffering expression on her face that made him smile.

She was wearing an ugly peasant dress and heavy Georgia Giant boots. He wondered fleetingly why she was doing everything in her power to make you over-look the fact that basically, despite an extra pound or two, she was very pretty.

"It's okay, Linda," Peter said to the receptionist. "I'll handle it."

"I just wish you'd let me know who can come up and who can't," Linda said in a martyred voice.

"Oh, God save me from receptionists who take their craft seriously," the girl said, rolling her eyes and shaking her head.

"You just call up here and ask, okay?" Peter said soothingly as he led Linda out of the office. "We're all having a rotten time of it."

The girl turned and flopped down heavily on the love seat in Peter's office. She let out a deep, businesslike sigh.

"Oh, boy," she said, "talk about the luck of the Jewish."

"Hello, Ivy," Peter said, walking back into the office, giving her an affectionate smile. "This is Bud Bacola. He's with the Beverly Hills Police Department. That's Ivy Greenwald."

She held out her hand solemnly, all the while studying him with a scrutiny worthy of a carnival weight-guesser. He wasn't quite sure what it was, but there was something touchingly comical about her, something that made it hard for him not to smile.

He stared back. She had a good face, good hair, thick, mouse-colored, unstyled, but somehow it worked, it looked fine. She had quick, intelligent eyes and a no-bullshit smile. There were so many freckles you didn't notice at first that she wore no makeup.

The dress was all wrong, but beneath the gathers and bunches he could see that she had a waistline and good knockers, and her upper calves above the terrible boots were slim and shapely.

"Are you a client?" Bud asked her.

"Christ, no," she said in a funny-sad voice, "after writing crud for years and years—fan magazines, the confessions, you know, utter garbage, I just got my first break. An assignment from *Esquire—Esquire!*" She repeated the name of the magazine in a pained, awed voice that made Bud smile. "It was to do a piece on Koenig, a taped-interview kind of thing. My ticket to the big time."

"Did you know him?" Bud asked her, looking down the front of her ugly dress, noticing the freckles on her chest, wondering how far down they went.

"No, I was going to meet him for the first time today. I had an appointment at three this afternoon. I would have done it yesterday, but I had an interview with— *get this*—Esther Williams for some geriatric magazine. *Esther Williams!* I could have done her any time. You see what greed gets you?"

"I've got a terrific idea," Bud said, smiling down at her. "I'll find the murderer and maybe you can get an assignment from *Esquire* to do a piece on him—or her."

"You're just saying that to cheer me up," Ivy said. "You know that Nora Ephron will beat me out."

"You're all heart, kid," Bud said, amused, wondering if anyone, anywhere, was actually grieving, mourning for the dead man. He was sure they were not.

Ivy got up and smoothed out her dress. Actually she was not as heavy as he had first thought. It was the dress that ruined her, and the goddamn dumb lumberman's boots. She was defiantly going out of her way to be funny-looking, and it touched him because he understood it so thoroughly.

"I'd like your home phone number," Bud said, taking out his notebook. He didn't even know why he was asking. She hadn't even met Koenig, and she was definitely someone who would not have profited by his death. But he believed she might be helpful to him in some way, or at least mildly entertaining.

"What for?" she asked. She was standing next to him and he could see that she was several inches shorter than he was.

"I don't know," he said. "Maybe you'll do a magazine article on the Beverly Hills Police Department one day.

Look, forget it. I don't need it." He slipped the notebook back into his pocket.

"It's 454-6553," she said quickly. "I'm in the phone book in the central section, and, in case you're interested, I did one hell of a research job on Koenig in order to get the assignment."

Bud took out his notebook again and jotted down her phone number. When he looked up she was no longer there.

The telephones were starting to ring and all hell was breaking loose as clients and customers heard the news. Bud was not interested in the people who were calling now, after they had heard about the murder. What he was interested in were yesterday's messages. The people who had called Koenig when he was alive and functioning, when he held absolute power over their professional lives.

"Peter, I want a record of all incoming and outgoing phone calls for Monday and Tuesday. I want to know who called him, and I want to know particularly the people who called and didn't get called back."

"Well, that's most of them," Peter said. He walked over to his desk and opened a drawer. Bud saw how meticulously neat everything was. He wondered whether all agents' secretaries were as neat—if it was perhaps a job requirement, along with being slim and well-dressed and evasive.

"Here," Peter said, handing Bud several sheets of paper from an office form with spaces for who called, when, the nature of the business, the return phone number. "But I don't think there's a name on that list that's capable of murder."

"I want their addresses and home phone numbers," Bud said. When he saw Peter was about to protest, he added quickly, "You know I can get the information myself. All you'll be doing is making it a little easier for me."

Reluctantly Peter fished around in a lower drawer, then removed two sheets of paper stapled together in the upper left-hand corner. There were two columns on each page, maybe thirty names. Bud felt his hands tremble as he took the client list from Peter. The name of the murderer was most probably in one of those columns.

"Thanks," Bud said as he folded the pages neatly down the center and slipped them into his pocket, along with the message sheets.

"How do you know it wasn't just a random crime, maybe some addict or junkie who just picked the first promising-looking house?" Peter asked.

"Because you have to be almost religious to feel someone like D. P. Koenig bought it accidentally," Bud said, smiling, "and I ain't got no religion."

"Amen," Peter said.

"About your alibi last night," Bud said. "Can you give me a name and a phone number?"

"Yes," Peter said slowly, his face troubled, "but I'd love for you to take my word for it."

"What's your problem there?" Bud asked. "A prominent Hollywood wife?"

"Try the happily married father of three children, who also happens to be on the Board of Education," Peter said, his voice quiet, pained. "He's absolutely frenzied right now."

Bud studied Peter's face. This information certainly came as no surprise to him. Peter didn't actually swish, but there was something off-center about him. Bud believed his story, believed that Peter was trying to protect a father and husband, a respected pillar of the community, whose cover was about to be blown by a murder that probably had nothing to do with him.

"If you leave him alone," Peter said slowly, "I'll cooperate with you in areas where normally I wouldn't. I will tell you things. I'll be very helpful."

"I'll give you forty-eight hours," Bud said, "but if I

don't find the murderer by then, I want your happy husband in my office to make a sworn statement, or I'll book you for anything from withholding evidence to obstruction to homicide."

The telephone rang and Peter answered it, turning away from Bud, his shoulder up, his voice low. Bud moved in closer so as not to miss anything.

"Oh, hello, Mr. Maxwell," Peter said. "Yes, it is a terrible thing, a terrible tragedy." It already had the insincere ring of a recorded announcement.

Bud recognized the name, was sure it had to be Richard Maxwell. He had seen Maxwell's picture in the paper a thousand times, always at an opening with a different starlet, or whatever they called themselves these days.

Richard Maxwell had made a killing in the fertilizer business in Des Moines. Some new way to process bullshit. So he had come out to Hollywood. But he had been good, had impeccable taste and a lot of drive, and had produced two quality low-budget pictures in one year.

The critics had tried hard to roast him with the fertilizer business, turned some cruel phrases at his expense. But the Hollywood community had risen in his defense, and one of the critics had been fired and the other reprimanded by the publisher, and the joke was over.

"Look," Peter said into the phone, shrugging apologetically, "I really can't talk to you right now. Can I get back to you?"

Bud smiled. Nothing like a good murder to have the pauper telling the prince he's too busy.

"I'll get back to you as soon as things quiet down here," Peter said. Then he added in a courtly voice, "And may I offer my congratulations to both you and your bride?" Obviously he couldn't, because Richard Maxwell hung up the phone hard enough for Bud to hear it six feet away.

"Is he a client?" Bud asked.

"They did some business together," Peter said in his best guarded voice.

"By the way," Bud said, stopping in the doorway, "what about Koenig? Was he gay?"

"Mr. Koenig could be anything that was advantageous to him," Peter said in a quiet, icy voice.

The phone rang and Peter picked it up, again turning away from Bud's curious gaze.

"This is Peter Lutz, may I help you?" he said, his voice soothing and unreal. "Look, I'll have to get back to you," he said quickly, his voice no longer soothing, just unreal. Then he hung up.

"Who was that?" Bud asked.

"Koenig's tailor," Peter said. "The poor guy is sitting there with two seven-hundred-dollar custom suits that haven't been paid for yet and he just turned on the news."

Bud smiled. He'd been wrong. Now he knew there was at least one person who was mourning the passing of D. P. Koenig.

"I'll get back to you," Bud said. As he walked out of the office, all the telephones started to ring at the same time.

He did not envy Peter Lutz one little bit.

2

Thirty-three thousand people live (most of them beyond their means) in Beverly Hills. Tour buses and out-of-state cars slip up and down its streets to observe the rich and famous in their natural habitat.

Everything north of Sunset Boulevard is residential with the exception of the Beverly Hills Hotel. Fanning out in an arc around and behind the hotel are the largest, most costly and desirable homes. Farther north and higher up into the hills is an area known as Beverly Hills Post Office. Residents here have the cachet of the Beverly Hills name on their letterheads, and they share post-office facilities, but their crimes are attended by the Los Angeles Police Department, their smoldering mattresses doused by Los Angeles firemen, and their children attend Los Angeles schools.

On the northwesterly tip of Beverly Hills are the Trousdale Estates, possibly the most expensive tract development in the world.

Everything south of Sunset Boulevard is known sim-

ply as The Flats. There are blocks of immense homes
built so close together that only a narrow driveway separates a chairman of the board's powder room from a
rock star's kitchen. The residential area south of Wilshire is known as Baja Beverly. Here the homes are
smaller, even closer together. There is a rundown seedy
industrial area that could be Pittsburgh a scant quarter
of a mile from Rodeo Drive with its three blocks of the
finest, most exclusive boutiques in the world. There are
four elementary schools and Beverly Hills High, with
pumping oil wells and a gymnasium floor that with the
pull of a switch separates to expose a vast swimming
pool beneath.

The Beverly Hills City Hall sits on a carefully land-
scaped block in the heart of The Flats. The police department takes up the lower floors, the municipal offices
and courtrooms are above.

From the outside the building is uniquely Southern
California, off-white and amorphous. The architecture is
somewhere between Italian and Spanish, with a touch
or two of Art Deco, but it had always pleased Bud, even
with its badly tarnished gold dome, its dingy teal blue-
and-turquoise mosaic tiles. He had added his name to a
lot of petitions passed around by zealous citizens to have
the building refurbished, repainted, another coat of gilt
for the dome, but nothing had ever come of it.

Inside it looked like any other police headquarters,
drab, functional, badly in need of fresh paint.

"Hey, Buddy-boy," Tom Edwards called across to
him, "got a biggie for you here."

Bud walked across to Tom Edwards' desk. The two
men had little use for each other, barely managed to
hide their hostility. Tom resented the fact that Bud was
the stationhouse celebrity. They were both detectives,
same rank, yet whenever a movie star was robbed,
mugged, or murdered, automatically the call went out to
Bud Bacola, the Hollywood *maven*. And then it was Bud

and Chuck who ran it all down, leaving the boring backup details for Tom.

There had been a call from Kenny Bartlett. He wanted to talk to someone about D. P. Koenig's murder. Right away. Bud took out the client list. Bartlett's name was second from the top.

Tom Edwards pushed the piece of paper with the information across to Bud, intentionally pushing too hard so that it slipped off the end of the desk and floated downward. Bud caught it midair, then looked up at Tom Edwards and grinned. It was no time to provoke. He did not want to make trouble and get taken off this case. He also knew there were some compelling reasons why he should be taken off the case. He just hoped no one else made the connection.

Kenny Bartlett had been a minor big-band vocalist in the forties who did some funny *shtick* between songs. He had routines about his mediocre voice, his large ears, his Basque heritage. His jokes, which weren't much, were still better than his singing voice, and by the late forties he had given up the bandstand entirely and worked most of the better nightclubs across the country as a stand-up comic.

He did a lot of inspirational flag-waving stuff at the end of each show which went over very big until the early fifties and the rise of comics like Mort Sahl and Lenny Bruce.

From then on, his blatant chauvinism started getting him booed off stage.

He gave up nightclubs and got into syndicated game shows and then into variety shows, then hit it big with a half-hour cowboy series which ran for five years. He followed this up with three more long-running series, one of which he starred in, all of which made him a multimillionaire and one of the major suppliers of journeyman television. He was generous with his time and could be counted on to perform or make an appearance at almost any charity function. He raised money for a university at the foot of the Pyrenees where for hundreds of years his family had tended sheep.

He was a party-goer, a party-giver, and barely a day went by when he and his wife of thirty-eight years were not mentioned in the society columns.

Kenny Bartlett lived in possibly the largest, most lavish, most vulgar house in the Trousdale section of Beverly Hills. Until the early fifties, the foothills north of Sunset Boulevard had been untouched, left in their natural wild state. Grayish desert scrub covered the steep slopes. Deer, rabbits, coyotes, snakes, and an occasional mountain cat roamed the area, and during spells of drought could be found late at night drinking uneasily from the more isolated swimming pools. On summer nights, the residents of The Flats could often hear the final terrified cry of a rabbit, or possibly a raccoon, brought down by a night predator.

Then, in the early fifties, a shrewd developer decided it would be feasible to do some heroic grading, to shave off the hilltops and create estate-sized building lots.

The main street running north and south through Trousdale is called Loma Vista. It is possibly the steepest grade in Southern California. The brakes and transmissions of cars owned by Trousdale residents need relining or replacing with triple the frequency of residents of The Flats.

For many years Trousdale was referred to contemptuously by people in The Flats as Marble Hill because of the garish over-use of every type of marble in all the homes: floors, walls, patios, pool decks, sink counters. It could also have been called Gold Filigree Hill, or Greek Column Hill, because there was no shortage of these either.

Kenny Bartlett's house was on a cul-de-sac high up in Trousdale. It had been designed and built for him nine years earlier, a lasting monument to how wrong you can go when money is no object. The house consisted of a graceless series of arches and columns, turrets and domes. The property was surrounded by a high pink wall.

The only thing simple about the house was the name: La Casa. But some mischief-maker had painted out the lower half of the s so that now it read La *Caca.* Bud wondered if anyone inside was aware of the vandalism, wondered if he could mention it to them without smiling.

Bud had driven by the house many times before, but he had never been inside. Six months earlier he and Chuck had gone on a call next door. The lady of the house had reported that her maid was acting "funny." By the time Bud and Chuck arrived, the maid had given birth to a perfect eight-pound boy. "I didn't even know she was pregnant," the lady of the house had said. "I just thought she was pigging out on my food."

Kenny Bartlett's butler opened the door. He was young and blond and dazzlingly handsome. Probably a failed actor, Bud thought, who decided to change his luck and try to bore from within.

He led Bud through what appeared to be five different living rooms on five different levels, each with differently colored carpeting, none of it cheap.

"Mr. Bartlett is having a haircut," the young butler announced. He opened an immense door that looked as if it could have dated back to the Spanish Inquisition. It was scarred, battered, overcarved. The handle was turquoise inlay and ugly, proving that they had bad taste even then.

Beyond the door was an expanse of vivid mosaic tile, and then the garden. Bud learned shortly that it was the "north" garden. There was also an "east" and a "west" garden. Bud knew unquestionably that he was looking at a house and property that had to have at least a five-million-dollar price tag on it, and he was impressed.

Kenny Bartlett was sitting on a portable barber's chair in the middle of the tiled patio. He was wearing pink-and-yellow bathing trunks. A matching terry cloth-lined jacket was resting on the knees of an eager, balding young man sitting in a director's chair directly across from him.

From where Bud was standing, Kenny Bartlett still looked like a young man, although he was rumored to be in his early seventies. He had watched his weight, and the California sun, coupled with his Basque blood, gave him the healthy glow of a man easily half his age. Up close, you could see the signs of erosion.

"Hi, kid," Kenny said, swiveling the chair around so the repressed-looking man who was cutting his hair had to walk in a half-circle to continue his work.

"Meet Barry, the corporate nephew," Kenny said, indicating the young man sitting across from him holding his jacket. Barry, the corporate nephew, a boy who had probably learned early that you don't have to be agreeable to underlings or civil servants, nodded minimally to Bud.

"You want a drink, kid?" Kenny Bartlett asked. "Something to eat, maybe? I know you cops never have time to eat." Before Bud could answer, he snapped his fingers at Barry. "Get Clyde," he said. Actually, Bud didn't want anything to eat or drink, but it pleased him to see the finger-trained nephew ordered around, and he let him go in search of the butler.

"Koenig loved me," Kenny Bartlett said. "He fuckin' idolized me." Bud barely heard what the actor was saying because of what was going on across the Olympic-size swimming pool.

Even from where Bud was standing, he could see that she was a knockout. She was stretched out on a golden lounger, her body glistening with suntan oil. She was lying on her stomach, wearing bikini bottoms only, and there was a large spotted cat (a zoo cat, not a domestic cat) sitting on the small of her back and rhythmically, methodically licking off the suntan oil. Her back, her arms, her armpits. The girl lay stretched out, abandoning herself to the cat's rough tongue. Bud wondered which of them was purring loudest.

"She's helping me with my autobiography," Bartlett said. Bud tried to look away, to re-focus his attention, but he kept staring at the cat as it changed its position on the editorial assistant's body searching for an unlicked area to work on.

"Is that her cat?" Bud asked. He couldn't help himself.

"No, he's mine. The trainer and I were on Johnny Carson the same night and I bought him on the spot."

"Is he tame?"

"He is if he gets what he wants," Bartlett said with a low and very dirty laugh.

Barry came back outside with a disagreeable look on his face. Behind him was the young blond butler. Bud asked for black coffee and Clyde disappeared back inside the house.

"Over there," Bartlett said to Barry. He was pointing to something on the costly tile floor.

"What is it?" Barry asked, his voice suddenly getting shrill. "I don't know what you're pointing at."

"There's some hair," Bartlett said. This time he pointed and snapped his fingers. Barry leaned down and brushed some of his uncle's newly cut hair into the palm of his hand. He took the hair almost reverently to a large brass frog and slipped the hair into the frog's opened mouth. There were some advantages, Bud thought, to having a rich and famous uncle. There were also some disadvantages.

"Mr. Bartlett," Bud said, deliberately standing with his back to the scene beyond the swimming pool, "you requested that I come by and talk with you about D. P. Koenig."

"Terrible, terrible thing," the actor said. He snapped his fingers again as a new tress hit the tile floor. Barry scampered to retrieve it. "He worshiped me, and I let this happen to him."

The barber was finishing up the haircut. He put the scissors in a back pocket, whipped out a thin comb and started back-teasing. Then he rubbed something black into the balding crown of Kenny Bartlett's head. Tricks of the trade.

"Why is it you feel responsible?"

"Not directly," the actor said impatiently, "but maybe if I'd forced him into coming over for dinner last night . . ."

The barber took out a spray can and gave an artistic spritz of pure white to the sideburns and temples of the black, black hair. A true work of art.

"The black dye looks unreal, so we touch up with a little white here and there," Bartlett said, generously sharing his beauty secrets.

"When was the last time you saw or spoke to Mr. Koenig?" Bud asked. Suddenly he heard a moan of joy from across the swimming pool. As a matter of principle, he was determined not to turn around.

"I talked to him yesterday afternoon," Bartlett said. "We were supposed to have lunch today. Christ, what a terrible thing."

The blond butler came out onto the patio with a mug of steaming coffee on a tray. Bud was amused to see it was a dime-store mug, chipped in several places. He was sure D. P. Koenig had never been served coffee from this mug.

"He liked being seen out with me," Kenny Bartlett said, touching his white, white sideburns, checking his fingers to see if there was any white on them. There was. He wiped his fingers on his pink-and-yellow print trunks. "I'm his biggest star, you know."

Bud edged around minimally, and out of the corner of

his eye he saw the girl now sitting on the lounger, her back to him. She was rubbing suntan oil all over her body again as the ocelot sat next to her, his tail twitching nervously, staring at her every move.

"Get the broom, kid," Bartlett said to his nephew, even though the butler was probably still within easy calling distance. He got up and brushed the excess hair off his dark, leathery body.

"You want to see the house?" Bartlett asked. "See what you could end up with if you had seven million dollars?" So he'd only been two million off. Not a bad guess.

Bud was about to protest, but Bartlett had pulled open the door leading into the house. Bud looked quickly over his shoulder at the cat-and-girl show. She was lying down on the lounger again, this time on her back, still naked from the waist up. The cat was earnestly licking her navel. It had to be more fun than writing.

Bud walked past Barry, who was now sweeping up his famous uncle's hair snips. He had a dark, grim set to his face, and he turned away to avoid eye contact with Bud.

"That kid," Bartlett said proudly from the doorway, pointing to his nephew, "is going to own this town one day. He's already an associate producer on two of my shows."

Bud tried not to look too skeptical.

"He's going to own this town because he knows how to eat shit and when to eat shit. I taught him that. It'll get you further than anything else in this town, except for maybe real talent."

It was not one house, Bud discovered; it was two houses, maybe three. There were upstairs kitchens and downstairs kitchens, upper dining rooms and lower dining rooms, dens and solariums on all levels, and windows that looked out on the north, south, east gardens, all with panoramic views of the city, limited only by the density of the smog.

47

There was too much furniture, too many accessories, too much marble, too much velvet. Everything cost too much. It was not so much tasteless as it was awe-inspiring. Although he had a lot of other things to do, a lot of other people to see, somehow Bud could not stop following the actor through the immense house, could not stop his own flow of polite, insincere praise.

Bartlett opened a door that led into a small, windowless hallway—a dark, airless grotto. At one end was a small Byzantine altar with tiers of flickering votive candles. There were two small velvet kneeling stools directly in front of the altar.

"This is where my wife and I pray every morning and evening," the actor said in a voice as natural as if he had been announcing where they ate their breakfast. Bud didn't know what the actor had left to pray for, but he was sure the wife, wherever she was, probably knelt there and asked God to let the ocelot sink his fangs into the editorial assistant's greasy throat.

"Do you have any idea who might have killed D. P. Koenig?" Bud asked. He pushed past the actor, out of the dark hallway that smelled of something like incense but was probably just the candles.

"I always said to him, get rid of those losers," Bartlett said, following Bud out into the upstairs living room, or possibly the downstairs living room. "All those hangers-on that kept whining for his attention and his time."

"Anyone in particular you suspect?"

Kenny Bartlett turned and looked directly into Bud's eyes. Bud looked down for a moment and was fascinated to see the actor's bare feet all but disappearing in the mauve carpeting, just the tops of his old man's thick horny toenails showing. It had to cost a hundred a yard at least.

"Can I trust you?" the actor asked, suddenly riveting Bud with his dark Basque eyes.

"Yes, I believe you can," Bud said.

"Do you have any idea how much money I make a year?"

"A lot, I'm sure," Bud said, wondering what the hell this had to do with anything.

"You bet your ass, a lot," Kenny Bartlett said.

"Is there anyone in particular you think might have murdered D. P. Koenig?" Bud asked quickly, trying to steer him back to matters at hand.

"The man worshiped the ground I walk on," Bartlett said.

"You asked to speak to me, Mr. Bartlett," Bud said, trying to keep the impatience from his voice. "I'd like to know if, in fact, you have any pertinent information because I've got a lot of places to go and people to talk to."

"I made him a rich man. The grandson of a Basque shepherd made him a millionaire." He leaned in close to Bud, who noticed for the first time the white roots of the black, black hair on his chest. What's left to believe in? Bud wondered, trying not to show his feelings, which now lay somewhere between amusement and contempt. He wondered if Bartlett used Grecian Formula on his crotch too.

"I've got to track down a murderer, Mr. Bartlett," Bud said, trying to head him off. "If you have any thoughts or ideas . . ."

"You know who was at my house for dinner last night?" Bartlett asked. "Streisand, Zanuck, Sue Mengers, you name it, they were here. Not even a major party. Just a usual Tuesday night get-together. My wife and I love people." He said it humbly, as if he were talking about just plain folks.

"Did he ever discuss his other clients with you?" Bud asked. "Ever mention a threat to his life, anything like that?"

"I invited him to dinner but he said no." He was already starting to repeat himself. It was a Hollywood affliction.

49

"Did he say why he couldn't come?" Bud asked quickly.

"He hated parties. He always said he didn't like to smile at night unless he had to."

"That was the reason he gave?" Bud pressed. "He didn't mention what he was doing instead, whom he was seeing?"

Barry, the corporate nephew, entered the room and walked silently through the lush carpeting toward his uncle. He had vacant, foolish eyes, and, as Bud studied his face, he believed despite whatever shit-eating talents this young man possessed, he would never own even a small part of this town.

"Shall I go to the studio now?" Barry asked. He tried to keep his head turned away from Bud, his voice down. Corporate nephews don't like civil servants watching them earn their keep.

"Is the hair all swept up?" Bartlett asked. He was sure getting his money's worth out of this nephew.

"My sister's only son," the actor said, pinching Barry's cheek perhaps a little harder than necessary.

Barry pulled away from his uncle's nipping fingers and headed grimly for the front door.

"As long as I'm alive, that kid will want for nothing," Bartlett said.

"What was it you wanted to speak to me about, Mr. Bartlett?"

"I just wanted you to know that if there was anything I could do to help you, you can call on me any hour of the night or day," the actor said, in a voice that indicated to Bud the audience was over.

"You mean, you have nothing to tell me?" Bud asked, barely able to suppress his annoyance.

"Would you like tickets to a new comedy pilot I'm doing?" Bartlett asked. "I'm doing the warm-up myself. Nobody does warm-ups like me. I'm the best in the business."

"No, thank you," Bud said.

"You can bring some of your police buddies," the actor said. "They worship me down there."

"I'm afraid we're all too busy tracking down a murderer," Bud said.

"Yeah, well, when you find him," Bartlett said, suddenly switching to his best street voice, "bring him around here first so I can punch his face in for him."

"I want to thank you for all your help," Bud said as politely as he could. The actor looked up instantly. He was out of it, but not so far out of it he didn't know he'd just been zinged.

Bud turned and walked toward the front door just as a woman he assumed to be Kenny Bartlett's wife shuffled into the room. She was wearing a limp brocade duster and satin slippers. Her hair was thin and dyed a pinkish color and you could see a lot of scalp through it. She walked past Bud with an impersonal nod and came and stood with her abused hair in front of her husband. She looked twice his age.

"What'll *she* have for lunch?" Bud heard her ask, icily enunciating each word. At least nobody had to ask what the cat was having for lunch.

"Well, thanks for everything," Bud said, and headed down the front path. For the first time he noticed that the privet hedges along the paths had been carefully sculpted to look like a double file of nose-to-tail sheep. A man definitely not ashamed of his humble heritage. Bud was willing to forgive a man a lot for that.

"He had a short attention span," the actor called out across the sheep-shaped bushes. "That's what got him killed." By the time Bud had turned around, Kenny Bartlett had closed the front door behind him.

Bud climbed into his car. He thought about Bartlett's parting words. A short attention span. What the hell was he talking about? Everyone in Hollywood had a short attention span.

A waste of time, he thought, as he descended the steep grade in low gear. A complete waste of time. But the phrase stayed with him, returned to haunt him over the next few days.

3

As Bud drove back down into the flats of Beverly Hills, he glanced at the names on the message sheet. One name leaped out at him.

Gordon Flemming had telephoned Koenig *five* times on the day he was murdered. There was nothing to indicate that any of the calls had been returned although they were all marked either urgent or important.

But he had to talk to Oliver Kelsey first, because he had telephoned the agent *six* times on the day of his death. His calls had not been returned either. Bud felt his gut muscles tighten involuntarily. He knew what that was all about.

Oliver Kelsey was a screen writer, part of the Old Guard. His face was familiar because over the years he had accepted Academy Awards for winning writers who were out of town, had often made warm and gracious speeches in their behalf. Bud had seen his name, his credit many times, but could not remember anything specific.

Bud smiled to himself as he noted the names of people whose calls had been returned promptly. Dustin Hoffman, Marsha Mason, Warren Beatty, Francis Ford Coppola. The Hollywood hierarchy. When you're hot, you're hot. Bud was glad he was out of it.

He drove out Sunset Boulevard, past the tourists still swarming around the Saudis' burned-out house with its bouquets of plastic flowers and the hand-painted privates on the Grecian statues, past the Beverly Hills Hotel, past UCLA.

Oliver Kelsey lived in Bel-Air. Bud turned right at the West Gate and wound up Bellagio Road. In the summer, when you enter Bel-Air, there is a noticeable drop in temperature. The lushness of the trees and shrubs, the glistening wet, eternally sprinkled lawns cool the air. There are some spots here where the sun never shines, moist bowers shaded by large costly trees and dense foliage.

It is a rich and private community. The only people you see in Bel-Air are the Spanish-speaking maids panting as they haul heavy trash cans out to the curb, or the Japanese gardeners squatting on their haunches, hosing down the garden paths, hosing down the streets, hosing down everything, even in the pouring rain.

This is *Old* Bel-Air. Farther up into the hills and closer to the San Diego Freeway is *New* Bel-Air, where developers with more greed than taste carved up the hillsides, created new streets with melodious Spanish names and built rows of small tract bungalows.

The only time the *Old* Bel-Air and *New* Bel-Air residents intermingle is in the fall when the hillside fires are raging out of control. Then everyone comes together on the highest vacant lot. They stand elbow to elbow, their binoculars raised, chatting pleasantly, united in danger, knowing they will not speak again until the next fire.

Oliver Kelsey lived in *New* Bel-Air. There were a dozen recently built houses on the street, half of them still under construction, only a few of them with lawns. A row of spindly saplings had been planted in the easements, but it would be years before they amounted to anything.

Bud pulled up in front of the house. He had taken a chance and not telephoned first. Writers were usually home in the mornings, and he didn't want to give Kelsey a chance to prepare what he was going to say.

There was an old Pontiac in the left side of the carport. There was no car on the right side, but there was a large smear of fresh grease on the cement floor.

As he walked up the steps to the house, he took out the message sheet and studied it. Six unreturned phone calls the day before the murder. Please call him at 282-4542. Bud felt his stomach churn. He'd sweated out those phone calls himself. In his other life.

He rang, rang again, and then he heard a woman's voice calling out for him to come around the back. He walked around the house and almost bumped into her. She was backing up, carrying a large burlap sack which enclosed the root ball of a small tree. It looked like it must have weighed a hundred pounds, but she was barely straining.

"Hi," she said, and carefully lowered the tree into a wide hole in the ground. He watched as she worked the burlap off the roots and eased the tree into the hole. She straightened up and reached for a shovel that was leaning against the side of the house.

"Can I help you?" She looked at him and smiled. It was a warm, easy smile, and Bud was struck by her serenity and her beauty. He figured she was somewhere in her early fifties. Her hair was soft and brown and the gray was starting to take over unopposed. She had kind blue eyes and her skin was clear but dry, almost leathery, probably from too much gardening.

There was something regal about her, something that made him think of deposed monarchs, exiled queens.

"I'd like to speak to Oliver Kelsey. Is he here?" Bud asked, as he took out his wallet and showed her his badge.

"I'm Vera Kelsey," she said. "May I know why?" As she spoke, she looked down at her hands. Bud looked, too, and was startled. They were the hands of a woman twice her age, spotted and wrinkled, and at the moment caked with dirt, and her unpolished nails were chipped and uneven. Definitely not a lady's hands.

When she noticed Bud was also looking at them, she smiled and quickly slipped her soiled hands into her pockets.

"I'd like to ask him some questions about D. P. Koenig," Bud said.

"Kind of a mess, isn't it?" Vera said easily. "But not exactly a loss to mankind either."

"Is Mr. Kelsey inside?"

"No, I'm sorry, he left just a few minutes ago."

"Do you know when he'll be back?"

"When he's having trouble with a story, sometimes he drives to the beach and walks for hours and hours trying to thrash it out. I have no idea when he'll be back."

"He telephoned Koenig a number of times the day before he was murdered. Do you know what it might have been about?"

She started to shovel the earth back around the tree she had just planted. He watched her as she forced the spade into the pile of dirt with her left foot, as she hauled the load up with both arms, her muscles straining under the cotton knit T-shirt she was wearing.

"Oliver has been his client for over twenty years," she said, working on another shovel of dirt. "They were on the telephone constantly."

"I don't believe Koenig returned any of his calls that day," Bud said. "Do you think there is any significance in that?"

"In an agent not returning a client's telephone calls?"

She let out a derisive snort. "That's what makes this town go around, waiting for agents to return your calls."

"Is your husband employed at this time?"

"As long as you're here, will you do me a favor?" she said. Without waiting for an answer, she turned and walked to the far end of the garden. She stood in front of a young tree, almost as tall as she was. It was planted in a corroded metal can. "The idiot from the nursery put my podocarpus here instead of where I told him to. Could you please help me carry it?"

Together they bent down and hoisted the tree. Bud strained under the weight of it and was awed to see the ease with which Vera Kelsey carried her share of the load. The woman was in very good condition.

"Just over there," she said, not even breathing hard. "We're putting a pool in and this is one of the few trees that doesn't drop too many leaves."

"In addition to the business relationship, did you or your husband have a personal relationship with Koenig?"

"I'm not sure I know what you mean by a personal relationship," she said slowly, her hands picking off the yellowing leaves from the young tree. "He used to be my agent many years ago, he comes to our parties, and we've played tennis at his house, but I don't think Oliver knows him any better today—or yesterday—than he did twenty years ago."

"What were your feelings for him, Mrs. Kelsey?"

"Quite frankly," she said pleasantly, "I grew to hate him. He was a cold, indifferent man, but Ollie had this strange, almost worshipful feeling about him. He trusted him completely. It drove me crazy because I don't think he deserved that much loyalty and respect."

"Are you in the business, Mrs. Kelsey?"

"I was an actress, not a good one, and I was always cursed with a weight problem. Now I'm just a housewife." She took a pair of wire clippers out of her back pocket and began cutting through the rusted metal can.

"Does your husband work at home?" he asked. He put his foot on the edge of the can to steady it while she cut. It was the least he could do.

"Yes, always," she said, "even when he's given a big office and a secretary at a studio. I do all his typing for him, and I make damn good coffee."

"Could you have him call me at the Beverly Hills Police Department when he comes home, please?"

"I have a few more trees to move around if you'd care to wait," she said and grinned up at him. Oliver Kelsey may have had a cold, indifferent agent, but he got lucky in the wife department, Bud thought. Vera Kelsey was a kind, warm, caring woman, and he was annoyed with himself for not believing a word she said.

"I'll help you move them if you'll show me around your kitchen," Bud said.

"Oh," Vera said lightly, "you think you'll find something important in my kitchen?"

"Just routine."

"I'm sure," Vera said, wiping her hands on the sides of her pants. She turned and walked to the back door and held it open for him, slipping out of her mud-caked sneakers as she entered the house.

The kitchen was cheerful, well-equipped. There were a lot of hanging plants and rows of African violets on the windowsills.

"If you could tell me what you're looking for, perhaps I could help you?" Vera said politely.

"Where do you keep your carving knives?" Bud asked.

"Oh, is that how he got it?" Vera said, making no effort to disguise a small, almost pleased smile. She opened two drawers and then stepped aside. Bud picked up one knife after another, studied them, looking for a set with a knife missing. The Sabatier trade name. But he found nothing to make him suspicious.

He closed the drawers and turned to Vera Kelsey. Her back was turned to him. She was picking dead leaves from the African violets.

"Thanks," he said. She turned to him and smiled.

"Everything okay?"

"So far." He started to walk out the back door, then turned to her. "By the way, what's your phone number here?"

"It's 476-3651," she told him, "and 3652. We have a rotary because Oliver thinks I talk too much, and he's not wrong."

Bud walked along the side of the house. He took the message sheet out of his pocket and checked the return telephone number Oliver Kelsey had left at Koenig's office. It was not the same number.

He drove down to the Bel-Air market and stepped into the telephone booth. He dialed the number Kelsey had given to Peter Lutz. It rang four times and then was answered by a young female voice.

"Yeah?" She sounded distracted, angry to have been pulled away from whatever she had been doing.

"Who's this?" Bud asked.

"Who's this asking?" The voice was now cold and suspicious.

"I'm just trying to find out what number I reached."

"What number do you want?"

"I'd like to speak to Oliver Kelsey."

"You have the wrong number," the voice said and the line went dead. He did not believe he had the wrong number. He called headquarters and told them to find out the name and address of whoever lived there.

Then, because he could put it off no longer, he went to pay a call on a director named Gordon Flemming.

4

$\mathbf{B}$ud was sure he remembered a house that Gordon Flemming had lived in back in the old days. It had been somewhere behind the Beverly Hills Hotel, a sprawling giant of a house with a five-car garage.

Well, times had changed, Bud thought, as he turned left off Sunset Boulevard. He followed the gentle upward curve of Doheny for half a mile. It was a nice community of attractive, well-maintained hillside homes squeezed together on jigsaw-puzzle lots far too small for their size, but it was definitely out of the high-rent district.

Bud took a sharp right on a street called Alta Verde, the name of which amused him because it was neither high nor green. Gordon Flemming's house was halfway down Alta Verde on the side of the street that didn't have even a passing shot at a city view.

Bud stopped the car in front of the director's house. It was a square, boxy two-story job and had no character at all. "Low on curb appeal" was how his real-estate lady friend would have described it. He got out of the car and tried to straighten the mailbox which was listing into the street at a forty-five-degree angle. The whole thing came out in his hands. He tried unsuccessfully to shove it back into the ground, then set it gently at the curb. It rolled over and several bills fell out.

As he walked up the path to the front door, Bud took in the flaking paint, the rusty, sagging gutters, the window shade in the living room hanging crookedly and rotted by the strong morning sun.

No five-car garage here, Bud thought. There was scant room for two cars, and the large overhead door was warped like a potato chip. As he walked by, a sleek gray cat jumped down from the curve in the garage door and slipped past his legs.

There was a note taped to the front door. "Bell out of order, please knock." The paper was frayed, yellowing. Bud had a strong hunch the bell hadn't worked for a long time. He wasn't sure why, but the shabbiness, the seediness, made him feel a little less tense.

Gordon Flemming came to the door himself. He was wearing a soiled terry cloth bathrobe and tennis shoes with no laces. Keeping the chain in place he peered at Bud through the crack in the door.

"Yeah," he said rudely, "what do you want?"

Bud held his badge up to the crack in the door.

"So?" Flemming said, making no move to open the door, but he didn't close it either.

"I'd like five minutes of your time to ask you some questions about D. P. Koenig," Bud said politely.

There was a brief struggle with the chain and then Gordon Flemming pushed the door open. Bud tried not to stare at the series of pecker tracks that dipped to the hem of his bathrobe. There was no invitation to come in. Flemming just turned and walked into a small, cluttered den, his left hand thrust deep into his pocket. Bud followed him inside.

61

He had changed very little in twenty years. Bud felt he would have recognized him anywhere. He was unwholesomely pale, his thin, bony face more weathered, but his hair was still all there, wild and coppery and unclean. There was a crust of flaking dandruff or worse around his hairline. Bud wondered how long it had been since he had seen a barber or given himself a shampoo.

His eyes were unchanged, bright blue and accusing, but his teeth seemed to be eroding, the edges serrated, almost transparent, possibly ground down from clenching, from repressed rage at his unanswered telephone calls.

He obviously did not recognize Bud, had barely even looked at him since that first hostile glare through the crack in the door.

Bud took in the room. It looked as dirty and uncared-for as it smelled. He wondered if it would get things off to a bad start if he asked to have a window opened.

The furniture in the den was good, expensive, old. But there was too much of it for the room—the finery from a larger home, more gracious days. Bud wondered if the sour smell came from the man himself or from a large calico cat that was now nestled in a corner of the sagging leather couch.

On every surface were leaning towers of manuscripts. There were rings from coffee cups or drinking glasses staining the top cover on each pile, some of them fainter than others, leading Bud to believe that the scripts had been there for months, possibly years, while some writer still waited hopefully by a telephone for word from the once-important director.

The walls of the room were ringed, in some places two and three deep, with cheaply framed eight-by-ten photographs of the movies that Flemming had directed. Right next to the door was a shot of Lyndon B. Johnson sitting in a canvas chair next to the director. They were both leaning back, laughing unself-consciously and Bud felt a quick stab of sadness that a man who had shared a joke with a president should now be living in such squalor, should be so badly in need of a scalp treatment.

Some of the pictures were head shots of famous or once-famous stars, all autographed, but most were unposed publicity stills taken on sound stages or on location. Bud moved away from the wall, away from the photographs, away from the past.

"The son of a bitch destroyed me" Gordon Flemming said, his voice casual, conversational. "I mean that literally." He flopped down in a worn damask chair and crossed his leg, his left ankle on his right knee, a laceless shoe dangling from his pale, prehensile toes.

From where Bud was standing, he could see that the director was naked under the now open robe, his limp mauve genitals crowded against the faded damask of the chair. Bud moved to the other side of the room to avoid the show.

"You want to tell me about it?" Bud asked, moving once more to try to escape both the view and the strong, sour smell of the room at the same time. He stood by the fireplace for a moment, but the odor there was overpowering. He looked into the fireplace and discovered the source of the stench. It was the cat's box bristling with grit-encrusted turds.

"What do you want to know about me?" Flemming asked. "I mean, do you want biographical stuff?" He looked eager, as if he were ready to launch into a recitation of his achievements.

"I know all about you professionally, sir," Bud said respectfully. He studied the director's face, his eyes, for a telltale sign of recognition, but there was none. Then he studied his own reflection in the mirror over the mantelpiece. Had he changed that much? He assumed that he must have.

"Then all you're interested in is where I was last night, the big night?" Flemming asked.

"To start with," Bud said, staring first out the door, then out the window. He knew that he could not look at the pictures on the wall. He would keep his gaze, if necessary, on the director's genitals rather than study the rows of photographs, because he knew with icy certainty what he would be looking for, knew that he would find it, knew that once having found it, he would not be able to do his work with a lot of authority.

"What are the chances of going into another room," Bud asked, "away from the cat shit?" It was only half the reason.

"Oh, sure," Flemming said, rising awkwardly to his feet, his left hand still deep in his pocket. There was something about the way he kept the hand in the pocket that aroused Bud's curiosity. The natural way to get out of a chair is to put one hand on each chair arm and push yourself up. What was unnatural was to keep one hand thrust into your pocket unless you were trying to hide something.

"It's that bitch of a maid of mine," Flemming said, walking across the dusty entry into an almost as stale-smelling living room. "She keeps telling me she's allergic to cat hair so she can't clean out the box. Those are the sort of things that keep happening to you when you fall from grace."

Bud looked around the living room. It was cluttered and musty, too. Bud figured that the bitch of a maid must have been allergic to Ajax and Lemon Pledge too.

"Where were you last night?" Bud asked, watching Flemming move around the room, his left hand still in his pocket, causing his left shoulder to rise almost to his ear.

"Right here, friend," Flemming said quickly, "in the cat-piss suite, all by myself. Of course, if I'd known it was going to happen, I'd have had a chic little party and invited all of his enemies, but the house would have been far too small."

"What's with your left hand?" Bud asked.

"None of your frigging business," Flemming said, a mirthless smile on his face. He sat down. This time he did not cross his legs, for which Bud was grateful, but his hand was still in his pocket.

"Just thought I'd ask," Bud said, getting annoyed, wondering if you could get a court order to make a man take his hand out of his pocket.

"Do you know how many times I've been nominated for an Academy Award?" Flemming asked.

"Is there anybody who can verify the fact that you were here last night?" Bud asked.

"Only my cats," Flemming said.

"What about the maid?"

"She comes on Mondays and Fridays. Sorry."

Bud suddenly lost interest in him as a suspect. He was enjoying it too much, center stage, the limelight. It was not the way the guilty come on. This man was weaving a drama about himself. The only thing Bud wanted to know now was about his left hand. It was more of a personal than a professional curiosity, a challenge to get him to withdraw the hand and whatever was in it.

"How well did you know Mr. Koenig?" Bud asked, walking around the living room, trying not to breathe too deeply.

"Do you know that he didn't perspire?" Flemming said in an awed voice. "The son of a bitch didn't sweat. Not a drop. Not ever."

Bud tried to remember, tried to recall the man from so many years before, leaning over him at studios under bright, hot lights, but all that came back to him from the past were the agent's pale, cold eyes, his impassive voice.

"He'd jog in place in his office while he was delivering some shit-ass news to you about your career," Flemming said. "A lot of agents are nice about it, will lie to you, but Koenig always wanted you to know about the producers and the studios who turned you down so you'd be humble and grateful and easier to handle."

Bud moved casually to the left side of Gordon Flemming's chair, then suddenly, deliberately, pretended to lose his footing and came crashing down on the director.

It worked. Flemming pulled his left hand out of his pocket to protect himself, and Bud saw what he was hiding. A bandaged hand. Only there was something missing and it looked to be the top half of his left middle finger.

"You want to tell me about that?" Bud said, indicating the bandaged hand.

"It has nothing to do with the murder," Flemming said, studying the bandaged finger stump impersonally, almost as if it had nothing to do with him, "but my hope is that the top half of this finger rides up Koenig's ass for the rest of eternity."

"What happened?" Bud asked. His curiosity was flying high now and he wanted to know about the missing finger, about the man's bitterness, even if it had nothing to do with the killing.

The telephone rang. Without a word or a nod, Flemming sprinted out the door and picked up the phone before the third ring, probably in the kitchen. There was an extension in the den, but the director had chosen not to answer it there, undoubtedly for reasons of privacy.

Bud walked back across the dusty entry floor into the den. He heard Flemming's voice raised high in protest. He kept repeating indignantly that he had sent a check the week before. It was nothing that could be helpful to Bud unless it was to generate more compassion for the man's failed life. Bud moved along the first wall, studying the pictures. He could hear the director's righteous voice rising and falling from the back of the house.

Two feet to the left of the fireplace he found the picture he was looking for. It was at eye level. He stood directly in front of it, staring at it, trying to believe that he was unaffected by it.

In the lower right-hand corner someone had printed *"The Little Renegade, 1960."* He felt his heart do something strange and alarming, but he kept his gaze on the overexposed photograph.

He could almost feel the intense, punishing heat of the desert. Everyone in the foreground had dark sweat rings on their shirts. D. P. Koenig was squatting on his haunches, talking to little Buddy Bacall, one hand raised to his forehead, shading himself from the brutal midday sun.

He saw Frank Bacola sitting on the first step of a portable dressing room. He was wearing cowboy boots and sunglasses and he was smiling. He had a large drinking glass in one hand. His other hand was resting easily on the bare shoulder of a young actress who was sitting next to him.

And over them all was Gordon Flemming, perched high on a camera crane, staring down at Koenig, his eyes riveted on the agent like a great bird of prey.

"I thought that was you!" Bud jumped involuntarily as he heard Flemming's voice directly behind him. He had been so absorbed in the picture that he had been unaware that anyone else was in the room with him.

"You little shit," Flemming said, grinning, pleased with himself. "Why didn't you say something?"

"That was another life," Bud said quietly.

"I remember how you used to follow him around like a little puppy dog," Flemming said, then added unpleasantly, "and you still are, only now he's dead and you're a full-grown bloodhound."

"Would you prefer I send another detective up to question you?" Bud asked formally.

"It doesn't matter," Flemming said with an awkward one-armed shrug. "I could care less who they send up here." His enthusiasm disappeared as quickly as it came. He studied Bud's face for a long time, walking around and around, his left hand still jammed into his pocket.

"I guess neither one of us is exactly knocking 'em dead these days," Flemming said morosely.

"I'm living in the present now, or I'm trying to. . . ."

"Here," Flemming said. He reached down and lifted some old newspapers from a large pile of scrapbooks. Bud could see the names of motion pictures embossed in gold on the spine of each book. He watched uneasily as the director's long, bony index finger traced each title.

Bud saw the *Little Renegade* scrapbook long before Flemming's finger got there.

"No, thank you," Bud said quickly. "I really don't have the time or the interest."

"Take it, take it," Flemming said. He started to pull the scrapbook from the center of the pile. "Put it in the trunk of your car."

As the scrapbook came free, the top two books slipped off the pile. The edge of the second book caught the rim of the cat box, sprinkling turds and grit over the floor, and partially exposing a large photograph that was being used as a liner for the cat box. Before Flemming had righted the box, Bud caught a glimpse of a young woman's face, hauntingly beautiful though blurred and warped by months, possibly even years, of cat piss.

"Say hello to Sabrina," Flemming said savagely.

Gordon Flemming liked young girls. He was no Humbert Humbert panting after twelve-year-old Lolitas, but once they passed eighteen he no longer found them exciting. The "Acne Lover," a not-too-close friend had dubbed him many years before. And the name had stuck.

He had been married twice, both times to girls well under seventeen, both times to girls with blotchy adolescent complexions and firm incredible bodies.

His first wife, Margie, was committed to a state institution for the insane six days after her eighteenth birthday. She was released two years later, and within a month her body was found washed up on a beach in Baja California.

His second wife, Jill, sued for divorce on their first anniversary. She married a Nebraska millionaire soon after, and she still sent Flemming a Christmas card each year, always including a recent snapshot of herself, more frumpily dressed with each passing season, always surrounded by her ever increasing brood of children, her waist encircled possessively by the beefy arm of her balding midwestern husband.

Gordon Flemming proposed marriage to three sixteen-year-old girls in the next four years. Two of them turned him down, one quite rudely, and the third accepted and then eloped with an Italian tile-setter less than a month before the planned nuptial.

And then D. P. Koenig introduced him to Sabrina LaFever. It had sounded to Flemming like a stripper's made-up name, but it was the name that appeared on her birth certificate. She was seventeen and crazy, her brain rotted with booze and dope and the other alternatives of the late seventies.

Koenig had spotted her on the Redondo Beach pier selling candied apples. She had a brooding, haunted face, dark and petulant, with a narrow, slightly too long nose that gave her face a character she did not possess. She was thin, with small, perfect breasts. Her legs were long and very firm, and she bit her fingernails.

Koenig brought her up to Brentwood and rented an apartment for her month to month. He took her to Elizabeth Arden and Georgette Klinger and Giorgio's, but there was no place he could take her to do anything about her brain. She was a fool, weak and vain and boring. But there was something unforgettable about her dark, pinched face, something that made you keep looking at it, and when you weren't with her, made you want to see the face again so that you could be sure you had it right.

69

Koenig used her badly. He did not sleep with her himself, but he fixed her up with disgruntled clients, gave them the key to the small Brentwood apartment, then telephoned her that she could expect company shortly.

He did not start her on drugs. She was already there when she sold him the stale candied apple in Redondo Beach. All he did was see that she was adequately, safely supplied so she would never have to go out on the street.

The community pacifier, she became known as in the business. The only requirement for her services was, according to Koenig, you don't have clap, you don't remove her from the apartment, pirate her away, but leave her as you found her in good condition for the next user.

When she wasn't fucking, Sabrina watched television, day and night, while she ate, while she bathed, while she was high on drugs or drunk on booze. Occasionally she found someone who didn't mind if she kept the television set on while they made love; then she would sneak glimpses of shows between their moist, plunging bodies.

Gordon Flemming was one of these. It amused him to thrust himself into her small, distracted body before Walter Cronkite, to ejaculate to reruns of "Happy Days."

For a long time he told himself that he wasn't hung up on her, that he could take her or leave her, but it was not so. When he was not with her, he thought of her constantly. Often he would leave a sound stage, with a cast and crew ready for action, while he would step to a private telephone just to hear her voice, to reassure himself that she was not with someone else.

He wanted to give her a screen test but Koenig refused. That was not what she was there for. Flemming offered her one anyway, but she turned him down. She was satisfied with her life the way it was. He became so enraged by this that he kicked over and broke her color

Zenith while she was watching "General Hospital." She burst into tears and raced into the bedroom to continue watching on another set.

Sabrina reported his violent outburst to Koenig. The agent telephoned Flemming immediately and told him that he had violated the terms of the understanding and that Sabrina was now off limits to him.

Flemming had laughed at this. He told Koenig to go to hell, the days of human bondage were over, and that he might even marry Sabrina, and then Koenig would once again have to pay off debts to his clients with Gucci briefcases instead of with Sabrina LaFever's flesh.

"I think not," was all that Koenig said. He hung up the telephone in Flemming's ear.

That evening, after he had dismissed the cast and crew early, Flemming drove to Sabrina's apartment. He tried to open the front door with his key. It didn't work. He stepped back to make sure he was on the right floor. He was. Then he rang the bell steadily for five minutes. The tenant next door, an out-of-work art director, grew weary of the noise and telephoned the landlord, who came up behind Flemming and removed his finger from the doorbell.

"She's gone," the landlord said. "The apartment's for rent."

"I don't believe you," Flemming said. "She was here just last night."

The landlord pulled out a large ring of keys. He searched through them methodically, trying one key after another until the door opened. The furniture was still there, clean and characterless, but the bric-a-brac was gone. Sabrina's memorabilia of months of impersonal sexual contacts had been removed.

Flemming ran through the apartment into the dark, shuttered bedroom. Sabrina never opened the shutters because it made the midday television images too pale. He pulled open the drawers in the bathroom. Everything was gone except for a thin film of face powder and a few pubic hairs on the tile floor.

"Where did she go?" Flemming asked the landlord, who was following him uneasily from room to room.

"How the hell should I know?" the landlord said, now wiggling his little finger in his ear. Flemming looked away quickly. "He came and took her away early this morning. Just her luggage, though."

"What about the furniture?" Flemming asked. "Where's the furniture going?"

"Bekins is coming out tomorrow to pick it up," the landlord said, now carefully examining the tip of his little finger. "It's going into storage, I think. The guy wanted to sell it to me, but I only rent unfurnished."

Flemming pushed past the landlord and ran back to his car. He drove through two traffic lights on his way to Koenig's office. He took the carpeted stairs three at a time and pushed past Peter Lutz, who had jumped up from his desk to intercept him.

"Where is she?" Flemming shouted. He tried to slam the door behind him, but Peter caught it and pushed it back open. He came in and stood somewhere halfway between Flemming and Koenig. It was so measured, so deliberate, that Flemming wondered if this were standard operating procedure. When an irate client confronts me, place yourself equidistant and stand poised for a quick karate chop should the meeting get out of hand.

"The matter is closed, Flemming," Koenig said quietly. "If you care to discuss your career with me, make an appointment with Mr. Lutz. If not, please leave now."

"You don't own her," Flemming said.

"Wherever did you get that idea?" Koenig said. "I do own her. Lock, stock, and barrel."

"White slavery is a fucking crime," Flemming shouted. "I could have you fucking arrested!" Out of the corner of his eye, Flemming could see Peter Lutz tensing, looking over at Koenig for a nod, a signal, to leap into action.

"I have an interesting feeler out for your services," Koenig said quietly. "It's a plum. A real plum."

"Where is she?"

"I know how you feel about doing television, but this is a quality two-hour. Top money."

"I love her," Flemming said in an unsteady voice. "For Christ's sake, Koenig, I want to marry her."

"Have you thought about seeking professional help?" Koenig asked. He smiled and moved around behind his desk and sat down. "She is an untrustworthy cunt and her head is fucked and always will be."

"Is she with someone else?" Flemming asked. "That's all I want to know."

"About this television project," Koenig said. "I think you should reconsider. Your career is not as viable as it once was." Flemming turned around and raced out of the office. He tried to slam the door, but Peter Lutz stopped it with his foot.

Sabrina LaFever was in Manhattan. The timing had been perfect for Koenig. The day that Gordon Flemming kicked in her television set, Koenig had signed Shamid Hakim as a client.

Shamid was the bastard offspring of a Saudi prince and his Syrian concubine. The prince had sired thirteen ugly daughters by assorted wives, and although his only son was not welcome in the royal household, his father took care of him generously. He was educated at Harvard, and although he was not a brilliant student, he graduated in the top half of his class.

His father bought the entire twenty-ninth floor of the Olympic Towers in New York City for him as a graduation present. In repayment for his father's generosity, Shamid wrote a five-hundred-page intimate history of the Hakim dynasty, filled with sordid and sexual reve-

73

lations told to him during his formative years by his vengeful and loquacious mother.

He had entitled it *The Curtain of Sand,* and although abysmally written, it was filled with such filth and degeneracy that Koenig knew he had a best seller by the time he had read the fourth page.

Shamid was twenty-five, with greasy, thinning hair and pockmarks. He wore black shantung suits and contact lenses and tended to touch his genitals when he was under a lot of pressure. There had even been complaints about this in the elevators of the Olympic Towers.

Shamid was signing his contract and requesting a date with a starlet when Sabrina called Koenig about Gordon Flemming's assault on her Zenith. Koenig turned instantly to Shamid, spoke lyrically of Sabrina LaFever's depravity, and suggested that Shamid buy her a first-class round-trip airplane ticket so she could grace his next few weeks in New York.

It was not difficult for Flemming to discover where his love had been stashed. All he had to do was read Radie Harris's column in the *Hollywood Reporter.* She referred to Sabrina LaFever as "a Cleveland heiress," which, had he not been in such a severe state of anguish, would have amused Flemming. The column hinted that she was in residence on the twenty-ninth floor of the Olympic Towers and that she looked bewitching in her Arabic wardrobe.

The moment Flemming read this, he packed a small overnight case and took the red-eye to New York. He went directly to the Olympic Towers, but was stopped at the desk by the manager, who, though well-dressed, looked as if he could have gone a round or two if he had to.

"I'm here to see Miss LaFever," Flemming said.

"Name, please?" Flemming gave his name, enunciating each syllable nastily. The manager looked up from a list of names he had been reading. "I'm sorry. I cannot allow you to go up to that apartment."

Flemming looked icily at the manager for a moment, then turned and walked toward the elevators. Suddenly three large men came from the office behind the desk and stood in front of Flemming, who looked at them, then at the manager, then turned and walked quickly out of the building.

He checked in at the Warwick Hotel, showered, shaved, and looked up Shamid Hakim in the telephone directory. Much to his surprise, he found the listing—no address, just a telephone number.

He was told by what was probably a secretary that Miss LaFever could not be disturbed. He called back seven times within the next three hours and was given the same message. It could even have been true. It was the midday block of time dedicated to the soaps, which he knew she never missed.

Then he telephoned Radie Harris, whom he had met once years before after the opening of a motion picture he had directed. He told her briefly about his obsessional love for the "Cleveland heiress" and begged her to arrange a meeting, to somehow get him together with Sabrina to plead his case.

Radie Harris told Flemming she was invited to a party that Shamid Hakim was giving that evening in honor of a visiting Persian Gulf potentate. She told Flemming that he could be her escort.

There was an Arab guard standing at the door with what had to be a gun bulging from under his tuxedo jacket. He had a list of names on a clipboard. As guests entered, he checked off their names after carefully examining their identification.

The door was opened by another Arab. He nodded courteously to Radie Harris and escorted them through the long travertine entry into the living room.

Flemming had never seen a room like it before. It was

enormous, and two walls were solid window from floor to ceiling with a view southward to Greenwich Village. The carpets were thick and lustrous, the furniture tasteless and costly.

Flemming looked around in the sea of Middle Eastern faces for a glimpse of Sabrina. He did not find her. But what he did find was D. P. Koenig's face glaring at him over the shoulders of two expensively dressed guests. Flemming nodded and smiled, then turned away. He excused himself from Radie Harris and headed for a long corridor leading to the bedrooms where he assumed he would find Sabrina stretched out on a bed watching television.

The corridor was lined with filthy *Arabian Nights* illustrations depicting every position known to man or beast. The veiled women's vaginas were freakishly enlarged and appeared to be suffering more from edema than sexual arousal.

He had opened only two doors by the time they got to him. He was led back into the living room. A heavyset man in a tuxedo had hold of his upper arm. He felt the pressure of the man's fingers. Once he tried to shrug off his hand, but the fingers tightened and Flemming knew it would be useless to try to free himself.

"It's all over, Gordon," Koenig said to him. "She doesn't want to see you anymore."

"Go fuck yourself," Flemming said, his voice almost conversational.

"She's not worth it. You must trust me on this."

Flemming mingled with the guests, trying to make small talk with the overly polite Arabs at the party, resenting their wealth, their presence in his country, the natural accident of oil beneath their uneducated asses that had miraculously changed them from camel herders to captains of finance.

He saw Sabrina the moment she walked into the living room. He checked his wristwatch and saw that it was

76

exactly seven-thirty. He smiled, knowing that her presence there at this exact moment meant only one thing. Station break.

Even across the room he could tell by her eyes that she was on something, probably cocaine. She was wearing a shimmering maroon-and-gold kaftan and he could see her small, dark nipples and her pubic triangle through the costly dress. She was barefoot, and he could see what appeared to be golden bells tied to her toes. She could make music wherever she went, which Flemming knew wouldn't be far because she was the laziest female he had ever come across, and he was still hopelessly in love with her.

She saw him almost immediately. She gave him a quick, vacant smile, then turned away from him and slipped her arm through the arm of a small, seedy-looking man who Flemming assumed was Shamid Hakim.

Flemming walked over to Sabrina. He stood next to her, wanting to reach out and touch her, to pull her toward him, to cover her near-nakedness so no one else in the large windowed room could see what he felt belonged only to him.

"Go away," she whispered to him. "Please."

"I just want to talk to you, Sabrina," he said, his voice low so as not to distract Shamid, who was speaking with two equally small, equally seedy-looking Middle Eastern types.

"Why did you do it?" she asked. He assumed she meant break her television set, the cardinal sin in her life. He wondered if she had ever asked Koenig the same question. Why did you do it? Why did you supply me with drugs, use my body to further your career? He was positive those questions would never have occurred to her. Only the Big One. Why did you break my television set?

Sabrina slipped around to the other side of Shamid and began talking to a dumpy dark woman with a pronounced mustache. She, too, was wearing a shimmering, see-through kaftan, but Flemming determinedly did not want to.

"I have to talk to you," Flemming whispered, looking around, fully expecting to be attacked bodily for daring to speak to her.

"They won't let me," she said.

"Who is *they?*" Flemming asked.

"Everybody," Sabrina said and smiled philosophically to show that she did not, would not, question this order. She is a dumb cunt, Flemming thought, undeserving of his or anybody's love, but as he thought it, he was filled with an overwhelming need to pull aside the gossamer gown and fasten his lips possessively over her dark, indifferent nipples.

He turned away from her long enough to help himself to a heaping tablespoon of Iranian caviar. He had never seen that much caviar at one time before. He figured that the glistening bowl probably cost more than his round-trip air fare from Los Angeles. He had three more helpings and smiled as he calculated the cost in air miles. He believed he had consumed enough to transport him to Kansas City.

Sabrina looked at her wristwatch. It was new, or at least Flemming had never seen it before. Lots of gold, lots of diamonds. Probably a gift of gratitude from the Arab. He watched her lips move as she strained to tell the time. She looked guiltily around, then, without a word to anyone, darted back down the hallway and disappeared into a room, closing the door behind her.

Flemming waited for a moment, then slipped out of the living room, down the hall in pursuit of his love. He opened the third door, having tried the other two earlier. She was bending over the TV set, adjusting the image. He could see her ass through the dress, see the lean, taut flesh. He walked quickly across the room and embraced her from behind, straightening her up, pulling her hard against him.

Flemming did not remember too clearly what happened in the next few seconds. He remembered only that the door to the hallway opened and there was Koenig, flanked by two unsmiling Arabs. Suddenly Sabrina burst into tears, something Flemming had never seen happen before, possibly because he had never interrupted her during "Laverne and Shirley" before. She pulled away from him and ran into the bathroom.

"Let her go," Koenig said, but Flemming paid no attention, believing insanely that he might reach the sanctuary of the bathroom and lock himself and Sabrina LaFever within its imported marble depths forever.

Just as Flemming reached the bathroom, Sabrina slammed the heavy oak door with a violence he had not suspected her capable of. Without thinking, he put his hand on the jamb to keep the door from closing him out, from keeping him away from her.

He felt for an instant a cold, stabbing pain in his hand, up his arm. Then the pain was replaced by a warm, sour surge that rose from his stomach to his head. Then he lost consciouness.

When he came to, his hand was wrapped in a satin pillowcase already soaked with blood. He was being helped to his feet by the two Arabs. He tried to unwind the crimson pillowcase, but one of the Arabs warned him, almost kindly, not to do it. As he was being led out of the room, he saw Sabrina leaning over once again trying to adjust the television set.

In the emergency room at the hospital an unshaven young doctor gently unwound the pillowcase from his hand.

"Christ," the doctor said wearily, "where's the rest of it?" Flemming looked down at his hand and it was only then that he discovered that two-thirds of his middle finger was missing.

Nobody seemed to know where the finger was. The two Arabs who brought him to the hospital spoke quietly to each other for a moment, then both of them turned to the doctor and shrugged.

The doctor looked once more at the wound, then told one of the Arabs to call and have somebody for Christ's sake find the finger, put it in a glass of salt water and rush it to the hospital immediately.

Flemming watched with dazed detachment as one of them telephoned. There was a lot of Arabic order-giving and a lot of waiting. Finally the men hung up the telephone and turned to the doctor.

"They can't find it," he said. Flemming thought the man might have been repressing a smile.

"Is there anybody there who might know something about your finger?" the doctor asked Flemming. He seemed unsure of himself suddenly. Sewing on a missing finger was one thing. Locating it was something else.

Flemming telephoned the apartment and asked to speak to Sabrina. He was told that she could not be disturbed. Then Flemming asked to speak to Koenig. He assumed he had started to pass out because the doctor held something acrid and stinging up to his nose.

"Yes?" Flemming heard Koenig's voice, clear and impersonal and impatient—the voice of a man who would not want to be pulled away from fresh Iranian caviar for something as unimportant as a man in the process of bleeding to death.

"Where's my finger, you fucking asshole?" Flemming said, moving his head away from the doctor's hand, away from the jarring odor.

"Oh, it's you," Koenig said. "Are you all right?"

"Get your ass over here with the rest of my finger," Flemming shouted.

"I told you she was a bummer," Koenig said, "that she was crazy and dangerous and depraved."

"I'm bleeding to death," Flemming said weakly. "Get over here with my goddamn finger!"

"I can't do that, old man," Koenig said, his voice soft, placating. "It can't be done."

"Why not?" Flemming asked, staring impersonally at his injured hand.

"It was Sabrina. She thought the sight of the finger would upset you when you came to, so she flushed it down the toilet."

"Is this a joke, Koenig?"

"I told you her brain was gone," Koenig said.

"I want a transplant," Flemming said. "Somebody owes me part of a finger." Flemming turned to the now attentive and curious doctor. "My fucking finger is in the fucking Hudson River."

"Too bad it's the middle one," the doctor said. "We get much better results on end fingers."

Gordon Flemming fainted again.

Bud tried to remember what Gordon Flemming had looked like twenty years earlier, tried to visualize him at the height of his vigor and success, but nothing would come except the eyes. He remembered the eyes that tried and convicted you in the same glance, the cutting edge of his voice. And that was it. His brain refused to let him churn up anything more.

"Have you seen Sabrina LaFever since that night?" Bud asked. Flemming did not answer. He continued sitting in his chair, idly studying the soiled bandage on his left hand. Bud repeated the question.

"I talked to her once after that," Flemming said finally, his voice thin, devoid of all energy. "I telephoned the apartment every station break for three days. Thank Christ it wasn't my dialing finger."

Finally she picked up the telephone herself. He could hear the sound of a commercial in the background. He could also hear a stern, male voice insisting that she hang up.

"Why did you do it?" Flemming asked her. "How could you do that to someone who loved you, someone who wanted to marry you?"

"The finger was just lying there on the floor," she told

him. "I asked Mr. Koenig what I should do with it, and he said to throw it in the john, so I did. And then, with all the excitement, I forgot, and I wee-weed on it and flushed it down the toilet."

"Where is she now?" Bud asked, making a major effort not to smile.

"The last I heard," Flemming said, his face breaking into a mirthless grin, "the Arab took her home with him. I like to think of her there being buggered by all those stinking savages with no American television to solace her."

"Have you made any further effort to get in touch with her?"

"No," Flemming said slowly. "Every time I start thinking about her, fantasizing about her, suddenly I get this really clear image of her sitting on the pot pissing on my finger."

"You no longer have any emotional feelings for Miss LaFever?" Bud asked.

"Christ, man," Flemming said impatiently, "how could a person of my taste and sensibilities remain in love with someone who actually says 'wee-wee'?"

"How long ago did all this happen?" Bud asked. "I mean, the party in New York, the accident with your finger?"

"Oh, three, four months," Flemming said. "I don't remember exactly."

Bud was shocked. He had estimated a month, possibly three weeks. He looked more closely at the bandaged hand and saw for the first time how crude, unprofessional, the gauze wrapping appeared to be.

"Why is your hand still bandaged?"

"Lest we forget," Flemming said lightly. "Lest we forget."

"When was the last time you saw D. P. Koenig?"

"About a month ago," Flemming said. "I ran into him at the City National Bank. It was awkward because

82

he hadn't answered my last four hundred phone calls."

"Why had you been calling him?"

"Why do you ever call your agent? Because you're staring at the four walls and you want to lay a guilt trip on him because he hasn't gotten you work."

"What happened at the bank?"

"I walked over to him and we shook hands. In a way, I almost admired him because he didn't make any excuses for not having returned my calls. I asked him about Sabrina, and he said he hadn't heard a word from her since the New York thing, but that somebody had tried to bump off Shamid Hakim, had sent a spray of bullets into his limousine on a street in Damascus."

"Did Koenig know who it was?" Bud asked.

"No, but he said, after that book, it was probably a literary critic."

"And that was all?"

"No," Flemming said slowly. "Just as he was about to step up to the teller, he turned to me and said, 'Since you're on a downtick professionally, how would you feel about directing a dirty movie?'"

"I asked him, 'How dirty? I mean, there's *Last Tango in Paris* and then there's *Trader Horny*.' He looked at me and smiled and said, 'Try *Trader Horny*.'"

"And what was your reaction?"

"If it were a hundred years ago, I'd have slapped him across the face with my gloves. I thought of hitting him with the letter telling me I was overdrawn, but it wouldn't have been quite the same thing."

"Why were you trying to reach him on the day before he was murdered? You called five times. Why?"

"If he had returned my first call, I assure you I would only have called him once."

"Did it ever occur to you to change agents?"

"In this town, you only change agents when you're

hot, when you're in demand, when other agents telephone you day and night, leave their cards under your
windshield wiper. That's when you make the move.
When *they* call you. If you have to call them, tell them
you're looking around, they treat you like dirt, tell you
there's no room in their stable for you, they have too
many similar 'genre' directors. Shit like that."

Flemming began pacing around, quickly warming to
his subject. Bud was sorry that he had sidetracked him
with the irrelevant question.

"I hate this town," the director continued. "If I could
make five thousand dollars a week laying carpeting, I'd
be out of here in a flash."

"What did you want to speak to D. P. Koenig about?"

"I was going to tell him that *Trader Horny* was starting to look good to me." The director let out a shrill,
hollow laugh. "A man who was nominated eight times
for an Academy Award couldn't get through to tell his
son of a bitch of an agent that he's been brought so low
he'd consent to directing a filthy flick."

"Did you go to D. P. Koenig's house any time on Tuesday night?"

"I told you," Flemming said, "I was here with the cat
turds."

"And you've never seen Sabrina LaFever since the
night you lost your finger?"

"Talking about cat turds," Flemming said, his grin
suddenly so wide that Bud could see his pale, receding
gums. Then he stopped smiling. "No, not since that
night. Three months, four months. Who the hell remem-
bers?"

"Did Koenig ever see her again?"

"Don't ask me. Ask that gung-ho fruitcake of a secretary of his."

"I guess I'll have to do that," Bud said. He closed his
notebook and headed for the front door.

"I happen to be a very good director," Flemming said.

"There's a whole cult of people who worship me in France and Belgium."

"You have a fine reputation," Bud said distractedly, flipping through his note pad.

"I'd just as soon nobody knew about the dirty movie," Flemming said. "I mean, it's not even as if I would ever have consented to do it."

"All interrogations are private," Bud said, still flipping through the pages. "Don't worry about it." He saw the word "knife" on a page all by itself just as he was opening the front door.

"They love me in Spain, too."

"I would like to look in your kitchen," Bud said.

"No problem," Flemming said lightly. He led Bud through a dark, sour-smelling hallway and pantry into the kitchen. By contrast to the rest of the house, the kitchen was dazzlingly clean and orderly. There were a top-of-the-line Cuisinart, a Mixmaster and an electric can opener lined up on the spotless tile counter. There was a large businesslike six-burner stove, also spotless. Hanging from the ceiling was a metal rack filled with fine pots and pans, wire whisks, a mesh basket filled with plump white onions.

"Who's the cook?" Bud asked.

"I told you they loved me in France," Flemming said.

Bud's eyes fastened on the wall over Flemming's right shoulder. He felt a quickening in his heart as he moved across the kitchen and studied a set of knives protruding from a mounted block of wood.

It was a set of five knives in graduating sizes. Bud removed the largest of the knives and studied it. He read the single word Sabatier. Then he picked up the second-largest knife. It looked the same as the others but it was not part of the set. The other three knives all had the word Sabatier on the wooden handle.

"Tell me about this knife," Bud said quietly, holding up the second-largest knife.

85

"What the hell are you talking about?" Flemming asked, a look of genuine bewilderment on his face.

"This knife is not part of the set," Bud said. "I would like to see the knife that belongs to this set." Flemming held out his hand for the knife. He studied it for a moment. Bud studied him studying it. How simple, Bud thought. It's all over. I've found the murderer.

"That asshole," Flemming said quietly. He handed Bud the knife and started searching through his top drawers, one at a time. "She never puts anything where it belongs." Bud decided he would let the director go through the charade of looking for the right knife for another minute or so, and then he would let him get out of his soiled bathrobe and take him to headquarters.

"I used to have only German help," Flemming said, still rattling through the drawers. "They respected *things*. Not like these uncaring wetbacks."

"I think maybe you and I are going to have to do a little more talking," Bud said.

"You know what a German couple goes for these days?" Flemming asked, his voice conversational, untroubled, as he moved his search to a series of lower drawers. "I understand Bob Evans is paying twenty-five hundred a month and they get the use of a Mercedes 280."

"For that kind of money," Bud said, "the least they could do is punch up his scripts."

"Well, it's not here," Flemming said, straightening up. "I'm so good to that bitch and I'll bet she walked off with one of my best knives."

"I'm afraid it won't wash, Mr. Flemming," Bud said softly. The director looked at him for a long, quiet beat, then he smiled.

"Wash, of course," Flemming said and walked around Bud across the kitchen and opened the door of the dishwasher. The knife was there, sticking out of the bottom tray. Flemming picked it up, studied it, his eyes indignant.

"That spic bitch," he said, then handed the knife to Bud. "You can tell them a million times not to put knives in the dishwasher and it doesn't do any good."

Bud studied the knife, was sure it was identical to the murder weapon, didn't know if he were relieved or disappointed.

"I'm going to have to take this with me."

"Fine," the director said easily. "Just don't put it in the goddamn dishwasher."

"Are you sure there's nothing that you've said you'd like to retract, change, add to?"

"Do you know that at the Spoleto Film Festival they stood up and cheered after my last movie was shown?"

"How long ago was that?" Bud asked, his voice overly polite.

"Go screw yourself," the director answered, almost good-naturedly.

They walked back through the acrid-smelling hallway. Flemming opened the door with his right hand. His left hand was jammed down hard into his bathrobe pocket.

"I used to be so frightened of you," Bud said gently.

"It's been a long time since anyone's been frightened of me," Flemming said with a wistful smile. "Now the most I seem to be able to inspire in people is a . . . sense of embarrassment."

"You're not planning on leaving town, are you?" Bud asked.

"I wish I were," Flemming said sadly. "I wish to hell I were."

Bud walked outside quickly and filled his lungs with the fresh midday air.

Bud climbed into his car and put the key in the ignition. He closed his eyes and tried to reach far back into his memory to see why Gordon Flemming had frightened him twenty years before, to see if it would serve as a clue as to why Gordon Flemming still unsettled him so profoundly.

I should get the hell off this case, Bud said to himself. Then he started the car, almost flooding the engine, and headed west on Sunset Boulevard to Brentwood.

5

Glenda Deering lived in Brentwood, just north of Sunset Boulevard. Because it is closer to the Pacific Ocean, it is cooler than Beverly Hills. The moisture content of the air is higher, resulting in greener lawns, denser foliage. It also has almost daily coastal fog.

Brentwood Park is on the west side of Brentwood. The larger, more costly and desirable homes are located here. Many of Hollywood's most famous stars live or have lived in The Park. As a child, Shirley Temple lived on Rockingham Drive in The Park. One of the more imposing homes on the street today was once Shirley Temple's dollhouse, built by the Temples so that their famous child could have a place of her own, somewhere to display the dolls and gifts that were sent to her from admirers all over the world.

Glenda Deering just lived in Brentwood, not Brentwood *Park*. Her house was small but elegant, a gray Regency with black trim and costly landscaping. Her

Mercedes was parked in a trellised carport next to a tricycle, a scooter and a box of children's toys.

It startled Bud. There was nothing of the mother about this woman with her sleek legs and demented green eyes. He wondered what the mother of a child who still rode a tricycle would be doing on her hands and knees looking under the bed of a recently murdered agent.

He walked up the brick pathway with its colorfully planted borders, trying to recall the few facts in the written report the Department had prepared for him. He had only been able to glance at it while he waited at traffic lights on his way up there. He took out the report again and studied it as he walked.

She was thirty-four, born and raised in Canton, Ohio, married twice. First husband, Milo Grooms (a suicide). Second husband, Roger Deering, deceased (natural causes). Two children: Monica, age seven, James, age five. Was left a sizable estate, contested by the Deering family. Moved from Ohio to Los Angeles in 1977. Had bit parts in three motion pictures. No talent, according to all three producers. Hired Jeremy Salters, a publicist, in 1978. Throws lavish parties. Has been linked in the columns with Maximilian Schell, Warren Beatty, Richard Maxwell—and the report went on to list an assortment of what Bud assumed to be directors, writers, producers, millionaires, merchants, many of whose names were not familiar to him.

He rang the doorbell, and when there was no response, he pushed the button again. Almost instantly the door was opened by a large black woman in a pink polyester uniform. Her eyes were blazing with hostility.

"I heard the first ring," she said, unwilling to let him off with just a dirty look.

"Mrs. Deering, please," Bud said, holding his badge up for her to look at. Over her massive shoulder he could see silver-framed snapshots of two redheaded children.

"She be right there," the maid said, still eying him suspiciously. She left him standing in the open doorway, did not invite him further into the house. He was used to it. It didn't mean he liked it. It just meant he was used to it.

As he stood in the doorway, he heard the telephone ring. It was picked up instantly somewhere in the back of the house. By moving across the entrance hall he was able to hear Glenda Deering's voice.

"Oh," he was able to make out, "I thought I'd hear from you." Even through the walls, he could hear the cold anger in her voice. There was a long pause, and then she said, "No, I'm afraid not, duckie, it wasn't there."

"You can wait in this room here," the black woman said to him. She came up behind him so quietly that he jumped when she spoke. She led him out of the hallway into a handsomely furnished den and then closed the heavy double doors behind her.

He walked around the room, touching the backs of chairs, feeling the heavy crewel drapes. He'd been around the decorators' showrooms enough to know that what she had here was the finest, the most expensive. No wonder she couldn't afford to get to Pasadena.

He took out the report again. As he was studying it, he heard the doors open, and Glenda Deering walked in, an artificial smile on her face, the gracious hostess greeting the guest of honor. It amused him, and he felt sorry for her, for the effort he knew this cordiality must have cost her.

She was wearing a long green dress, thin and gauzy, more suitable for a Roman orgy than a late-afternoon interview with a cop. But it was tasteful, and obviously expensive, and he wondered if he'd be able to ask the right questions with her nipples standing out like two jelly beans. She was barefoot and her toenails were painted bright red. She was wearing a thin gold ring on

91

the second toe of her left foot. He was determined not to ask her about it.

"Hi," she said. "I'm fixing myself something to drink. Can I fix you something?"

"I'll take a Diet Pepsi, something like that."

"Are you serious? That stuff gives you brain damage. How about plain soda?"

"Fine."

"With some Scotch in it?"

"Just soda's fine."

She fixed the drinks, served them in cut-glass tumblers that he knew had to cost over twenty bucks apiece. Then she sat down on a chair across from him and swung one leg up on the arm of the chair. It was a floor-length dress, but he ended up seeing a lot of thigh. So it was going to be that kind of interview. He probably wouldn't learn much, but getting there was half the fun.

"What was your relationship to Koenig?" he asked.

"Very weird," she said finally. "Sweet, sort of, in a way, but really weird."

"Do you have any idea who might have killed him?"

"No. Do you?"

"All right, then, do you have any idea who might have had a motive for murdering him?"

"Oh, I don't know," she said. "Just about everyone, I guess." As she spoke, she moved her leg so that he could see up past her pale thighs, could see that she was wearing absolutely nothing under the green gauze dress. Doesn't anyone in this fucking town wear underpants? Bud wondered, but he did not move or shift his gaze.

Suddenly she burst into tears, sobbed noisily there on the fine tapestry chair, her white thighs flashing at him from across the room.

He waited for her to compose herself, even got up and poured himself another soda, while she sniffed and sobbed and dabbed at her crazy green eyes. Her mascara blurred and ran, making her look like a Barbi doll that had been left out in the rain.

She made no effort to look in a mirror or repair her stained face, and he found himself liking her for that. She even took her leg off the arm of the chair so that he could no longer look up her skirt, a hopeful sign, he felt, that she might now start to tell him the truth.

She let him fix her another drink; he made it a stiff one, and then she told him how she had come to know D. P. Koenig.

She met him at a party in Malibu during the summer of 1977. She had only been out there for a few days and had telephoned a friend of a friend because she had grown tired of sitting in her room at the Beverly Wilshire Hotel crying and ordering piña coladas from room service.

At the time she was thirty-two, twice widowed, and, until she arrived in Hollywood she believed she was rich. In Canton, Ohio, she was rich. Out here she knew that she would run out of money long before she could parlay it into something meaningful. That is, if she could manage to hang on to it at all, what with those crazy Deerings nipping at her heels since the day of the funeral.

Nobody thought Roger Deering would ever actually marry her, even though she bore him two children out of wedlock. He took good care of her, though, bought her a nice little house just outside Canton, and sent a black woman there twice a week to do the heavy work.

He visited the children at least every other day, took them to the circus, and on holidays he would take them to his mother's home, staring stonily at the old woman until she smiled at them, embraced them, offered them candy from the milk-glass dish on the coffee table.

Roger Deering had started out as a crop duster, and ended up owning five planes with five pilots working for him full time. Everybody believed he would never marry—this exemplary boy, and then man, who supported his mother and his three sisters and their families. So when, at the age of fifty-four, he told them that he was going to marry for the first time, make Glenda Grooms his wife, legitimatize his two children, they were understandably shocked, and demanded to know why.

"Because she's never asked me for a thing," he told them.

He married her, and less than two weeks later he was dead. An aneurism. And, as the Deerings all said for years to come, "the *slut* got all the money." He had changed his will the day before the wedding, and Glenda got it all.

The day after the will was read, Glenda took the children to her aunt's house and then got on an airplane and flew out to Los Angeles. She had never been there before, had never even been out of Ohio—but a year after the suicide of her first husband she had slept with a man, an ABC executive, who had told her to call if she ever got out to Hollywood, and had given her his card.

Nobody else had ever given her his card, so she flew to Hollywood. She telephoned the man, who was no longer at ABC, but they gave her a new telephone number. He had an answering machine with an annoying announcement. She left her number with the vague message about being the redheaded girl from Canton, then hung up, never expecting to hear from him.

The following day, however, he telephoned her and told her he was living with someone, but he had a friend, Jeremy Salters, a press agent, who'd just been booted out by his old lady and could use some good Ohio cheering up. She told him he could give his friend her phone number.

Jeremy Salters called her within ten minutes and invited her out to lunch. She didn't like the way he sounded, too loud, too eager, so she said no, but asked for his phone number.

94

Two days later she called him. He was quieter, even admitted to her over the phone that he had been crying, and he asked her if she wanted to go to a party at the beach. "An A party," he told her, and, at the time, she didn't even know what that meant.

She put on slacks and a shirt over her bathing suit, and picked out a dress to change into later. She telephoned her aunt to find out how her children were. She talked to the children, one at a time, and then her aunt told her that the Deerings had just hired the best law firm in Canton to fight the will.

She stared uneasily out the window onto Wilshire Boulevard until the desk called and told her that a Mr. Salters was waiting for her out front in his car.

It had been a slight exaggeration. It was only a B party, but to Glenda Deering from Canton, Ohio, the realization that she was stretched out on a Brown-Jordan lounger with William Windom, pink and perspiring, on one side of her, and Rosemary Clooney on the other, was heady stuff.

Jeremy sat at the foot of her lounger and stopped people as they passed to introduce her, to show her off. She knew that she was far and away the best-looking woman at the party and she found herself turning each time she heard the glass doors slide open to see if someone with a prettier face, a sexier body, had shown up to displace her.

She went swimming in the ocean, careful not to get her hair wet. As she paddled just beyond the breakers, she saw a white-haired man swimming toward her. He was moving in a straight line, parallel to the shore, his strokes strong, his form perfect. She did not move out of his way because she was sure he had seen her and would avoid her at the last moment, but he swam right into her. He stopped and looked up at her, startled, and then treaded water next to her.

"This is my ocean," he said smiling, and she saw that

the face under the white hair, now flattened down over his forehead, was lean and clear and did not seem to belong with the white hair. "What the hell are you doing in here without my permission?"

She told him that she had never seen an ocean before that day, except in movies, and had never even been in salt water before.

"Okay, then, you get a pass because you're the prettiest person in Malibu today." He smiled at her, then swam away. She watched him rise on a wave, and only when he was twenty yards away from her, when she saw the sun reflecting off his pale, lean ass, did she realize that he was naked. Maybe it is his ocean after all, she thought.

When she came out of the water, she changed into the dress she had brought along with her. It was from the best store in Canton. It was a vivid print, slit on both sides from the floor to her upper thighs, and she wore a wide gold belt decorated with rhinestones and high-heeled gold evening sandals to match. She found a hibiscus bush near the dressing room and broke off a flower and pinned it in her hair.

When she joined the party again, Jeremy was already drunk and noisy. He had spilled some cocktail sauce down the front of his expensive sport shirt and either didn't notice it or didn't care, because he was making no effort to clean it off. She decided that she did not like him and joined a group of people as far away from him as she could get.

He spotted her and lurched over to her across the used-brick patio. He draped his arm possessively over her shoulders, letting his finger tips rest on her bare collarbone, and it annoyed her. She moved away from him, but he followed her and tried to kiss her on the mouth. His breath stank of scotch and his lips were greasy from the cocktail franks.

She pushed him away so hard that he lost his balance,

took several steps backward, and then went down. All the guests turned instantly to stare at the drunken young man on the ground and the overdressed woman who had pushed him there. They remained where they were and continued talking animatedly, either out of tact or indifference.

Glenda bent down to where he was lying on the sandy bricks.

"Are you okay?" she whispered. He did not answer. She was sure he was not dead, just passed out, and she was filled with rage toward him. When she looked up, she saw him—saw the naked white-haired man who owned the ocean. He was looking at her from next door and he was wearing blue jeans and a sweatshirt. He scaled the low brick wall that separated the two houses and walked across the sand to her.

"Are you with him?" he asked her, indicating the unconscious man still lying at her feet.

"Yes, goddamn it," she said. "He's been drinking since we got here." The white-haired man leaned down and grabbed Jeremy's hand and pulled him into a sitting position.

"All right, Jer," he said, shaking him, his voice loud and commanding, "shape up, now."

"Oh, you know him," Glenda said, startled.

"Yeah, he used to work for me. How do you know him?" The white-haired man picked Jeremy up and effortlessly slung him over his shoulder. By now the host and hostess and most of the guests who weren't too smashed themselves had gathered around them.

"I just met him today," Glenda said quickly, disavowing any responsibility, any affiliation. Neither of her husbands had been drinkers, had never been even slightly tipsy in her presence, so she found Jeremy Salters, who was drooling complacently down his ex-employer's back, weak and contemptible.

With barely a nod to the host and hostess, the white-haired man turned and walked down the sand, almost to the high-tide mark, to where their mutual wall stopped; then he turned with his burden and walked back up toward his own house.

She did not know whether to remain at the party and hope someone would drive her home, or follow the white-haired man and try to revive Jeremy so that she could drive him home.

She walked down onto the sand, her high-heeled evening shoes sinking with each step. She walked around the wall and followed the white-haired man up onto his patio. She looked through the opened doorway, past the expensive potted trees, into the living room, where she saw the white-haired man bend forward and let his dead-weight burden roll onto a large rattan couch. As he fell, Jeremy's head hit the curved rattan arm with a blow loud enough for her to hear all the way out on the patio.

She walked into the living room and stood leaning against the door frame, watching the white-haired man as he took off Jeremy's shoes. She wondered if it were thoughtfulness or just a concern that he might get sand on the upholstery.

"Go fix us something to drink," he said without turning around to look at her. "The bar's on the way to the kitchen. I'll have straight bourbon." Then, still without looking at her, he walked down the dark hallway leading from the living room and disappeared. She walked over to the bar and poured his drink, wondering if straight meant with or without ice cubes, then decided to let him get his own ice if that's what he wanted.

She believed she heard him talking to someone in another part of the house, believed she heard a woman's voice also, raised in protest about something. A few moments later she heard a side door open and then slam shut. She walked into the kitchen and looked out the window over the sink. She saw a tall, thin girl in a bikini walking toward the street. She had a pair of sandals in one hand and car keys in the other.

Glenda walked to the refrigerator and found a Coke, which she opened and started to drink right out of the can. She picked up the glass of bourbon and went back into the living room. She turned a chair away from Jeremy's slack, drunken face and sipped thoughtfully on her Coke.

A moment later she heard a car engine start. She believed whoever was behind the wheel must have been angry because they gunned the motor all the way down Malibu Road.

"Do you have to go out of your way to look trashy," he asked, walking up behind her, "or does it come naturally to you?"

"What do you mean, trashy?" she asked, turning quickly to look up at him to see if he was smiling, to find out if this was just some cruel Hollywood come-on. But he was not smiling. He reached down and picked up his drink.

"That dress, the belt, those shoes," he said. "Individually they're bad enough, but together they're unspeakable."

"Who the hell are you?" she said finally. Only then did she realize how tired she was, and how bewildering and frightening she had found the entire day, how much she hated the town, the beach, the rude, uncaring people.

She rose to her feet, set the Coke on the coffee table, and started to walk out of the house. He caught up with her at the door and took her firmly by the arm and led her back into the house.

"My dear girl," he said, his voice gentle and soothing, "in a town filled with nothing but flashy, trashy types, we're just going to have to see that you do better for yourself."

"I'm only visiting," she said. "I'm only here for a few

99

days." She felt tears spring to her eyes and she turned away because she desperately didn't want this cold, indifferent man to see them.

"Now I want you to sit down and tell me about yourself," he said, leading her back to the chair she had been sitting in. "Start from the beginning and tell me everything."

"Why?" she asked, but she sat down obediently and picked up her Coke again although she was no longer thirsty. He pulled up another chair and sat directly in front of her, their knees almost touching, and then he smiled at her and introduced himself.

"What does the D. P. stand for?" she asked.

"It depends on whom you ask."

"Well, what do people call you for short?"

"Koenig," he said. "You may call me Koenig if you wish."

"What do your best friends call you?"

"*Mr.* Koenig," he told her, and she laughed, believing that he was kidding, but he did not smile. He waited patiently for her to stop laughing, and then he urged her to start talking about herself.

She talked. She told him about Canton, about being grindingly poor, about Milo Grooms, her morose first husband, who drank a formaldehyde cocktail the day he got the doctor's report informing him he was sterile. And she talked about Roger Deering, who left his entire estate to the *slut*.

"How much?" he asked quickly. "How much have you got?"

"I don't know," she said, and she didn't because there were land holdings and stock options, confusing things that made her brain float when they talked to her about it.

"Give or take a hundred thou," he asked, "how much?"

"Why does it matter?" she asked, wary now, wondering if he were a fortune hunter, this person who swam naked in the ocean and preyed on gullible widows.

"Do you know how to act?" he asked. "Have you ever been in a play, a movie, anything?"

"In Canton?"

"Do you think you could?" he asked, looking at her, twisting his head rapidly from side to side to view her from different angles.

"Why?" she asked.

"I don't know. I just have a hunch about you."

"Tell me," she said quietly, "did you also have a hunch about the girl in the bikini you just threw out of your bedroom?"

"No," he said lightly, "I don't get hunches about tramps."

"I may be from the Midwest," Glenda said, "but I'm not a fool."

"I know. That's what intrigues me the most."

Jeremy started to stir in his sleep, making unpleasant grunting noises. He turned over and tried to burrow his face deeper into the couch. They both turned and looked at him.

"He's a creep," Koenig said, "but he's a good press agent." He got up and poured himself another bourbon. As he passed the couch, he picked up a copy of *Daily Variety* from the coffee table, lifted Jeremy's head, and slipped the trade paper between his drooling mouth and the couch fabric.

"Okay," he said, sitting down again. "Now tell me about your plans. What do you want, what are you looking for, what are you going to do for the next, say, forty-five years?"

"I don't know," Glenda said slowly. "All I know is that I don't ever want to be poor again. Not me, not my children."

"Do you photograph well?" he asked, as if he had not

101

heard what she had said. "Do you have any pictures here with you?"

"Oh, you're going to make me a star?" she said, her voice hard, the laughter brittle. "What a really original approach." She walked over to Jeremy and felt around in his pants pockets until she found his car keys. "You know, I always thought that was a gag, that nobody really pulled that crap."

"I can't guarantee that I'll make you a star," he said, quite unruffled by what she had just said, "but I can make you a Hollywood celebrity. That I promise you."

"Why me?" she asked, heading for the door and the dark night air.

"Because you bring out the Pygmalion in me," he said.

She did not know who or what a Pygmalion was and assumed it was something vile and sexual. When he saw her indignant, blazing eyes, he laughed delightedly.

"Get lost," she said, and walked out onto the patio.

"Burn the dress," he called after her.

She walked down to the wet sand and stood looking up at his house, saw him walk across the room in the direction of the bar. She looked down at her dress and was confused. It had cost a lot of money and she liked it, liked the vivid hot colors and the way the wide gold belt cinched in her waist.

She started to walk up the beach. She thought she would slip out by the side of the house without saying goodbye to anyone and take Jeremy's car back to the hotel. She would pack the following day and take a taxi to the airport and fly back to Canton, where people didn't confuse her and frighten her.

But instead she walked back up to Koenig's house and stood in the doorway and watched him trying to rouse the sleeping press agent.

"What's a Pygmalion?" she asked. He turned quickly and smiled at her.

"I am, my dear," he said, and he held out his hand to her, "and it's nothing terrible, I promise you." She walked across the room and he took her hand in his. He raised her knuckles to his mouth and kissed them lightly, and then dropped her hand.

"All right, now I'm going to ask you again," Koenig said. "How much did the crop duster leave you?"

"After taxes and everything, my lawyer says it'll probably be just under a million."

"Not bad, not too bad. Now tell me," he said, "is your taste in everything as flashy and trashy as that dress and those shoes?"

"Probably," she said slowly and she found she was not even angry. She had never really thought about it much. Roger had made her return the wedding dress she had picked out. He had said only that it was unbecoming, but he had told her to select something plainer. She liked bright colors and sequins and lamé and rhinestones and low-cut and side slits and ruffles and gloppy jewelry. Yes, flashy and trashy was probably just what she was.

"All right, then, we'll have to start from scratch," he said. He walked over to a small, elegant desk, opened the top drawer and took out a business card.

"Here," he said, placing the card in her hand and closing her fingers over it. "Be in my office tomorrow morning at ten-thirty."

"What about him?" she asked, pointing to Jeremy. She was already starting to feel guilty about taking his car keys, stranding him here with this unpredictable man with no first name.

"He will be very useful to you one day, when he sobers up," Koenig said, and he led her to the sliding glass door, shook her hand formally, and then slid the glass door closed, almost on her nose. A moment later, the drapes slid by her face, too.

She had been dismissed.

103

The telephone rang.

She kept on talking and made no effort to answer it. On the sixth ring it was picked up somewhere else in the house. A few moments later there was a militant rap on the door.

"Tell them I'll get back to them, Mona," Glenda called out in her most gracious voice.

"It's for *him*," Mona said through the door. There were no receding footsteps, and, as Bud crossed to pick up the telephone, Glenda called out again in the same unreal voice, "Thank you, Mona, that will be all." Then there were angry footsteps and a door slammed somewhere in the back of the house.

"That you, Buddy-boy?" It was Tom Edwards.

"What's up?"

"Gilbert Ritner, you know, the fat kid next door, says he remembered something and he'll only talk to you."

"Where is he now?"

"He's right here."

He was sitting right there and Tom had called him 'the fat kid.' No wonder he wasn't talking.

"Tell him to go home and I'll catch up with him in about an hour," Bud said.

"He says it's very important."

"Put him on," Bud said wearily. He knew the moment he had set eyes on Gilbert Ritner that he was going to be a pain in the ass. He might even help him solve the case, but he'd still be a pain in the ass.

"Hi," Gilbert said brightly. "I went back to my bedroom and I closed all the windows and pulled the drapes and I sat in the dark and concentrated until I remembered something."

"Give somebody else down there your business, huh?" Bud asked, trying to keep the irritation out of his voice.

"No," he said firmly. "I don't like their attitude. When are you coming back?"

"Are you jerking me around, kid?" Bud asked, sure that when he got there Gilbert would not have anything for him.

"I'll wait for you right here," Gilbert said.

Bud hung up the telephone and looked over at Glenda. The rest of her story would have to wait now. He believed that she was innocent, believed that nobody that self-involved could possibly be capable of murder. He had been listening to her for over twenty-five minutes and they were still only on the first night she had met Koenig some two years before.

"What the hell were you looking for over there?" he asked, thinking maybe he could get lucky and skip over a year or two in her recitation.

"Oh, I forgot to tell you," she said. Suddenly her eyes went blank. They looked the way the green light on a traffic sign looks when the sun is shining directly into it, dazzlingly empty. And he knew that whatever she told him now would be a lie. "I found it. It was in the trunk of my car and I just didn't know it."

"Yeah, what was it?"

"It's so silly," she said, and even managed a blush. "I'd really prefer not to tell you."

He didn't care any more. He knew whatever she told him now would be a lie, and whatever he found there in Koenig's house she'd deny was hers. But it would probably have her fingerprints, so she'd be trapped anyway.

"What was it?" he asked again as he was heading for the door. He was only curious now to see what kind of lie she'd tell him. He knew she couldn't come up with anything mundane like a tennis racket. It would have to be something embarrassing or mildly incriminating.

"Well, if you must know," she said, her eyes modestly focused somewhere in the vicinity of her lap, "I'd been using a foreign product for a couple of weeks and he thought it might be unsafe so I gave it to him to check out. That was a few days ago. He must have driven by and put it in my trunk. He's done that before."

105

"May I see it, please?" He didn't give a damn, but he was sore now and he wanted to humiliate her.

"It's still in the back of my car." She rose gracefully and walked out the front door with him. She took the shortest route to the car. She stepped over the flower beds, lifting her hem above her ankles, and crossed the lawn.

She opened the trunk of her Mercedes and handed Bud something the size of a cigar box. He opened it. He couldn't read French, but he was pretty sure the contraption had something to do with toning breasts. He'd seen them advertised in the backs of magazines and always wondered who bought them. Now he knew. He turned the box over and saw what was left of a price tag. All that remained was what looked like the upper loops of a B and/or a P. He handed the box back to Glenda.

"I think it's really touching that such a busy man would have been so deeply involved in the care and upkeep of your tits," Bud said to her. "I'll get back to you tomorrow. Don't leave town."

On a hunch, he stopped at the Brentwood Pharmacy on his way back to headquarters. He covered the bottom part of one of their price tags with his thumb. He spoke to the pharmacist's helper, a short, intense-looking woman with bad skin, who remembered selling the French gizmo to a nervous redheaded woman a few hours earlier that day. She had paid cash for it, although she was a regular charge-account customer.

He drove back to Beverly Hills. He still had the message sheets in his pocket. He would get rid of Gilbert Ritner in a few minutes and then would study the messages, make a few phone calls, and see who sounded frightened or angry enough to have driven a kitchen knife deep into an agent's heart.

6

Gilbert Ritner was driving everyone crazy by the time Bud got there. He was asking a million questions, using the phones, trying to get information about his neighbors.

"Get him out of here," Tom Edwards called out, right in front of the kid. Gilbert looked at Edwards, gave Bud a world-weary shrug and one of those spiral gestures with the finger to the forehead to indicate that he knew he was dealing with a crazy man.

"Come on, Ritner," Bud said, beckoning to him, "let's you and me go for a walk."

"No," Gilbert said. "I want to see pictures. I want to see mug shots."

"Terrific," Bud said, grabbing him firmly by the arm. "We'll go down to Doubleday's and get a copy of *Silver Screen*, and then you can point out the murderer to me."

"I don't know why you don't take me more seriously," Gilbert said. He shrugged off Bud's hand and trotted eagerly by his side.

"All right, what've you got?" Bud asked as they started

to walk toward Little Santa Monica, "and it better be good."

"Two days ago, Monday afternoon, about four o'clock, just as I was coming up the street, there was a camper parked in his driveway."

"So?"

"So," Gilbert said impatiently, "I noticed it because it was different, not like the usual Excaliburs and Rolls-Royces that come up to his house. This camper was old and cruddy and there was a pretty girl sitting in the front seat, and the engine was running."

Is that all? Bud thought wearily. Probably just someone lost, asking for directions, and he dragged me back here for this.

"The girl wasn't driving. She wasn't sitting behind the wheel," Gilbert said excitedly.

"So what?" He was beginning to lose his patience.

"So that meant somebody was in the house. Whoever was driving was in the house because there was nobody at the front door."

"Was Koenig at home then?"

"I didn't see his car."

"Well, who would have let him in?"

"Probably Hernando or Adelina. That's his couple," Gilbert explained. The way he said "couple" irritated Bud. The Beverly Hills vernacular. "They'll be at his house tomorrow. They have Tuesday and Wednesday off. Most of *them* have Sunday and Monday off. Whoever killed him probably knew about their having weirdo days off. Wouldn't you think?"

"What's their last name?" Bud asked, taking out his note pad.

"Who knows?" Gilbert said, looking at him with surprise. This was a land of Hernandos and Adelinas, of Juanitas and Rosarios, of olive-skinned domestics who did not need last names because they were paid in cash, more often than not, to avoid detection by the immigration authorities.

108

"Did you happen to get a license number?" Bud asked, now mildly curious about the camper that had been idling in the dead man's driveway two days before he became a dead man.

"It had a few J's in it, I think."

"Do you know what make?"

"No, but if you drive me to a lot where they sell used ones, I could show you."

Bud was not ready for that. He had a pocketful of solid leads to go on. He did not have to go chasing down to a used-camper lot with a kid who was already starting to bug him.

"Did you see who was driving the camper?" Bud asked.

"No, but when he got back in the car, he pulled out of the driveway with a lot of noise. Like he was mad, and he burned rubber going down the street."

"Are you sure it was the camper?"

"No, but it probably was."

"And why are you so sure it was a man driving? Did you see him?"

"No, but I figure it was a guy because the camper was so dirty, and because the girl was very pretty."

"You said Hubie, the guy who found Koenig's body, was crazy. What exactly is crazy about him?" Bud asked, purposely changing to another subject. He was getting the feeling that Gilbert was starting to make up things, embellish the few facts he did know, to keep Bud's interest level up.

"I don't know. He's always angry and shouting at you about something. And he drinks on the job."

"Is that it?"

"Somebody on the block reported him recently for pissing against a telephone pole in the alley. He got into a lot of trouble and now he gives out citations on this block for lots of dumb things."

"Do you know who reported him?"

"I don't think it was Koenig."

"Did he think it was Koenig?"

"He thought it was everybody."

"What's his last name?" Bud asked, taking out his note pad again.

"Who knows?" Gilbert said, shrugging. "Crazy Hubie is what everybody calls him."

No wonder he pisses on their telephone poles, Bud thought, but made a note to check with Sanitation, to check Hubie's records, to talk to Hubie's partner, another man with no last name, he was sure.

"Can you get home from here all right?" Bud asked. They had walked all the way to Camden Drive, but he didn't want to hear this kid's snotty, knowing voice any more that night.

"I'll buy you dinner," Gilbert said eagerly. "I got my allowance check today, but I'll blow it all on dinner. You name the place."

"Why don't you go home and curl up with a carton of yogurt instead?" Bud asked. It came out crueler than he had meant it to, but the invitation annoyed him, a rotten rich kid's invitation.

Gilbert didn't respond. He stood there for a moment, then he turned around and ran up Camden toward Santa Monica Boulevard. He ran across the street against the light, bouncing heavily with each step. He kept running north until he hit Carmelita, then he disappeared around the corner.

Bud walked back to where he had parked his car. He was hungry, almost sorry that he hadn't grabbed a quick hot dog at Throckmorton's with the kid. He wondered as he headed toward his apartment if Gilbert Ritner would have shrugged if someone had asked him what his own last name was. Cops and maids and maintenance men were probably one and the same to him.

Ivy Greenwald was sitting in her dusty VW by the entrance to his apartment house. She tooted the horn as he pulled up to the garage and waited for the electric door to open.

"Hang on a minute," she called. She ran over to his car and hopped in beside him. "Remember me?"

"Yeah, I remember you," Bud said as he pulled into his parking space.

"Most people don't," she said. "It's that kind of face."

"How long have you been waiting?" he asked, wondering if she had driven straight over from Koenig's office, how she got his address, and why she was there at all.

"Not too long," she said. "About three hours and twelve minutes. Do you have anyone stashed up there or can you ask me up?"

"I can ask you up," he said, smiling at her. She was not unlike Gilbert Ritner, whom he'd just dispatched into the darkness, lonely and eager and overweight— not even that much unlike himself.

She came into his apartment and looked around. He waited for her to compliment him, to say some flattering things, but she just dropped her purse and briefcase on a chair and then flopped down on the couch, her large boots stretched out in front of her.

"You want something to eat?" he asked.

"Yeah, but don't bother," she said, reaching for her purse. "In fact, I bought enough for both of us." She fished around in the depths of her leather purse and brought out a large bottle wrapped in a brown paper bag. She rolled the paper bag down around the neck of the bottle like a Skid Row wino, then politely offered it to Bud first.

He accepted the bottle and pulled the bag away to read the label. It was liquid protein. Cherry flavor. He'd tried it once the year before, after a week of hard-core eating, but it had made him gag and he threw the whole bottle out after the first mouthful.

"How long have you been on this?" he asked her.

111

"About an hour and a half," she said, grinning at him. "I stopped over at the health food store and bought it. I have the folic acid pills, the potassium, the whole number."

"Why?"

"I want to be thin for you," she said, then when she saw him start to pull away from her, she added, "but don't get clutched. I go around looking for people I'd like to be thin for because I can't diet on spec."

He handed the bottle back to her untouched. Solemnly she took off the cap, then held her head back and took five large swallows with her eyes tightly shut. She put the bottle down and shuddered.

"Are you sure you couldn't learn to like me just the way I am?" she said. She held the bottle out to him again. He looked at it for a moment, tipped his head back and took a series of deep swallows, then rushed into the kitchen for some water.

"It sure does kill the old appetite," he said, working on his second glass of water.

"Along with the old desire to live," she said, following him into the kitchen. "Shall we stay on it? Shall we try it for, say, a week?"

"I've got a better idea," he said. "Let's go on it and stay on it until whoever killed Koenig is found. No kidding around, no back-sliding, no cheating. How does that sound?" He suddenly believed that, vile as the predigested protein was, he might be able to do it, stay with it this time. Maybe she was right. Maybe you had to have a reason to diet. Maybe nobody could take off weight on spec.

"Okay," she said eagerly, "but what if you find the murderer tomorrow?"

"I'll be too weak."

"And I've got another rule," she said, "and I think we should stick by it, no matter what."

"Yeah, what is it?"

"No making love, no going to bed, until we've both lost our first five pounds." Her voice was so business-like, so conversational, that he started to laugh. He knew that he had at least six prettier, sexier women who would jump into bed with him unconditionally at any time, but he suddenly found himself aroused as he gazed across at her. He wondered what she looked like without the terrible dress, the heavy boots. He had often been surprised by the grace and beauty of overweight women once they had stripped down.

"Okay, you've got yourself a deal." He looked at her and smiled. He wondered how staunch she'd be if he reached over and ran his hand up under her unbecoming dress. He thought seriously of doing it, but as he moved toward her, she got up and crossed to her briefcase. She opened it and pulled out a legal tablet with a lot of scribbled notes.

"Now back to business," she said, flopping down heavily on the couch. She studied her notes. "As I see it, there are three prime suspects in this town, three people with super reasons to have scragged Koenig."

"I'm listening," he said, trying to peer over her shoulder to see what she had written on the yellow page.

"One of them is Oliver Kelsey, one of them is Gordon Flemming." She stopped and looked up at him. "And the third one is you."

He waited for her to say something else, but she just sat there, tapping her legal pad with her pencil, waiting for him to respond.

"You've been very busy since I last saw you," he said, and he was startled at the unsteadiness of his own voice.

"Not only that," she said, grinning at him. "I had my legs waxed, too. You know, just in case."

"Fat and hairy," he said quickly. "What a parlay." He wanted to punish her for digging into his life, for finding out about him, but there was something so vulnerable and achingly hopeful in the way she sat across from him, in the way she wore the goddamn boots, that he was instantly sorry for lashing out at her.

"I'm just . . . fastidious," she said, her voice quieter than he'd heard it before, and she had stopped smiling.

"Did Lutz put you onto this?"

"Yes, he told me who you were."

"How do you know him?"

"He used to be my brother's whatever-you-call-it," she said, then added in a too-brittle voice, "and weren't my parents lucky, though? A gay son and a fat, hairy daughter."

"How come you don't have Peter Lutz down on your hit parade?" Bud asked.

"Are you kidding?" Ivy said. "This is a disaster for him. One or two more years with Koenig and he'd have probably been the head of a studio, if not the world."

"An agent's secretary?"

"Things have changed around here since your day," she said. "Agents run this town now. They're the real superstars. Nothing happens here without the agents, and a hell of a lot of them started out as those wind-up secretaries in three-piece suits."

"Why do you single out Kelsey and Flemming?" Bud asked her.

"Because of all his clients, their careers are just about back to zilch," she said. "And that can make you very crazy very quickly."

"Did Lutz tell you that, too?"

"He wouldn't give me the time of day when it comes to clients. I had to dig this up myself."

"What for?" he asked. "Your assignment's dead, isn't it?"

"Listen, I had to have a reason to come here, didn't I?" She crossed to her briefcase again and this time pulled out a stack of Xeroxed newspaper clippings. She dropped them in his lap. "There's a pretty good case in here. Gossip-column items, trade-paper stuff."

"But that kind of thing is all phony promotion, isn't it?"

"What isn't?" she said, smiling at him. Then she picked up her purse and her briefcase and stood over him. "Do we still have a contest?"

"Sure."

"I'll leave you that bottle of stuff. I have more in the car."

"Shall I pay you for it?" he asked.

"No, but the next dose'll be on you."

"Weigh-in tomorrow night at seven-thirty?" he asked.

"I'll be here."

"My scales aren't very accurate."

"I'll bring mine," she said and she started out the door.

"You don't really think I'm a murderer, do you?" Bud called out, but the door slammed shut. Either she didn't hear or chose not to respond.

Bud waited until he heard the elevator door slide closed. Then he took the stairs three at a time, climbed into his car and drove all the way downtown on Beverly Boulevard.

The preliminary report from the coroner's office would be waiting on his desk the next morning, so there was no reason for him to go to the morgue. He seldom did, relying on the professionalism of the pathology department. Occasionally a detective could turn up something that had been overlooked by a coroner, but it was so rare, so unusual, except in the movies, that most detectives didn't waste their time and depended totally on the written reports.

But Bud wanted to see the corpse for himself, felt somehow cheated at having arrived at the North Bedford house after D. P. Koenig's body had been removed. Just like him, Bud thought. I wait all these years and then he gets himself scragged on my day off.

He shivered involuntarily as he stared down at D. P. Koenig's naked body, the name tag hanging from his rigid toe. Bud would have known him anywhere. His body was trim, not an extra ounce of flesh on him.

Bud studied the fatal knife wound. One neat lucky thrust had done the trick, entering between the ribs, instantly puncturing the lungs and probably the heart. There would have been a moment of stunned surprise as the pale, bubbling blood filled his mouth. And then, death.

The entry wound was incredibly thin and small, and in no way looked as if it could have brought a man down forever, particularly a man like D. P. Koenig.

He stood looking down at the body, still wondering why he had come, why it had been important for him to be there, to see for himself. He had not planned on coming downtown until he heard Ivy mention his own name as a possible suspect. He assumed she had been kidding.

Nobody on the Beverly Hills police force knew about the connection, not even his partner. They all knew he had been a kid star and that something bad had happened. They didn't know who had been responsible or what scars he carried around with him. And they didn't care, because he was good, one of the best.

Because he had once been in show business, all the crimes involving the Hollywood famous were automatically turned over to him. It was believed that he understood their needs, their hang-ups, that he could relate to them better than anyone else in the department. So he knocked on their doors, wandered around their homes, jotting down their complaints or checking out their alibis. Some of them remembered who he was, but for the most part they treated him with the same polite indifference they reserved for any other civil servant, and it always hurt.

Bud knew if anyone suspected the cold rage and fury he carried with him for the man whose corpse he now stood over, he would be taken off the case instantly. He did not want that to happen.

Up until that day, if anyone had accused him of keeping an eye on, actually *stalking*, D. P. Koenig, Bud would have laughed. But now he had to admit to himself, it wasn't that far from the truth. The kid had seen him passing the North Bedford house, slowing down, looking through the occasionally opened windows.

And then there were the Hollywood trade papers. He subscribed secretly to both of them, had for years. He would slip them out of his mailbox, furtively flip through to the obituaries. He would scan the names for *the* name, for D. P. Koenig's death notice, he realized now, then he would toss them both into the trash, making sure to cover them with a bag of greasy garbage lest someone discover his guilty practice.

Once a woman he was fooling around with had come upon both papers stashed at the bottom of his garbage can. She asked him why a detective read the Hollywood trade papers. He felt a quick and unreasonable surge of anger toward her, but managed to conceal it.

"You read that, say Neil Diamond has just signed a multimillion-dollar contract, or Jimmy Stewart is in London, so you keep closer tabs on their houses," Bud lied easily.

"You mean you think that burglars and robbers read *Variety* and *Reporter*, too?" she asked.

"I would if that were my line of work," Bud said. He led her back into the bedroom, and the subject was closed.

He had actually seen Koenig a number of times over the past years, observed him getting in and out of cars, had once stood behind him in a line at Thrifty Drug Store on Canon Drive. Bud had peered over his shoulder to see what he was buying. On the counter in front of him was a box of glycerin suppositories. Bud had grinned all the way back to headquarters.

On his days off in the summer he would often go to

the public beach next to the Malibu Colony. There were a lot of better swimming beaches closer in, but somehow he always ended up there even though there was no surf, too many rocks, too many people.

He would put down his blanket, his suntan lotion, his paperback, and he would walk past the chain-link fence into the Malibu Colony, playland of the rich and famous, just so he could stroll in front of D. P. Koenig's second home.

The Malibu Colony is one of the great tourist disappointments of Southern California. It is a narrow, flat strip of beach with enormous houses built so close together that from the street side you cannot see sand or ocean from one end to the other.

Some of the houses are old, lovely, tasteful, a few of them are new, lovely, tasteful, but most of them are new and ugly. As the years went by, the original houses were leveled by the new owners and replaced by garish Moorish monstrosities with arches and domes, too large, too opulent for the small, narrow lots they were built on.

Although it is a private community (a guard at a gate must have proof of your right to be there before you are permitted in by car), anyone can walk along the wet sand in the Colony and look up at the costly homes, look up through the salt-water scum on the glass windbreaks, and possibly see Robert Redford sipping his morning coffee; Ryan O'Neal studying a script; Candice Bergen photographing the sunset. They are all either owners or renters or guests, and they can be seen partying up and down the Colony, tossing Frisbies with their children, seemingly oblivious to the rubberneckers who wander just below the high-tide mark in search of famous faces.

Bud could never quite admit to himself that he walked through the Colony expressly to see D. P. Koenig. Occasionally he caught a glimpse of a gray head bobbing up and down beyond the breakers or would see a cluster of handsome, expensively dressed people gathered on the agent's used-brick patio. Once when there was a strong offshore breeze he heard the mirthless laugh that he remembered so clearly from his childhood.

Bud stared down at the gray, rigid body, a gasp of fear or pain or possibly just astonishment frozen forever on the face. He tried to figure out what it was that gave him the feeling of heaviness in his chest. All those early fantasies, those evil dreams of standing over D. P. Koenig's corpse were now realized. Yet he felt no pleasure, no satisfaction, not even guilt. It was what he had waited for, had prepared himself for, and now that it had happened, he realized how unimportant it was to him, to his life, and that was what shook him the most profoundly.

"Are you through?" the pathologist's assistant asked.

"Yeah," Bud said slowly, "I'm through."

"Amazing how some people who get all smashed to hell recover, and he got one tiny puncture and it's all over."

"Just lucky, I guess," Bud said quietly. "I mean, unlucky." He wasn't really sure what he meant. He turned and walked out into the brightly lit offices, into the warm world of the living. He did not stop shaking until he left the building and got into his car.

The telephone was ringing as he let himself into his apartment. It was his mother. He slipped out of his jacket and lay back on the bed.

"I heard about it on the television," she said quietly. "Is that why you didn't come to lunch today?"

"That sure is why," Bud said.

"Who killed him?"

"Don't know yet."

"He finally got what he deserved." He could not remember hearing his mother's voice so cold and punishing.

"What does that mean?" Bud asked quickly, sensing

119

that now, after all these years of silence, she would talk, she would tell him all the things he wanted to know, or believed he wanted to know.

"He killed your father. He tried to kill you."

"If he killed my father," Bud said quietly, "why didn't he go to jail?"

"Famous people don't go to jail so fast."

"There was not even a trial, Mom," Bud said, measuring each word carefully, fearful of going too far, of driving her away from him. "It was just a tragic . . . accident. That's what people said."

"You listen to the wrong people. You always have."

"Mom," Bud said urgently, "talk to me."

"He killed your father."

"Mom, I don't know what that means anymore."

"He killed your father."

"You've gotta do better than that."

She hung up the phone so softly that he didn't realize she was gone until he heard the buzzing in his ear.

He had long since given up trying to find out anything about his earlier life from his mother. Occasionally when he was at her apartment having lunch he would try to get her to talk, to open up, about the brief days of his fame and stardom.

"There's nothing to tell," she would say stonily, her eyes turned away from him. "We were a family before then. He killed your father. He almost killed you." That was the extent of her litany. If he asked her, that was all he could get from her. If he pushed harder for more information, she would walk away from the table and busy herself in the kitchen.

Even as a boy he began to believe that digging deeper into his past was an act of disloyalty to her, the last betrayal. One day, after he had already left home and was visiting, when he had followed her into the kitchen and cornered her, she had turned around and slapped his face very hard, then turned back to scrape the dishes.

120

His face—and his heart—stinging from the blow, he turned and walked out of the house. He did not come back for lunch the next Saturday. He did not telephone her and she did not call him.

Three weeks later he came for lunch without telephoning first. She kissed him as if nothing had happened, and he could smell white clam sauce simmering in the kitchen. He wondered if she had prepared lunch for him on the two Saturdays he had chosen not to come. He wondered what she had done with the lunch for two. Then, studying her waistline, he assumed that she had probably eaten it all herself.

The curse of the Bacolas.

Frank Bacola owned a small Italian grocery store on Santa Monica Boulevard. He was a large, heavy man with lots of black hair. There were swirls of it in his ears, and sharp bristles protruded from his nostrils. He was a quiet, almost somber man, scrupulously honest, often running blocks after shoppers who had left without their change.

Connie, his wife, worked in the market with him, a resigned, once beautiful woman who gained a hundred and two pounds during her only pregnancy. She delivered a ten-pound son but never lost the remaining ninety-two pounds.

When little Buddy Bacola was four, a beautiful, wide-eyed toothpick of a child, he was permitted to run around the store and play quietly among the counters and rows of canned goods. Shoppers admired him, praising him enthusiastically to his proud mother and father.

One day an attractive, well-dressed man came into the store to buy some Greek olives. His name was D. P. Koenig. He was thirty-four years old, his hair almost completely gray.

He followed the child with his eyes, even bending

down once or twice to get a closer look. He bought the olives and asked Frank Bacola to bring the kid to his office the next day. A part in a motion picture.

Frank Bacola took the card the man handed him, studied it for as long as it took the man to walk out with his olives, then tore up the card.

Two days later, the man came into the store again. This time he said he would drive them both, father and son, to the studio for a screen test. Solemnly Frank Bacola hung up his apron and took his son by the hand and together they drove to the studio in the back seat of D. P. Koenig's Buick.

Little Buddy was winning and adorable, a natural. He smiled when the director told him to smile, and he waved. He scampered up to the cameraman. He had no self-consciousness.

A severe-looking woman in a man's suit was summoned to take Buddy to the wardrobe department. She removed his cheap Sears sweater and replaced it with a striped T-shirt from Saks which was far too big for him. First she tried a beret on him, then a baseball hat, which was also too big for him. She twisted it so the visor was in the back.

And Buddy Bacola, son of an immigrant grocer, turned into Buddy Bacall, impish all-American kid, star of the silver screen.

More and more, as his son became famous, worked in one motion picture after another, Frank Bacola took to accompanying him to the studio, leaving his wife to manage the store. Not that they needed it anymore with the kind of money Buddy was earning. But the store was for dignity.

He was known as D. P. Koenig's kid. Everybody, even the directors of the movies he was in, knew that if you wanted something out of Buddy and for one reason or another you couldn't get it, you got hold of the agent, who'd come over to the studio on the fly. He'd take the kid on a walk around the set. He would sit knee to knee with him, talking with unsmiling earnestness. And then you ended up getting exactly what you wanted.

"Don't let me down, kid," the agent would say to him. "You're going to make me rich and famous." They both knew that it was an awesome burden for a five-year-old boy.

In the beginning, Frank Bacola was a non-presence on the set. He wore dark funereal suits and sat in Buddy's dressing room, speaking only when he was spoken to, smiling nervously at members of the crew who came in search of his son.

Then suddenly it began to change. The black suit gave way to vivid sport jackets, loud shirts, fringed suede, and ultimately, tooled-leather cowboy boots. The initial shyness gave way to nonstop talking, nonstop complaining about the dressing room, the script, the food.

Often he would step over to the script girl or even the director and suggest that Buddy wouldn't say this or Buddy doesn't talk that way. Sometimes Buddy would overhear the crew make terrible, cruel jokes about his father and he would blush with humiliation.

If there were any problems on the set, if the camera was jammed or a light shorted out, someone was usually heard to suggest, "Why don't you ask the grocer about it?"

His mother never came to the studio and would not accompany the father and son to Sunday brunches given by studio executives. They made her feel uncomfortable and she believed she never had the right thing to wear or to say. And she was not wrong.

Buddy's sixth motion picture was called *The Little Renegade*. It was to be his biggest part, D. P. Koenig told him solemnly. Big movie. Big budget. A western to be shot entirely on location in Utah.

The only thing D. P. Koenig didn't tell him was that it would be the last movie he would ever make, because there was no way, at that time, anybody could possibly have known it.

The telephone rang. Bud reached over for it, grateful for the interruption, eager to be pulled away from his thoughts, his memories, because the old headache was starting up again, as he knew it would.

"Yeah?" Bud said, sitting up on the edge of his bed.

"Are you in the middle of anyone?" Chuck's voice was nasal and drugged and in no way apologetic. Bud smiled and settled back on the bed again.

"You know I don't pick up the phone when I'm in the middle of anyone."

"Hey, Buddy," Chuck said lugubriously, "I'm worried about you."

"It's a small world," Bud said evasively, "because I'm worried about you, too."

"Don't crap me, Buddy," Chuck said, sounding less drugged by the moment. "You're in a little trouble out there, aren't you?"

"How's the old schnoz?"

"I saw all about that cowboy on television," Chuck said. His voice shifted so slightly that only someone who had worked side by side with him for five years would have noticed it. "He's the *guy,* isn't he?"

"Do you look like Robert Redford yet?"

"Christ, Buddy, you're not on this one, are you?"

"Yeah, I'm on this one. So what?"

"So, I think you ought to come to Santa Barbara with us, that's all."

"That was a million years ago," Bud said finally.

"I've got two bedrooms, ocean view, washer, dryer, trash compactor . . ."

"I'm in good shape," Bud said quickly. "No sweat, no hassle." It was not entirely true, and both men knew it.

"When we saw him getting out of a gray Rolls in front of the Beverly Wilshire about a year or so ago, you

124

turned to me and said, 'There's the guy that blew me away.' "

"Has anyone ever told you you'd make a good cop?"

"That's the same one, isn't it?"

"I'm a very overdramatic person," Bud said. He could hear the tension growing in his voice. "Remember me? Ex-boy, ex-actor?"

He tried to remember how much he had told Chuck over their years of working together. Not much, he was sure. Just that Koenig had been his agent, had been there at the beginning and at the end. His voice always got funny when he talked about it, so the subject didn't come up much.

Anybody who wanted to know what had happened could have studied the Los Angeles *Times* microfilms at the Beverly Hills library. It would all be there, features, wire service stories, the whole number. He'd never gone through them himself, and he assumed nobody else would bother.

"Why don't you come over here right now?" Chuck said, his voice sounding bombed again. "Pay a call on a sick friend?"

"Actually, I do have someone here," Bud said, lowering his voice, lying convincingly. He wanted to get off the telephone, take a hot shower, go to sleep, and blot out the next six hours.

"There are a lot of good guys down there who could handle this one."

"I'm on it. I'm staying on it."

"It may just be a skillet full of snakes you ought to let alone."

"I met a girl today who has me down as a prime suspect."

"Tell you what," Chuck said. It had a touch of the voice he used with psychotics who might have a concealed weapon. "Come with us and we'll give you the bedroom with the ocean view."

"Christ, that sounds like you think I'm a prime suspect too."

"No, but I'm not sure you're the A Number One honcho to track down the guy who did it."

"In one minute I'll come over there and break your nose for you myself," Bud said lightly.

"You've always been jealous of my good looks," Chuck said. "Why don't you admit it?" They both laughed too heartily. They knew they were on uneasy ground and they were anxious to get off as quickly and gracefully as possible.

7

ernando Ramos was a slight, graying Guatemalan with a gentle face and shaking hands. His wife, Adelina, had probably once been pretty, but was now heavy, with coarsened features and the dark, watchful eyes of a grazing animal. They were both wearing uniforms, his a black suit with a white shirt and a black bow tie, hers a gray cotton dress with a starched white apron and sensible shoes.

When Bud arrived at the house, they were walking around the living room with Tom Edwards, who was asking them rapid-fire questions without waiting for answers.

They claimed they had not heard about the death of their employer until they arrived at the North Bedford Drive house and were told by the patrolman on duty there. They had been shocked, the patrolman reported, but no tears, no hysteria. They had asked to go to their quarters and pack, but were told they had to remain there until somebody came to question them.

The couple had gone into the kitchen and made a pot

of coffee. They sat at the table and drank coffee until Tom Edwards arrived. He had gone on a tour of the house with them, and he reported later that they were helpful, but not *overly* helpful. Bud chalked it off to Tom's basic distrust of blacks and Latins.

"Did anyone come to the house on Monday afternoon?" Bud asked them.

"No one, sir," Hernando said thoughtfully. "No one came."

"Maybe your wife spoke to someone?"

"No," Adelina said. "No one came to the house on Monday, except for the Sparkletts man. And the gardener comes three times a week, but nobody special came to the house on Monday."

"The kid next door said he saw a camper parked in the driveway on Monday afternoon. Are you sure you don't remember?"

The two of them looked at each other, genuinely confused. Then they turned to Bud and shook their heads politely. They did not remember anyone coming to the door on Monday.

Bud's stomach started to growl. He wondered if the dark, rich chocolate cake was still in the kitchen under the heavy glass dome. He had had nothing but the protein drink since the night before, and he felt irritable and lightheaded.

"Could you please show me where Mr. Koenig put Mrs. Deering's property?" Bud said, trying a new tack. They both looked at him blankly and shook their heads. He wondered if they were dense or just loyal employees.

"It was something personal and I know he would want her to have it," Bud said. "You know who Mrs. Deering is?"

"Yes," they both assured him, their heads bobbing up and down this time.

Adelina suddenly got up and walked into the entrance

hall, with Bud following close behind. She opened the closet door and turned on the light.

"That's it," she said, pointing to a Bonwit Teller shopping bag which was barely visible under an array of costly overcoats. "I started to pick it up on Sunday morning, and Mr. Koenig got upset and told me it wasn't his; it belonged to someone else."

Bud eased Adelina out of the way and bent down. He grabbed the carrying loops and pulled. He could tell immediately that it was empty. He looked inside. There was nothing, no sales slip, not even a piece of tissue paper.

"What was in it?" Bud asked, holding out the bag to her.

"I don't know," Adelina said nervously. "He wouldn't even let me pick it up. He put it back there in the closet by himself."

"And you're sure somebody didn't come by here to pick it up on Monday?"

Hernando and Adelina looked at each other quickly, then looked away. Then Hernando cleared his throat and smiled. Adelina cleared her throat and didn't smile.

"We weren't here all day on Monday," he said grinning uneasily. "We went to see about another job on the next block around four o'clock."

"So someone might have been here while you were away."

"We were only gone a few minutes," Hernando said righteously.

"You weren't happy here?" Bud asked lightly. He wondered if this polite couple could have been driven to an act of violence by their cold, demanding employer.

"No, we were happy here. We just like to . . . look."

Bud smiled. It was the Beverly Hills fox trot, started by the Arabs, who paid their domestics almost double what the locals were paying. If word got out that some

129

oil-soaked Saudi needed help, every maid, butler, chauffeur, and cook from Doheny Drive to the Pacific Ocean came running.

"The murder weapon's here," Tom Edwards said, taking Bud aside. He led Bud into the playroom where the body had been found. He opened a box and pulled out the knife. He studied it for a moment, testing the sharpness, then handed it to Bud, along with the written report from the lab.

The knife, according to the report, was a Sabatier, a French trademark, but licensed to a lot of domestic manufacturers. It was made of high-carbon steel, had been repeatedly sharpened, possibly by an amateur, as it had irregular erosion along the blade edge. It had been through multiple dishwashing cycles, ruling out the possibility of its having been purchased expressly for the murder. The only fingerprints found were those of the victim, who may have reached for it prior to his decease. Such knives were sold either individually or as part of a set.

Following this was a list of stores within a twenty-mile radius of Beverly Hills that carried this knife. There were some seventy outlets—cookery shops, hardware stores. If the purchase had been a recent one, he would have sent men out to talk to the shop owners, but a used knife was a needle in the haystack nobody had the time for.

Bud walked back into the living room where Hernando and Adelina were standing side by side, with taut, guarded expressions on their faces.

"Have you ever seen this knife before?" Bud asked, holding it out to Adelina. She just stared at the knife from where she stood, and shook her head. "Here," Bud said, putting it gently in her hand. "Look at it closely. Is this knife from your kitchen here?"

"No," she said finally. "This is a good knife. Nice, sharp. We don't have any good knives here." She handed the knife back to Bud, holding it by the blade, the way you're taught to do in school or scouts.

Bud handed Hernando the knife. Hernando studied it carefully, running his finger along the blade. Bud knew that even if he recognized the knife this man would not go against his wife's testimony.

"No, this does not belong in this house."

"Maybe somebody brought it over here for a party? Or a caterer left it here?" Bud suggested.

"I have never seen this knife before," Adelina said. Then added, almost wistfully, "it is a very good knife."

Bud believed them. He had seen the shabbiness of the kitchen contrasted with the elegance of the rest of the house. A man who would let his kitchen run down like that would undoubtedly buy his cutlery at the dime store.

They walked into the kitchen. The chocolate cake was still there. What Bud felt in his stomach was very close to pain. Adelina opened a drawer by the sink and Bud looked inside. There was no knife there to compare in quality to the murder weapon.

Now he knew that this murder was no act of passion, but a carefully premeditated crime. Somebody had brought this fine French knife into the house with the express purpose of driving it deep into D. P. Koenig's heart.

"Did you overhear any arguments, any fights, that Mr. Koenig might have had here in the house or over the telephone?"

"No, he was a quiet man," Hernando said. "He never raised his voice."

Amen, Bud thought. He remembered that. He remembered the icy voice that you had to strain to hear, that when you heard it, you wished you hadn't. It made him appreciate the red-faced screamers of the world. You could live with that: a noisy blast of fury, and then back to normal. But the other, the cold, quiet hostility, did

131

something permanent to your soul and your sense of yourself.

From what they told him, Bud pieced together a picture of the last years of Koenig's home life. It was spent primarily on the telephone. Day and night. Talking quietly, giving orders. He entertained once or twice a month, usually a Sunday buffet after a day of tennis.

As far as the couple knew, no one ever spent the night with him unless they slipped out early in the morning. And he never spent the night away from home unless he was traveling.

He usually ate alone, sitting by himself at the long, formal dining-room table, a telephone to his ear, a pen and note pad by his silverware. After dinner he would go to bed, in the summer often while it was still light out. He would spread the Hollywood trade papers, the *Evening Herald,* and whatever magazines came in the mail on his satin quilt. He would have the remote control to his television set on the nightstand and the telephone at his elbow.

Sometimes he would buzz the kitchen to bring him something to eat or drink, but usually they would not hear from him until early the following morning, when he would appear at the long dining-room table, the telephone before him, to make a series of calls to New York City. He would eat his omelet or his kippered herring talking quietly, often with his mouth full of food.

Bud pulled the list of telephone messages from his pocket. He moved away from Hernando and Adelina because he knew that his stomach was about to growl, undercutting his role as an authority figure.

He had taken half of Ivy Greenwald's liquid protein and put it in a small flask in his glove compartment. It was still mid-morning and he knew with a sinking feeling that he would go off the diet before noon.

He recalled the joke about the reformed alcoholic who

complained that the worst part about being dry is that when you wake up in the morning, you know that's as good as you're going to feel all day.

He stood over by a far window studying the message sheet, grateful for the nearby hum of a power lawnmower that drowned out his complaining gut.

"Oliver Kelsey," Bud said, turning back to Hernando and Adelina, "do you know who he is?"

"Oh, yes," Hernando said. "Mr. and Mrs. Kelsey used to come here very often. He's a good tennis player."

"When was the last time they were here?"

"Oh, a long, long time," Hernando said, turning to his wife for corroboration. She nodded her head affirmatively and smiled to show that they were both telling the truth.

"Did they have a fight? Mr. Koenig and Mr. Kelsey?" Bud asked.

"I never heard Mr. Koenig fight with anybody," Hernando said.

The front doorbell rang. Tom Edwards left the room, then came back in a few moments followed by Peter Lutz. Peter was wearing a navy blue suit and black shoes with a dazzling high shine, but his face looked as if it hadn't slept for a couple of nights.

"I just talked to Howard Gottlieb," Peter said. He nodded minimally to Hernando and Adelina, who nodded minimally back. "That's Koenig's lawyer. He just read the will to me."

Bud touched Peter's shoulder, guiding him into the playroom. He thought it would be amusing to hear about the murdered man's will as close to the scene of the crime as possible.

"His only relatives are twin cretins in St. Louis. Dennis and Emmet Crowder. Second cousins. They've been calling Gottlieb since the first wire-service stories, but Gottlieb says Koenig stiffed them completely."

"Who got it?"

"The Motion Picture Fund, a couple of thou for Hernando and Adelina in there."

"Is that it?"

"No," Peter said, a troubled look on his face. "He left a sort of small trust fund for Glenda Deering."

"Oh," Bud said quickly. "The plot thickens."

"No, it doesn't," Peter said. "Trust me on that."

"Why would he have left money to Glenda Deering?"

"It was sort of a moral commitment. He felt guilty about her, about running through her money and not being able to produce for her, about losing interest in her just as her money ran out. Maybe even because she wasn't actually in *the business*."

"What kind of an arrangement did they have?"

"Weird," Peter said. "I'm not even sure what it consisted of, I mean, I don't think he ever touched her, but he cost her a lot of money. Talk to her about it."

Bud took out his pad and made a quick entry.

"When was the will drawn?"

"About a month ago," Peter said. "Actually, it was revised then."

"Why so recently?" Bud asked. "Did he ever receive any threats against his life?"

"No more than any agent," Peter said, laughing. "I don't know of any threats, but I do know some people who were plenty sore at him."

"Who?"

"They're on your message sheets," Peter said.

"I don't want to play guessing games with you," Bud said irritably. "Just tell me who you suspect and let's get it over with."

"All I can say is that there is a possibility that someone on that list might have been angry or crazed enough to have done it. I will not pick out any one or two names because that could be . . . irresponsible, and could cause an innocent client undue anguish."

There was something stiff and rehearsed about Peter's

words, as if he were reading a prepared statement, but Bud found himself respectful of his businesslike attitude. He was like Deep Throat. He wouldn't come right out and finger someone, but he sure knew how to hint.

"What about them?" Bud asked, indicating the Guatemalan couple.

"Not a chance," Peter said.

"They just said they had been out on Monday looking for another job. Why was that?"

"Go on and arrest them," Peter said, "but you're barking up the wrong suspects. Look on your list. Go talk to the people on your list and leave the couple alone."

"You're just not going to make life easy for me, are you?" Bud said, letting out a deep sigh, not sure himself if it was from frustration or just hunger.

"How come they let you on this case anyway?" Peter asked. "I mean, isn't it like a doctor operating on a member of his family?"

"Not quite," Bud said, but he was shaken by the question.

"Do they know about your relationship with Koenig down at headquarters?"

"Maybe not as much as you do," Bud said, "but they know."

It wasn't true, of course. If they had any idea about what he was carrying around, had been carrying around for so many years, they'd have had him on the next bus to Santa Barbara with his partner.

"How old were you when it happened?" Peter asked.

"About nine," Bud said. There was the voice again. Choked, unsteady.

"Christ, then you probably remember everything," Peter said.

Bud looked up at him, saw something between concern and curiosity on the young man's face, and found that he could not speak, or did not trust himself to say anything further. He turned quickly and walked out of the room, out of the house.

Bud had come perilously close to the truth about himself several years before. He was having Sunday brunch at the Fiasco at the Marina with a girl he'd slept with the night before. She was an actress, ambitious, self-involved, humorless. The brunch was his way of kissing her off, as he did not intend to continue the relationship. She talked too much and she had faked an orgasm—two of his least favorite numbers. He also figured, if she couldn't even fool him in bed she must be some lousy actress.

Just as the bill came, she called noisily to three men who were starting to sit down at a nearby table. They were electricians, part of the crew of the last movie she had worked on. Bud was irritated by her sudden burst of vivaciousness, her newfound desire to be winning and charming.

She introduced Bud, then turned to the two younger men, gossiping and joking with them. The older electrician, bald, with a red, freckled scalp and thick-lensed glasses, kept staring at Bud. Then he started to smile.

"Bud Bacola?" he said slowly. "Buddy Bacall! Christ-almighty, you must be Buddy Bacall!"

"A long time ago, yeah," Bud said uneasily. "A long, long time ago."

"If that doesn't make me feel about a million years old! I'm Chet Wolburton," the older man said, holding out his hand eagerly. "I was Best Boy on your last movie." Then he quickly added, "I mean, your second-to-last movie."

"Best Boy." Bud had not heard, had not thought of that term in longer than he could remember. He suddenly felt dizzy, disoriented. He wanted to rush out of the restaurant and fill his lungs with the fresh coastal air.

In motion pictures, the Best Boy is the chief electrician on the set. The Best Boy is directly under the Gaffer, who is the assistant to the first cameraman. It is an unalterable chain of command and a competent Best Boy or Gaffer is requested by a director or a cameraman almost immediately upon signing his contract. The outstanding ones seldom have more than a few days off a year, running from movie to movie, from location to location.

"It's nice seeing you again," Bud said, almost rudely. He picked up the check and ducked away from the table, leaving the now animated actress and her movie crew behind.

"What are you doing with yourself these days?" Bud turned away from the cashier and saw Chet standing close behind him, smiling benignly.

"I'm a cop," Bud said minimally, then added, "Beverly Hills."

"No kidding," the Best Boy said.

Bud paid his bill quickly, nodded and hurried outside. The sun was shining, and the haze hurt his eyes. He wanted to jump into his Porsche and drive away, and keep driving, but the fucking actress was still in the restaurant.

"Your father was an okay guy," Chet said, almost defensively, almost as if he expected an argument. He had followed Bud out into the sunlight and was standing next to him, looking out over the rows of expensive pleasure boats.

"I hardly remember him," Bud said. He could feel the dryness in his throat, as if it were closing up, as if he could no longer swallow.

"A lot of people didn't understand him," Chet went on, "but he and I had kind of a friendly thing."

Suddenly Bud wanted to turn to this stranger from his former life, to grab him by his double-knit Dacron lapels and hurl him over the railing into the murky water below.

"I try not to think about that whole number," Bud

137

said. He stepped to the window of the restaurant. The actress was still talking animatedly to the two young electricians who were standing by the table with polite smiles on their faces.

"Is she your girl or something?" Chet asked.

"I just met her last week."

"Ernie Waco, the cameraman on the movie we were all on together just now thinks he might have gotten the crabs from her."

Great, Bud thought grimly. A boring, bad lay and now he'd probably wind up with a crotchful of crabs.

"But we're getting married next Thursday," Bud heard himself say. He wanted to punish the man for his loose tongue, for his quick character assassination. But most of all, Bud wanted to make him pay for daring to scrape at the scar tissue that protected him from his past.

"Oh, damn," Chet said quickly, "I'm sorry. Maybe it wasn't her. Now that I think about it, I'm sure it wasn't. It was the other actress. Joanne Weller. That's who it was."

"Joanne Weller is my ex-wife," Bud said, now starting to enjoy the Best Boy's mounting discomfort. Bud turned and headed for his parked car as the actress came out into the street. "I'm kidding," he called over his shoulder. He began to feel an itching around his genitals. He put his hands in his pockets and scratched himself discreetly.

"You know who was on that last movie with you?" He heard Chet's voice close behind him and turned quickly.

"You don't seem to understand," Bud said, trying to smile, "I don't care. I don't even want to know. I'm a cop now."

"It was Murray Erdman. He was Gaffer out at Utah. He says he used to play catch with you between takes."

"Yeah, well, I don't remember him," Bud said, almost pushing the actress into the car. He got into the driver's seat quickly, slamming the door after him.

138

"He's out at the Motion Picture Home in Woodland Hills," Chet said, leaning down and smiling in the window at Bud.

"Thanks," Bud said. He wanted to roll the window up, to back out and leave Chet Wolburton in his vapor trail, possibly even run him down.

Bud had lied. He remembered Murray Erdman, who was warm and noisy and eternally sunburned. He would make the crew give little Buddy Bacall a round of applause each time they printed a take, and would let out catcalls of protest to Gordon Flemming if he reprimanded Buddy or made him repeat a scene or accused him of overacting. And he remembered playing catch with Murray Erdman with a hard black ball that would sting his hands each time he caught it.

"A camera boom fell over on him and crushed his legs about a year ago," Chet Wolburton said. "Maybe you could go cheer him up sometime."

"Maybe," Bud said, turning on the ignition.

"Do you ever see D. P. Koenig anymore?" the Best Boy asked, but Bud revved his engine and backed out of the parking space and pretended he had not heard.

He dropped the actress off at her apartment and stopped at a drugstore in Westwood for some Cuprex, but before he got home, the itching had stopped completely. And he had successfully pushed from his mind any further thought of Chet Wolburton or Murray Erdman put out to pasture at the Motion Picture Home in Woodland Hills with his crushed legs.

When he got home, he changed into his sweatsuit and jogged faster and longer than he had ever jogged before.

About three months later, on his day off, he picked up the telephone and called the Motion Picture Home. The operator said that Murray Erdman was in therapy and asked Bud to call back in an hour. Ten minutes later he got a call from Tom Edwards telling him the new guy on

139

the force was sick and couldn't work that day. "Any chance you can cover for him?"

"Give me ten minutes," Bud said. He slipped the phone number of the Motion Picture Home into his pocket and raced out the front door. He was too busy for the rest of the day to think about calling Murray Erdman. The next day he used the paper with the phone number on it to discard his chewing gum.

Two weeks later, he read in the trade-paper obituaries that Murray Erdman was dead. Bud went around for the next couple of days with a sense that something heavy and nonspecific had been lifted from him. He didn't even bother to figure what it was or how it had been lifted from him. Or by whom.

8

When he returned to headquarters, he found Ivy Greenwald and Gilbert Ritner at his desk. Gilbert was sitting in the swivel chair, his dirty sneakers on Bud's desk blotter. Ivy was sitting on the desk, her Georgia Giants dangling a foot from the floor. He was startled by how pleased he was to see them, almost touched by the animated way they were talking to each other, like two old, overweight friends.

"How'd it go?" Ivy said, smiling at him as he covered the distance to the desk.

"Nothing yet."

"I mean the diet," she said quickly. He put his hands on her waist and moved her off his desk. She felt firmer than he had believed she would.

"Oh, that," he said, signaling Gilbert out of his chair. "I'm still on it, but fading fast."

"You'll never last," Gilbert said, rising reluctantly from the chair. "No way."

"What do you want, Ritner?" Bud was annoyed at the

positive way the kid assumed he couldn't stay on the diet.

"I came by to find out how you were doing, hotshot," Gilbert said, "and now I know. Zilch."

"Get lost, will you?"

"No, he just said something interesting to me," Ivy interceded. "I think you should pay attention."

"What is it this time, Ritner?"

"The girl's hair was wet."

"What girl?"

"The girl in the camper in the driveway on Monday?"

"How do you know?"

"If you told me someone had wet hair," Gilbert said patiently, "I'd believe you knew what wet hair looked like."

"All right. So what if her hair was wet?"

"Who drives around with wet hair?" Ivy asked, "unless it was someone who'd just been in the ocean or in a pool."

"Or just washed it," Bud said.

"Now that I think of it," Gilbert said eagerly, "it was sopping wet, not drying out or anything."

"Long or short?"

Gilbert pointed to just above his shoulder. Bud thought about it for a moment, thought about a young woman with sopping wet hair idling in the dead man's driveway. He looked on his desk for the report on Oliver Kelsey's telephone number. It was there with only a small smudge from the kid's sneaker.

The telephone had been installed four days earlier at a private residence on Rose Avenue in Venice, just a few blocks from the beach. The phone was listed under the name G. Dunn.

"I'm going to the beach," Bud said to Ivy. He looked at his watch. In another ten minutes he'd be off duty. "You want to come along?"

"Can I come, too?" Gilbert asked eagerly, but his eyes

142

were guarded as if he were used to being turned down, left behind.

"Some other time, kid."

"Oh, let him come," Ivy said, then turning to Gilbert, she said, "You're coming. You're my guest."

"Is that okay?" Gilbert asked.

"Yeah, yeah, yeah," Bud said, "but just keep the talking down."

They had to drive in Ivy's VW because she had a back seat. Gilbert leaned forward, his head bobbing happily between them, all the way to Rose Avenue.

It was a small stucco bungalow. There were mauve hollyhocks on one side of the house and a dog run on the other. The lawn needed mowing, to say nothing of watering.

Bud rang the doorbell and waited. After a few minutes, he walked around the house, peering into the windows. The house was neat inside, sparsely but tastefully furnished. In the breakfast nook there was an IBM Selectric typewriter. It was sitting in the center of the small table, the cord neatly coiled and fastened midway with a fat rubber band, as if it had just been brought there but never used.

He heard a noise at the back, the sound of a garage door opening. He walked around the side of the house just as the garage door closed. He walked uneasily across the driveway and pushed the garage door open. He was glad there was no dog in the dog run.

It was his new partner, Gilbert Ritner. Damn, the kid had really had him going there.

"I thought I'd see the camper," Gilbert said. "That's what you're looking for, isn't it?"

"Yeah," Bud said, "I guess so."

"Are we going to stake out?" Gilbert asked eagerly.

"Haven't got time," Bud said. He walked to the side of the house with the hollyhocks and looked into a bedroom window. There was a large mattress on the floor

143

covered by a slightly soiled bottom sheet. There was no top sheet, just a limp quilt in a pile at one end, and several pillows. There was no other furniture in the bedroom, not even a bureau. There were lint balls on the bare floor. And a television set.

"Okay, sport," Bud said as they stood under an open bathroom window. "Do you want to let me stand on you to look inside, or do you want to stand on me?"

"I'll look," Gilbert said excitedly. Bud got down on his hands and knees and Gilbert jumped on his back.

"Not in the middle," Bud said. "You want to cripple me?" Gilbert moved so his weight was primarily on Bud's ass, then cupped his hands around his eyes and peered into the bathroom.

"There's a woman's robe hanging on the door," Gilbert said, "and there's something on the floor that's probably a man's shirt. And there are two wet face cloths on the towel bar."

"Will you hurry up?"

"And there are a lot of little black hair stubs on the bar of soap over the sink."

"Not bad, kid," Bud said, impressed by his eyesight.

"And there's a container for some kind of prescription on the back of the toilet."

"Made out to whom?" Bud asked.

"I can't read it from here."

"Go see if Ivy has binoculars," Bud said, "before you maim me for life."

Gilbert jumped off and started to run out front. As Bud struggled to his feet, he saw Gilbert stop, then turn back to him.

"Did you find the ball, Dad?" Gilbert called out. As Bud scrambled to his feet, he saw a white-haired woman peering at him from the front garden. Her eyes were frightened, suspicious.

"I live next door," she said. "What do you want?"

"My kid hit his ball too hard, from the next street,"

Bud said easily. "It either landed here or in your yard."

"What did he hit it with?" the white-haired woman asked suspiciously. "I don't see any baseball bat." (Everybody wants to be a detective, Bud thought wearily.)

"My mom has the bat in the car," Gilbert said—a born liar—and Bud was impressed. As he walked past Gilbert, he gave the kid as close to a loving pat as he had ever given anyone he didn't want to go to bed with.

The white-haired woman looked from Bud to Gilbert, then turned her scrutiny on Ivy, who was leaning against the car. Ivy waved to the white-haired woman. The white-haired woman nodded briefly, then started to walk back to her own property.

"Is it all right if we check your back yard?" Bud asked, figuring that she would hover over him and he'd be able to get a little information while he rooted around in her flower beds.

"This neighborhood isn't what it was when I was growing up here," Bud said, as he walked along next to her, moving aside some of her flowers with his foot.

"I've only been here four years," she said, "and I've been here longer than almost anybody else." Bud got down on his hands and knees and pushed aside the ground cover.

"Big turnover, huh?"

"The house next door where you were," she said, now getting into the game and poking around for the ball herself, "there've been three different people in there in the last year."

"From the look of the front lawn," Bud said, "it sure seems like you've got some losers in there now."

"A slut," the white-haired woman said, "and sluts don't know what it is to keep up a garden."

"Amen," Bud said, still rooting around in her plants. He stood up and wiped his hands on his pants. "But

145

maybe the neighborhood'll get lucky and she'll take up with a gardener."

"Not while he's there," she said, a pleased, mean little smile on her face.

"While who's there?" Bud pretended to be walking away, barely interested in her conversation.

"She's got someone right now who looks like he'd be too old for me."

"Things are tough all over," Bud said. He turned and waved to her as he walked back to the car. "Thanks for letting me look around."

"So?" Gilbert demanded, leaning up between the front seats.

"So, you're brilliant," Bud said.

They pulled into a Shell station. Bud got out and headed for the phone booth, with Gilbert hot on his heels, filled with suggestions as to how Bud should proceed with the investigation. A real pain in the ass.

When he telephoned headquarters, he was told that Vera Kelsey had just been involved in an accident on the Ventura Freeway. She had a couple of broken bones, but her condition was stable. She had asked to speak with the "short, stocky detective" who had been by her house to question her.

"Figured that might have been you," Tom Edwards said, chortling to himself. Another pain in the ass. The candy machine was right next to the phone booth. Bud had been eying the Hershey with almonds. He turned away quickly.

"Screw you," Bud said. "Where is she?"

"Balboa Hospital."

Bud hung up and stepped out of the booth. He saw that Ivy was bending over, pumping gas into her car. He also saw that the backs of her legs above the ugly boots were trim.

"Good news? Bad news? What?" Gilbert asked.

"It depends on where you're sitting," Bud said. He

146

walked over to Ivy and took the pump handle. "Any chance you could drive me to Balboa Hospital, out in the valley?"

"Sure," she said, "if the Beverly Hills P.D. picks up the tab for my gas." Bud took the receipt for the gasoline and paid the attendant.

"I know the best way to get to the valley from here," Gilbert said. "I'll sit in the front and tell you just how to go."

"Forget it," Bud said. "I'm sending you home in a cab." He reached for his wallet. He'd give him ten bucks and get the kid out of his hair for a while.

"No way," Gilbert said and climbed quickly into the back seat of the car.

"Don't you have anything better to do?"

"Naw, I've seen every movie in Westwood. Some of them twice," Gilbert said. "And, besides, I'm brilliant, a real genius, and I'm going to help you crack this case. You're lucky to have me around."

"Yeah, lucky," Bud said, but he turned around and smiled at the self-avowed genius.

A block or two later, he felt Gilbert's fingers resting lightly on his upper arm, and he knew it was not an accident. Even baby geniuses could be very needy. Bud kept his arm where it was until he no longer felt the pressure.

"Tell me everything you know about Vera and Oliver Kelsey," Bud said to Ivy.

"It's all in there," she said, pointing to a fat manila envelope on the floor. "Trade-paper items from the fifties. Louella Parsons' columns, like that."

"Why is Oliver Kelsey on your list?" Bud asked.

"Well, over and above the fact that his career has really hit the skids," Ivy said, "Vera Lakin Kelsey and D. P. Koenig seem to have been an item before she ever met Kelsey."

"Are you sure?" Bud asked. He settled back and

147

smiled, pleased with himself, with his ability to sense, even in Hollywood, who was lying and who wasn't. But why had Vera Kelsey lied to him? He fingered the envelope, then dropped it back on the floor. He would wait and hear what she had to say to him.

9

The Balboa Hospital parking lot was full, so Ivy dropped him off right at the entrance. Bud leaned over and kissed Ivy Greenwald's forehead.

"I'll get a ride back to Beverly Hills," Bud said.

"How long do you think you'll be?"

"I don't know. Not too long."

"Then we'll wait," Ivy said, and Bud was pleased that she was going to wait for him, that they would both be there when he came out of Vera Kelsey's hospital room.

Vera Kelsey was hooked up to an I.V. She had a broken arm and a lot of facial swelling. Other than that, she was in pretty good shape. Cheerful, almost. Bud wondered if she might be on something, some mood elevator.

"The short, stocky detective is here now," Bud said, standing at the end of her bed. "What can I do for you?"

"When you were at my house," Vera said slowly, "almost everything I told you was a lie."

"Yeah, I kind of figured that."

"Find my purse down there and put it up on the bed, will you?" Vera said. Bud opened the cabinet door of the nightstand. There was a worn leather pouch resting in the stainless steel bedpan. Bud put it on the bed next to Vera. With her good hand, she tried to open the purse, then quickly gave up.

"My car keys should be in there," Vera whispered. "Get them and find out where my car was towed. There's something in the trunk."

"I understand your car was totaled, that you're lucky you're alive."

"Oh, yes," Vera said, a hard edge in her voice. "Lucky me. How could I forget?"

"Tell me about the accident," Bud said, now sitting on the edge of her bed, going through her purse. He found the keys and slipped them into his pocket.

"I was following *them* and the car went out of control, that's all." Vera moved and her purse fell off the bed, emptying the contents out onto the floor. As Bud put everything back in her purse, he saw a slip of paper with the Rose Avenue address in Venice scribbled on it.

"Who's *them*?" Bud asked, pocketing the slip of paper.

"My husband and his *cunt*," Vera said, her voice light, almost conversational so that Bud thought at first that he had misunderstood her.

"What's in the trunk of your car?" Bud asked.

"Something of *hers*, the *cunt's*," Vera said. "I saw it at Koenig's house and just sort of took it for spite, threw it in the back of my car and didn't do anything about it, even look at it, because it was locked."

"When were you at Koenig's house?"

"I was there Monday night, a day before the murder."

"Why did you go there?"

"Because my life had turned to garbage." Suddenly her face paled, then turned greenish, and she put her hand to her throat.

"Are you all right?" Bud asked. "Shall I call a nurse?"

She asked him to hand her a bowl, anything, and then get the hell out of the room. But he didn't leave. Instead he held a small metal pan for her while she vomited. When she was through, he put the pan in the bathroom and wet a face cloth and came back to her bed. Very gently, he wiped her face, her forehead, and was not surprised when she started to cry.

"I'm so frightened," she whispered. "I've never been so frightened in my life."

Bud waited for her to stop crying. He walked to the window and looked out over the parking lot. At the far end he saw Ivy's VW. Just beyond it on the grass, he saw Ivy and Gilbert sitting cross-legged facing each other. They appeared to be talking animatedly and laughing. He wanted to be sitting there with them, talking and laughing, too.

"I think there's every possibility that my husband killed D. P. Koenig," Vera said. Bud turned around and took his note pad out of his pocket.

In 1955, Oliver Kelsey wrote a movie about the Korean war. It was a low-budget, high-message B picture shot in the Malibu mountains. The second female lead was played by an unknown, a young actress named Vera Lakin, a large-boned, slightly awkward girl with a strikingly pretty and intelligent face.

She got the part through the perseverance of her agent, a man named D. P. Koenig. Koenig had come to Los Angeles several years before from Chicago where he had booked cheap musical acts, dancing bears, like that. There were rumors that the D. P. stood for Dwayne Percy, but no one had ever seen a birth certificate and all his official documents bore only the initials.

Because the agent was sleek and dark and unpredictable, a columnist for the *Hollywood Reporter* claimed the D. P. stood for "Doberman Pinscher." Even without the mystery of this name, he would have made it, but it helped catapult him to the top very quickly, just as the nickname Swifty helped turn Irving Lazar from journeyman agent to a superstar.

During his rise, Koenig had dated most of the starlets in Hollywood. It was said that he could make love all night without coming, without losing his erection, that the moment he withdrew, he would rise, shower and go home, or rise, escort the young lady to his front door, then shower.

Vera Lakin had acted in a few plays on Broadway, small walk-on roles, and had done a season in summer stock. The first day she came to Hollywood, she telephoned D. P. Koenig. Her last director had suggested she call the agent and said to use the director's name. Koenig said he'd never heard of the director, but consented to see her anyway.

She had a two o'clock appointment. She came five minutes early. He came two hours late. He did not call or leave a message with his secretary for her. The secretary kept apologizing and suggesting Vera leave, make another appointment.

"No, I'll wait," Vera said, smiled politely at the secretary, and continued flipping through the pages of *Look* magazine.

At a few minutes after four, the secretary told her that Koenig had returned, that he would now see her. Vera put the magazine down, straightened her skirt, and strode into D. P. Koenig's office.

He was reading *Variety* when she came in. He looked up for a moment, then looked back down and continued reading. He had to look up again almost immediately because she had pulled the paper away from him, had wadded it into a ball in her hands, and then dropped it on the floor at his feet.

"You are a rude prick," she said quietly, meeting his startled gaze. He looked at her, took her all in, her face, her large body, her blazing eyes.

152

"And you are an actress without representation."

"Do you know that I was sitting out there waiting for you for over two hours?"

"You could have left."

"No, I couldn't," she said, leaning across the desk, "because I wanted to see what someone who keeps you waiting for two hours looks like." Suddenly she reached across the desk and grabbed his chin and tilted his head up, twisted it roughly to one side, then, before he had time to react, she pulled her hand away. "Okay," she said, "now I've seen it, and now I know what that kind of a face looks like. And if I want to keep my sanity and any sense of myself, I'll steer clear of that kind of face from now on."

She turned and walked out of his office and down the street to her rented car. She looked up once and believed she saw him standing at his window, looking down at her.

The following day, a large bouquet of out-of-season roses was delivered to her. The card read "A thousand pardons." And was signed D. P. Koenig. She did not write a note to thank him for the flowers. She did not telephone him. She even forgot to add water before she went to keep an appointment with an agent at William Morris, who only kept her waiting four minutes and rose to his feet when she entered his office.

Two days later, Koenig telephoned her early in the morning, woke her up. She yawned and told him that she was thinking of signing with William Morris because they were kind and they did not keep her waiting for two hours. She did not thank him for the flowers.

"Make me a cup of coffee and I'll come over and tell you why you shouldn't sign with them," he said, then hung up before she had a chance to turn him down. She smiled and got out of bed and went into the bathroom.

She met him at the front door wearing a man's shirt with nothing under it. She was still damp from a shower or a bath and her breath smelled of toothpaste.

153

"Did you really want coffee, or was that just a come-on?" she asked. His arms were around her, under her shirt, his hands pulling her toward him.

She led him into her bedroom. She helped undress him, none too gently, popping two buttons in the process. She pulled him down onto her still unmade bed.

She came almost immediately, then sat up and looked at him. She nodded approvingly.

"You'll do," she said grinning down at him. Then she climbed out of bed, leaving him lying there unsatisfied, suspended. He suggested to her in an amused but annoyed voice that the job was only half done.

"Oh, do agents come, too?" she said, and walked into the bathroom and closed the door behind her. He heard her turn on the shower.

He was still lying in her bed when she came out of the bathroom. She was fully dressed, all business, and wanted him to look over the William Morris contract.

Without looking at it, he tore it in two and dropped it at her feet.

"You're a rude prick," he said. She looked at him, studied his unsmiling face, then started to laugh.

"Don't ever keep me waiting two hours again," she said. She let him undress her, and they made love again.

"You want to be the greatest actress in the world, right?" he asked her later on that morning as they sat together in her small, cheaply furnished living room.

"Wrong," she said. "It's all dangerous, destructive nonsense to me. What I really want is to find somebody brilliant and sensitive and sexy, and walk off into the sunset with him."

"What about rich?"

"If he's that brilliant and sensitive and sexy, and he isn't rich already, we'll get rich together."

"Your ass is too big, your shoulders are too broad, you'll probably have a weight problem all your life," he said quietly, "but I think you could probably have a halfway decent career out here."

"I'm a mildly interesting type," she said matter-of-factly, "a young character actress, that's all."

"And you'd throw it all over to be somebody's wife?"

"You bet," she said. Then she made him a proposition. She told him that she would just as soon not have the reputation for being an easy lay, the town pump, especially if she was hoping one day to land someone brilliant, sensitive, and sexy.

"How would you like to service me, very discreetly, until something more . . . suitable comes along?" she said, smiling impersonally at him. "No strings, no obligations. You could fool around with anybody you wanted to as long as you were available to me on, say, six hours' notice."

"And you?" he asked. She knew he was shocked, and also knew that he was trying hard to conceal that fact.

"Oh, I would go out and date," she said, "but I'd be faithful to you physically, if that's what you mean."

"Why?" he asked her. "How did I get so lucky?"

"Because you're mean and rotten and there's no possibility I could ever fall in love with you," she said. There was no viciousness or cruelty in her voice. She was merely telling him the truth.

He got up slowly and walked to the front door.

"Well?" she asked. He didn't stop, didn't answer her. He walked out the door and closed it quietly after him.

But ultimately he took her up on it. She would summon him every three or four days, usually in the early morning hours after she got home from a date. If he did not hear from her, often he would telephone her or appear on her doorstep between midnight and dawn, his finger on the bell until she came sleepily to let him into her bed, if not her heart.

Although there was no contract between them, he was

155

her agent. He took her to openings, to parties. He talked her up everywhere, set up interviews and auditions for her.

He got her several small parts, one or two lines, which she handled ably, but not memorably. She let it be known to him that their business relationship was one thing, their private arrangement was another. She either did not know or did not care to know the pain that this relationship was causing Koenig. Often, in bed with him, she would tell him about her intense feelings for this actor or that director.

Once, after a date, she came by his house and rang the doorbell. He came to the door in his robe and told her that she couldn't come in, that he had someone with him.

"I'll wait in the car," she said.

"No, not tonight."

"Take as long as you want," she said lightly. "I'll be out there." She turned and walked down the path to her car. He walked back to his bedroom. A perfectly nice girl in his bed held out her arms to him.

He made love to her joylessly for the next half hour, then told her to stay where she was, go to sleep. He got dressed quickly and walked out his front door, down the path to Vera Lakin's parked car. He stuck his head in the window and told her that he would follow her home.

After they made love in her bed, he asked her how she would feel about moving into his house with him, living with him. Just for convenience, he assured her.

"Then how could I date?" she asked him. "How could I keep looking for Mr. Right?"

"What is it you want that I'm unable to give you?" he asked, poised on one elbow, staring guardedly down at her in the semi-light of the new day.

"Do you know that you have never called me by my name? Never. Not once," she said quietly. "That you've never kissed me hello or goodbye or without putting your tongue down my throat."

156

"Are you forgetting whose idea this very tender relationship was in the first place?"

"The only reason you're even slightly interested in me is because I've bullied you. I mean, God help me if I ever stopped."

"You may go screw yourself," he said, then added nastily, "Velma."

"Even the D. P.," she said, unable to stop herself now, "it's so dehumanized."

"You are some prize to talk about dehumanized," he said, slipping out of bed, gathering up his clothes. "A hybrid like you, with a man's brain, a woman's genitalia, and the morals of an Algerian pimp."

He turned and walked out of the bedroom, his clothes in his arms. He did not once look back at her. She heard the front door open and close so quickly that she wondered if he might not have walked to his car naked.

She planned to telephone him in a few days, resume the illusionless relationship, but two mornings later, in the Malibu mountains, she started working on a war movie written by a man named Oliver Kelsey.

It was a good part, a noisy bitch of a nurse, but Vera Lakin was having trouble with it.

"I can't seem to make it come out rotten," Vera told the director, a man named Gordon Flemming, whose charm and courtliness had impressed her from the first time she had read for him. Flemming linked his arm through hers and led her into the tent that was serving as her dressing room. As he lifted the flap of the tent she saw him smile fondly at a young schoolgirl with a lovely figure and blotchy complexion who Vera assumed was his daughter.

She told the director what she perceived the problem to be. The character, as it was written, was not so much a cold bitch as a deeply disturbed woman who was basically okay, likable. She asked if she could play the scene as a neurotic rather than as a bitch.

Gordon Flemming considered what she said, then suggested they shoot around the scene until the writer showed up and perhaps they could all agree on how the character should be played.

Oliver Kelsey was a lean, spare, weathered man, often mistaken on the streets of Beverly Hills, Hollywood, for Robert Ryan. He had a quiet, repressed air about him, a droll, often cruel sense of humor. He also had the reputation for being the worst-dressed man in the entertainment industry, given to loud Hawaiian shirts and Jesus sandals over white sweat socks.

When Oliver Kelsey came to the Malibu mountains, Flemming took him aside and explained that the pain-in-the-ass actress playing the bitchy nurse was having trouble with the concept of the role. Oliver Kelsey's jaw stiffened, his eyes narrowed. He had never related well to actresses, and particularly to thinking actresses.

He walked into Vera Lakin's dressing room and introduced himself. Less than an hour later, he had made the decision to divorce his wife. He had been married for three years to a physicist whose brain had awed him initially, but after living with her he had discovered that she was an earthbound bore.

He decided he wanted to marry Vera Lakin because she was bright and funny and sexy; and because she had the rare ability to tell him that something he wrote didn't work and at the same time made him feel like the leading stud in the industry, if not the world—a truly remarkable gift.

He rewrote the pivotal scene while Vera paced around him, occasionally touching the back of his neck with her long, cool fingers. He felt ten feet tall when she read the scene, then looked up at him, her eyes brimming, and said merely, "Oh, yes."

When she returned from filming the scene, he was lying fully clothed on her day bed, the opened script across his loins, unsuccessfully hiding an erection.

She picked up the script, then, looking down at him,

grinning, she took off all her clothes and lay down on top of him. He came before he entered her, and she announced solemnly that it was the most flattering thing that had ever happened to her in her entire life.

Then he asked her to marry him. When she saw from his eyes that he was serious, she suggested he ask her again when he was no longer married to someone else.

Three weeks later he was in Juarez dissolving his marriage to the physicist, and a week after that, Oliver Kelsey and Vera Lakin were married in Santa Barbara.

One of the guests at the wedding breakfast was the bride's agent, D. P. Koenig. She had not wanted to invite him, had suggested when she telephoned to tell him she was getting married that he be busy and not come up to Santa Barbara.

"And miss this coupling of giants?" he said to her.

"Please don't come," she said.

"I think I have a right to meet this brilliant, sensitive, sexy gentleman who replaced me."

"He doesn't know about us," Vera said. "I'd like to keep it that way."

"It was a mutually degrading relationship," Koenig said finally. "I'd be unlikely to talk about it."

She could not dissuade him from coming to Santa Barbara. He brought his wedding gift with him and presented it to the bride and groom after the ceremony.

It was an old English tea service easily worth several thousand dollars. The groom was impressed. The bride was embarrassed, uneasy about the excessively extravagant gift.

"Your agent's a pretty classy guy," Oliver said.

"He's not my agent anymore," Vera said quickly.

Later that morning, D. P. Koenig invited Oliver Kelsey to go for a walk on the beach with him. If Vera had known about it, she would have accompanied them, but she had been in another room and did not know that the two men had gone off together.

When they returned, Oliver announced that he was

changing agents, that D. P. Koenig would now represent him, had guaranteed to make him the most important, sought-after writer in Hollywood. Vera looked over her new husband's shoulder at Koenig. He smiled impassively back at her.

"Just think of it as a sort of bonus wedding gift," Koenig told her.

"Nice," she said. "Very nice." And she turned away from him.

The following week, Oliver Kelsey dismissed his own agent and signed a three-year contract with D. P. Koenig, despite the fact that his new bride seemed dead set against it.

Vera's acting career was over. It was what they both wanted. Oliver had barely been able to handle his first wife's distractions, which had only been irritating, but nonthreatening to him professionally. He knew that if Vera pursued an acting career it would both irritate and threaten him.

Vera slipped into the role of author's wife with ease and grace. She upgraded his wardrobe, she learned to type and to laugh convincingly at stories she had heard many times. She discovered she could not have children, and he did not want children, so she spent her days moving contentedly from the kitchen to the typewriter to the compost heap in her garden, a happy and fulfilled woman.

Vera had been convinced that Koenig would run her husband's career into the ground, but she had been wrong. Oliver Kelsey worked steadily for the next seventeen years. The fact that her husband had not become the most important, the most sought-after writer in Hollywood had more to do with his own creative limitations than with Koenig's effort in his behalf.

They were Hollywood's happiest, most compatible couple. Other marriages came and went, but theirs grew strong, and their devotion, their affection for each other was so real, so genuine, that after several years it stopped getting on people's nerves.

They were public hand holders and face touchers and never permitted hostesses to separate them at dinner parties. They had often been discovered making love in their swimming pool by guests who arrived too early. And once on a clear, sunny day on Mulholland Drive a policeman booked them for performing oral sex in the front seat of their car.

Three years ago it all started going bad for them. The young, hip, bearded, blue-jeaned writers began to take over the industry. D. P. Koenig was representing seven of them, all under thirty, all making six figures a year. Oliver Kelsey was getting harder and harder to sell.

"He's old, he's tired," the youthful, laid-back producers would tell Koenig, and then would ask him who else he had. Several times Koenig suggested to Oliver that he seek other representation, but each time, Oliver would tell him, "You have my X-rays, I'll stay with you."

Vera Kelsey watched her husband's sense of himself shrivel, almost totally disappear. She saw him sit by the telephone and stare at it for hours. She would urge him to come for a walk, but he would say no, that he couldn't leave, that he was waiting for Koenig to return his call. The calls did not come, or if they did, they would come several days late. There would be a note of irritation in Koenig's voice, a taxi meter running.

Sometimes the return call would be made by Peter Lutz, who would give him the message that Koenig was too busy to deliver himself. Nothing new. No job. No interest.

At Vera's insistence, they moved from the big Brentwood house into the newly carved out tract home in the unchic section of Bel-Air. She had wanted to move to an apartment to save money, but, knowing her love for and need to work in a garden, Oliver insisted on moving into a house.

The first night they spent in the new house marked the third anniversary of Oliver's unemployment. For face, he had been telling people that he was writing a novel. The year before, Vera had typed the first forty pages of the novel and knew in her heart that it was dreadful, but still encouraged, even nagged him to keep working on it.

He then told people that he was writing a play. When he was away from home, she would go through his desk drawers, his files, to see if, in fact, he was writing a play. She found one sheet of yellow typing paper with a paragraph of stage directions.

From where she worked in the garden, just outside Oliver's office window, she could hear the new ingratiating tone in his voice as he tried to get through to his agent, and it pained her, enraged her.

"It's you-know-who again, Peter," Oliver would say, and the forced, apologetic joviality chilled her heart. "I've been out all morning and I thought maybe the Big Honcho tried to call me, so I'm beating him to the punch."

It was a lie, of course. He had been in the house all morning, all day, waiting for the phone to ring, for Koenig to get back to him. Her husband had started calling Koenig three days before. He had not left the house in those three days, but had sat in his office in front of his typewriter, staring at the telephone, waiting, waiting.

Vera had tried to get him to come for a drive to the beach, a walk up into the hillside, but he refused, said he was working. When she tried to urge him, he snapped at her and closed the office door in her face.

She had seen it happen before to other writers who had been cut loose emotionally, if not contractually, by their agents. Once a close friend of Oliver's had driven in from his home in Malibu after five unreturned telephone calls to his agent. The writer burst into the agent's office, lifted him up from his suede swivel chair and punched him so hard that shards of the man's hearing aid had to be removed from his chest in the emergency room of Cedars-Sinai.

The writer had felt so good afterward, so existentially liberated, that he rented a banquet room at Chasen's and invited forty people, including the assaulted agent, who turned down the invitation but got the writer a two-hour television movie at Paramount the following week.

Vera begged her husband to fire Koenig, to find another agent, someone young and hungry who would go out and fight for him.

"I've been in this business forty-two years," Oliver said to her, his jaw tight, his eyes cold. "I'll kill myself before I go back and start over again."

"Changing agents is not starting over again."

"What do you want me to do?" he said disagreeably. "A few episodes of 'Mork and Mindy'?" He turned and walked back into his office. She heard the door lock behind him. She knew he was going to call Koenig again, make feeble jokes with Peter Lutz about being in and out that morning.

The lies at cocktail parties became worse. He was now telling other writers that he had a pilot at NBC, a movie deal pending at United Artists. Vera had to move away from him, could not bear to see the looks of compassionate disbelief on people's faces. It was a town where everyone knew who was busy, who was working, and whose agent had stopped returning phone calls.

Then he refused to go to cocktail parties altogether, shouted abusively at her when she told him about the invitations. He spent more and more time in his office, the door locked, the television set on with the sound turned very low. She knew he was watching the morning game shows, then the afternoon soaps.

When she could stand it no longer, she drove down to

the Bel-Air Market and called D. P. Koenig from a pay phone. Peter Lutz told her politely that he was in conference.

"I have not telephoned him in twenty years," Vera said, enunciating each word icily. "You tell him to get his skinny ass on this phone."

"Are you at home?" Peter asked.

"I'm in a phone booth because my husband would quite literally murder me if he knew I was making this call."

Peter asked for the phone number of the booth and said he'd have Koenig get right back to her.

Four dimes later, she hung up the phone, climbed into her car and drove to Koenig's office. Peter Lutz told her politely he could not be disturbed for another five minutes. She strode past Peter's desk and threw open the door to Koenig's office before Peter was able to get around his desk and try to block her way.

Koenig was alone, jogging in place. He turned and looked at her but did not break stride. Peter interposed himself, but Koenig nodded that it was all right, that he could handle it.

"Do you realize," Koenig said, his knees moving up and down, "this is the first time you and I have been alone in twenty years?"

"You're killing him," she said quietly. "You know that, don't you? Little pieces of him are dying every day."

"I've told him that I will release him any time he wishes," Koenig said, still pumping up and down.

"He wants you, he trusts you, he is depending on you to get him something, anything."

"His last three scripts were garbage," Koenig said impatiently. "You know that, and I know that. He's lost it."

"Then answer his telephone calls," Vera said quietly, "the same day he makes them, even if you don't have anything to tell him."

164

"He calls here three times a day, for Christ's sake!" Koenig said. "I'm too busy for that."

"I have never in all these years asked you for anything, but I'm asking you now. Do something for him. Save his life."

"He's still got money," Koenig said, still keeping up the pace. "Why don't you both be realistic and buy a chicken farm somewhere?"

"You always were a prick," Vera said.

"You just backed the wrong horse, that's all."

"You were a piece of ass to me then," Vera said, smiling impersonally at him, "just as I was to you. And that's all there ever was." Koenig suddenly stopped jogging and crossed the room. He stood very close to her. His face was flushed, but papery dry.

"In a lifetime of using people," Koenig said, "you were the only person who ever used me. I didn't like the way it felt."

"I'll tell you this now, twenty years after the fact—for sheer mechanics, you were the best. It's just too bad they couldn't have slipped a real person inside while they were at it."

"I would have married you," Koenig said, his voice light, teasing, but he looked away, could not meet her unwavering gaze as he spoke.

"Bullshit," Vera said gently.

"I was stunned when you told me you were marrying a second-rater like Oliver Kelsey."

"He wasn't a second-rater when I married him," Vera said. "You made him a second-rater. All these years he stuck by you, hung on your every word. You were his guru."

"It may please you to believe that I scuttled him over the years," Koenig said, walking away from her, standing at his window, looking out over Beverly Hills. "What you don't know is that I carried him, protected him, and you, from the truths, the direct quotes, the savage turndowns."

165

"Do something for him now," Vera said. She walked up and stood behind him. He did not turn around. "I'm begging you."

"There's never been a whisper about you," Koenig said, turning suddenly and facing her. "I listened. I asked. It would have amused me to think that you hadn't lost your . . . voraciousness, your lewdness."

"Find him a job, an assignment, something, anything."

"I remember how you felt," Koenig said. His voice was unsteady.

"And, if you can't do that, answer his phone calls the same day he makes them."

"How did a second-rate man and a third-rate writer end up with you?"

"He has not touched me voluntarily for two years," Vera said. "Has he touched anyone else? I must know that, and I believe, if he has, you will tell me."

Koenig moved away from her, walked across the room and stared out another window. Then, without turning around, he shook his head.

"I would swear on my life that he's not had anything to do with anyone. And nothing would have pleased me more than to tell you that he had."

"Then he's dying. He is quite literally dying. He is almost all gone." She turned away so that he would not see that she was crying.

"I'll have something for him before the day is out," Koenig said, his voice once again clipped, professional, guarded.

"Thank you," she said quietly. "Thank you very much."

"It will not be *Gone With The Wind*, however."

"Call him immediately, please."

"I fantasized that one day you'd come to me for something—I just didn't know it would take you twenty years."

"Hey," Vera said gently, "he's my life. My whole life." Koenig walked her, almost formally, to the door. She stopped suddenly and turned to him.

"One last favor," she said.

"I will not tell him who shook the plum out of the tree."

A young intern came in, followed by a severe-looking nurse who told Bud he had to leave.

"Just one more question," Bud said, but the nurse had already started to pull the white curtain around the bed.

"It'll have to wait," the nurse said. The young intern shrugged and smiled to indicate that he, too, knew that the nurse was a rigid bitch, but confirmed that Bud had been there too long already, that he could come back later, or preferably the next day.

"Mrs. Kelsey," Bud called around the white curtain, "does your husband know you're here?"

"She can't talk," the nurse said. "She has a thermometer in her mouth."

It was starting to get dark when he stepped outside the hospital. He filled his lungs with fresh, unmedicated air and looked around for the VW. He was sorry now that he had permitted them to wait because he was going to have to dump them almost immediately.

He looked out over the parking lot, but could see no dusty VW, no happy pair sitting on the grass. He figured they had grown tired of waiting for him and had driven away. As he was turning to find a pay phone, he saw Gilbert Ritner running toward him, his hair bouncing up and down, and even at a distance Bud could see his face was flushed, his eyes bulging. The kid was obviously in terrible shape.

"She went after them!" Gilbert called across the remaining distance. "She followed them!"

"After who?"

"The van was here!" Gilbert stopped in front of Bud, hardly able to catch his breath. "The one I saw in front of Koenig's house the other day. The same girl was driving it."

"Was there a man in the van with her?" There was no doubt about it, this kid was going to solve the goddamn case for him.

"Yeah, a gray, skinny guy," Gilbert said, still panting. "Ivy and I crawled up near where they were double-parked in front of the entrance here. They were fighting about something, and then they drove off together."

"You mean, he didn't even get out of the car?"

"He started to. He opened the door and started to get out, then she said something to him and he got back in the car, and they drove off."

"Why the hell did she follow them?" Bud said, annoyed at the inconvenience this was going to cause him. "We know where they live."

"Maybe they weren't going home," Gilbert said in an infuriatingly patronizing voice. "Maybe they were going somewhere that would tell us something."

At that moment, Ivy's VW pulled up in front of them and stopped. She leaned out the window, a grim look on her face, and then put a traffic ticket in Bud's hand.

"There is no justice in this world," Ivy said. "The van went right through a red light and nobody stopped *her* and gave *her* a ticket."

"Did you get a good look at her?"

"Not really," Ivy said. "Do you have enough juice to take care of the ticket?"

"Don't sweat it," Bud said, holding the seat so Gilbert could climb in the back.

"It might humble you to know that the Encino Police Force has never heard of you."

"Yeah, well, my fame is very localized."

"I'm sorry I lost them," she said gently. Bud smiled over at her. He meant only to pat her hand, but ended

168

up holding it until she next had to shift gears. He felt Gilbert's fingertips on his shoulder.

If it were not for the heaviness settling nearer and nearer his heart, he believed that he might actually start to enjoy this case.

10

Bud turned over Vera Kelsey's car keys to Tom Edwards.

"Can you find out where her car was towed and have
someone get over there and bring everything in the
trunk except the repair tools back here to me?" Bud
said.

"Is tomorrow okay?" Tom said, staring reluctantly at
the keys. "The garage'll probably be locked up."

"If tomorrow were okay, I'd have given you the keys
tomorrow."

"Okay, okay," Tom said, and got up to look for someone lower down the ladder to do the job.

Bud sat down at his desk and tried to sort out what he
had. A failed writer was cheating on his wife. The wife
racked up her car and herself trying to follow her husband and his girlfriend. The wife had taken something
of the girlfriend's from the agent's house and had locked
it in the trunk of her car. The writer wouldn't even go
to the hospital to see his bruised and broken wife of
twenty-two years. The wife and the agent had a sick

relationship at one time. The agent represented the husband for twenty years.

The agent was dead.

He still didn't know where the hell he was, so he telephoned Peter Lutz.

"I'm just on my way out," Peter said.

"Where'll you be in twenty minutes?" Bud asked. There was a long silence.

"Damn," Peter said finally.

"I have about five questions I want answers to. Where will you be?"

"Have you heard of the Blue Parrot?"

Bud had heard of it. It was in the gay section of West Hollywood, an eight-block stretch of Santa Monica Boulevard known as Boys Town. The Blue Parrot was a homosexual bar with lots of hanging plants, lots of raw wood, lots of loud music, and wall-to-wall gays.

"I'll meet you in the parking lot," Bud said.

"You'll be safer inside, believe me."

"I'll see you there in twenty minutes."

"Who knows," Peter said lightly. "It might change the course of your life."

Bud had never seen so many elegantly dressed men. There were at least seventy of them packed in there, and not an over-thirty-inch waist in the bunch. As he walked in, each man he passed eyed him, sized him up. Some of them smiled, one or two of them tried to stop him, to offer him a drink.

The first face he recognized was Mr. Edwin from Cannell and Chaffin. He was tempted to go over and chew him out about the down in his couch, but he didn't want to be observed in a heated argument with a queer in a queer joint.

"Over here," Peter called to him from the bar, "unless something better presents itself."

"Christalmighty," Bud said, as he sat down next to Peter, "where do you all come from?"

"Just good mothering, I guess," Peter said lightly. He was still wearing an expensive three-piece suit, but his tie was loose, his top four shirt buttons undone, his vest completely open. Bud wondered if this signaled availability or just end-of-the-day relaxation.

"What'll it be, fellas?" the bartender said. He appeared to be straight, but probably wasn't.

"I'll have a screwdriver," Peter said in a too-loud voice, "and my friend here will have the usual." Peter laughed noisily and several young men turned and looked at Bud with new interest.

"I'll have club soda," Bud said, smiling grimly at the bartender, "and I ain't never been here before."

"How's the old investigation coming?" Peter asked, casing the bar, casing the entrance as a group of graying business men walked in. "You unearth anything worth anything yet?"

"Vera Kelsey's in the hospital," Bud said. "Automobile accident."

"Yes, I know," Peter said, his voice suddenly guarded. His gecko-like eyes stopped rotating for a moment and he focused his attention on Bud.

"How do you know?" Bud asked.

"Because I know everything," Peter said lightly.

"Vera Kelsey said some very strange things."

"She's a very strange lady."

"Did she ever telephone Koenig, come by the office?"

"Never," Peter said, shooting a torrid look at a man down the bar, then turning back to Bud, "except for once about six weeks ago when she barged into his office loaded for bear."

"What did they talk about?"

"I don't know, but he was kind of jumpy and distracted for the rest of the day."

"What were Koenig's feelings for Vera Kelsey?"

"Unusual," Peter said. "More than met the eye."

"What does that mean?"

172

"Be back in a second," Peter said and walked three barstools down and started talking quietly to the man he had exchanged the torrid glances with. Even Bud had to admit he was a good-looking son of a bitch with his Kennedy-type hair and his soft suede windbreaker.

The man swiveled around on his stool and smiled at Peter. As they spoke, Bud saw the man reach out and brush what had to be imaginary lint from Peter's lapel because Bud had noticed earlier how immaculately clean and lintless he was. The two men touched hands, and Peter came back and sat on his barstool. He took a sip of his screwdriver, still looking over Bud's shoulder at his new pal down the bar.

"What happened to the love of your life on the school board?" Bud asked, irritated at being there in the first place, and at the distractions.

"Right now he's in Aspen with his wife and children doing cleancut all-American things."

"Scared, huh?" Bud asked.

"Yeah, I guess," Peter sighed. He slumped lower on the barstool and looked away—not at his friend down the bar, but just away. "He will never see me again, never speak to me again. I'm never to call him again. Something else to thank the corpse for."

"Well, in the meantime, you've got a new buddy, so what's the big deal?"

"Are you kidding?" Peter said. "The little prick called me down there to ask me your name and number."

"Can we get the hell out of here?" Bud said, angry now and uncomfortable.

"You really want to be seen leaving this place with one of the town's most eligible gays?"

"Okay, then, quit fooling around and start talking to me."

Peter finished his drink and signaled the bartender for another one. "There was a manuscript," Peter said. "It was a rough draft, barely readable, no title page, no author. When I was cleaning out the files about a year ago, I found it and I brought it in to Koenig and asked him whose it was, what he wanted me to do with it, and he got very upset. He said it was just a piece of crap by an ex-client. He grabbed it out of my hands and threw it in the wastepaper basket."

The man with the Kennedy hair and the suede windbreaker got off his barstool and came and stood next to Bud.

"Can I buy you a drink?" he said, throwing his arm over Bud's shoulder, giving him a real locker-room grin.

"Tell you what, pal," Bud said. "I'll show you mine if you show me yours." Bud took out his wallet and flashed his detective badge.

"I get the picture," the man with the Kennedy hair said, and walked away.

"Now what about the manuscript?" Bud said.

After D. P. Koenig had left for the day, Peter went into his office and looked in the wastepaper basket. He was curious to see what piece of crap by an ex-client could have made the blood drain from his employer's face.

The manuscript was no longer in the wastepaper basket. His curiosity aroused even more, he made a thorough search of the office and finally found the manuscript hidden under the jogging platform in Koenig's closet.

Peter slipped it into his briefcase and went directly home. Even before he had taken off his tie, he started to read it. While still on the first page, he began to suspect that the author was D. P. Koenig himself. It was poorly written, melodramatic, with long, emotional, punishing monologues. But despite its amateurish quality, its stilted syntax, it had grabbed him with its undiluted anger and anguish.

"It was about an agent," Peter said, "a guarded loner, who falls passionately in love with a bitch of an actress who uses and abuses him, ultimately abandoning him to marry a successful writer."

"Do you know," Bud said, "that's the first thing worth a dime you've ever said to me."

"None of the characters were named," Peter said. "He just referred to them as *The Writer, The Actress, The Agent,* like that."

"Anybody get murdered in it?"

"It started with the meeting between the actress and the agent and ended with the funeral of the writer, with the agent delivering the eulogy."

"You're sure it wasn't the agent's funeral?"

"No, but it was an interesting eulogy. The agent said, as the writer's body was being lowered into the ground, 'Those whom the Gods wish to destroy, they first stop returning their phone calls.' "

"Where is the manuscript now?" Bud asked.

"The next morning, I slipped it back under the jogging mat," Peter said. "Then, that evening, as Koenig was leaving, I saw a manila envelope under his arm. I asked him if he wanted me to mail something for him, and he said, no, he'd do it himself; and since he never did anything like that for himself before, I figured it was the manuscript."

"Damn," Bud said, "I wanted to take a look at it."

"You still can," Peter said, now smiling and nodding warmly to a man with very blond hair on the other side of the bar. He started to slip off his barstool and mumbled something to Bud about being back in a second, but Bud pushed him back on the barstool.

"Arrange your sex life on your own time."

"Okay, okay," Peter said, shooting one last burning glance down the bar. "Anyway, just on a hunch, when I went to get my car, I looked in the trash bin in the garage, and, sure enough, there it was. The manila envelope Koenig had been carrying."

"Where is it now?" Bud asked.

"My place," Peter said, "under lock and key."

"What were you planning to do with it?"

"Damned if I know, but I always figured if he wanted

175

to get rid of it that badly, it had to be worth something to somebody one day."

"Do you know if anybody ever saw it or if it was submitted to a studio, producers, something like that?"

"My guess is, no, that this was a first draft that he thought better of, that it was some kind of purge for him, but for some reason he couldn't burn it."

"I want to read it," Bud said.

"I won't let you take it away from my apartment, but you can read it there if you want." Bud looked up quickly to see if this was an invitation, a come-on, but Peter was once again looking down the bar at the very blond man.

"What time will you be home?" Bud asked. Two men turned and stared at him as he spoke, and suddenly he realized that he sounded like a gay making a date with another gay.

"It depends on how lucky I get this evening," Peter said, "but, if you're there at eleven-thirty, I'll make a point of being there."

Peter handed Bud his business card just as Mr. Edwin of Cannell and Chaffin sidled up to the bar.

"If I'd only known," Mr. Edwin whispered to Bud, "I'd have stuffed your cushions myself." Bud didn't answer, didn't react. He wanted to tell the little fruit to go screw himself, but he also wanted his reupholstering done without hassle. It was just another of life's small compromises.

"By the way," Bud said to Peter, as he was starting to leave, "where can I reach Oliver Kelsey?"

"You haven't spoken to him yet?" Peter sounded genuinely surprised.

"He hasn't been home for days, and there's nobody at the address of the phone number you gave me."

"Well, you'll hear from him sooner or later," Peter said. "I know he wants to talk to you."

"Will you stop being so goddamn mysterious?"

"All right," Peter said finally, "he's out there some-where with Gypsy Doniger."

"Who the hell is Gypsy Doniger?"

"I always suspected you were a lousy detective," Peter said. He looked at his wristwatch, then back up at Bud. "Eleven-thirty, then." And Peter was down at the other end of the bar standing very close to the blond young man.

There was a pay phone in the parking lot. Two short thin men in identical windbreakers were standing very close together in the booth. One was talking on the telephone. The other was socking it into the man who was talking on the telephone.

Bud waited for a minute, then walked up to the glass door of the booth and held his detective's shield at eye level. The man talking on the telephone hung up instantly and they both scrambled out of the booth and disappeared down the alley like two silver bullets.

Bud stepped into the booth which smelled faintly of after-shave lotion and not so faintly of sweat. He telephoned headquarters and asked for Tom Edwards, who told him there were a lot of messages for him.

"A guy named Oliver Kelsey has called you three times. He won't talk to anybody else."

"Who is Gypsy Doniger?" Bud asked.

"Sounds like a made-up name," Tom said.

"You mean, you've never heard of her?"

"Should I have?"

"Get me a rundown on her, huh? Address, phone. Whatever."

"What is this, I have to check out some piece of ass for you?"

"Where can I reach Oliver Kelsey?"

Tom gave him the phone number. It was the Rose Avenue telephone number. Bud was not surprised. He hung up and drove to his apartment.

After he stepped over the threshold, he saw a note on

the floor. It was from Ivy, in bold, no-nonsense block letters. She said she had waited for him for over an hour, that he should come to her apartment, that she had some incredible news for him.

He smiled, folded up the note with her address on it, and dialed Oliver Kelsey. There was no answer. He showered, changed, and drove to Ivy's apartment.

She lived just off Fountain Avenue in West Hollywood. The building was fake Hawaiian with colored lights focused on two unworthy palm trees. A wall of corrugated plastic shielded the swimming pool from the street. He walked around the pool, around a noisy middle-aged couple on aluminum loungers sipping tropical drinks. It made him grateful for his own apartment house with no pool, no patio, no lanai, no public areas.

It took her over a minute to come to the door, although she called out to him almost immediately. She was wearing a white terry cloth robe and hot rollers and probably not much else.

"All right," she said, grinning at him, "now you know that I'm not a natural beauty."

"I have to use your phone," he said, walking into her small, cluttered living room. It was not spare and tasteful like his own, but the posters on the wall were good and she had books coming out of everywhere. It was a warm jumble of what looked to be garage-sale purchases, hand-me-downs from friends.

"Don't officers of the law say hello or anything like that?" Ivy said as she bent down to follow the telephone cord to the side of a worn but once-good couch.

"Not when they're off duty," Bud said. He sat down on the couch and dialed Oliver Kelsey's number. Still no answer. He hung up the phone and looked at her, saw that where her robe separated, her legs were good; short, freckled, but shapely.

"Hi," he said, wondering what she'd do if he tugged on her terry cloth belt, pulled her down on top of him.

"I have lost two and a half pounds," she told him, her voice awed, almost childlike. "Two and a half pounds. What about you?"

He thought over his intake of the past twenty-four hours. He'd had nothing but the liquid protein crap, and he had to admit that he felt lighter, even more alert in a strange, almost mystical way.

"I don't know," he said. "Have you got scales here?"

A lean, tense young man with troubled eyes and a black beard walked into the living room from the back of the apartment. He was wearing blue jeans and that was it, except for a yellow towel draped around his neck.

"Oh," Ivy said, turning around, smiling warmly at the intruder, "Bud, I'd like you to meet my good friend, Gil Rudolph. Gil, this is my good friend, Bud Bacola."

Bud was up off the couch like a shot. He was more angry, more put out than he could have imagined possible. He was aware of Ivy, looking from her one good friend to her other good friend, a pleased smile on her face. He wanted to grab her, slap her, do something other than just stand there. The intensity of his feelings frightened him.

The two men shook hands politely. Ivy flopped down on the couch, hugging her robe around her, not noticeably uncomfortable or embarrassed, which angered Bud even more.

"Gil reviews movies for a Marin County newspaper," Ivy said, almost formally, to Bud. Bud nodded politely.

"Bud is a detective with the Beverly Hills Police Department," Ivy explained to Gil. Gil nodded politely. Bud picked up the telephone and dialed Oliver Kelsey, but hung up after the fifth ring. He put the telephone down and headed for the front door.

"If you have any information for me, Miss Greenwald," Bud said in an icy voice, "you can reach me through the Beverly Hills Police Department."

He turned and was out the door, resisting the urge to

179

slam it hard. She caught up with him at the foot of the stairs.

"Hey," she said, "wait a minute and I'll explain." He stopped and turned and looked at her. She smiled. He did not smile back. "What it is," she said quietly, "is that I've kind of been sleeping with him. Off and on."

"That's an explanation?"

"Yeah, that's an explanation. It's exactly what it is. He comes down here on press junkets and he drops by, and, if he isn't hung up on somebody or I'm not hung up on somebody, we sleep together."

"And have you already been in the hay with him this evening?" Bud asked, trying to sound like someone who didn't care one way or the other, but not altogether succeeding.

"He showed up unexpectedly about seven minutes before you did," Ivy said.

"Well, he certainly made himself at home in a hell of a hurry."

"We're very old friends. We've been through a lot together."

"And I guess you'd have been through a little more if I hadn't shown up when I did." Bud knew he sounded like a jealous lover, hated the role, but didn't seem to be able to do all that much about it.

"Well, you are some crummy detective," she said, starting to lose her temper for the first time, "because if you were any good, you'd have seen the sheets and blankets and pillow on the other side of the couch in the living room. That's where he's sleeping tonight."

"Oh," Bud said, starting to smile, "then he's hung up on someone now. Is that it?"

"Yeah, right," Ivy said. "It's his problem. Thank God it's not mine." She turned and walked back toward the stairs to her apartment. He smiled as he watched her pick up the hem of her robe as she walked through some puddles of water on the pavement. He caught up with her and stopped her at the bottom of the stairs.

"Are you not sleeping with him tonight because of me?" Bud asked.

"Yeah, something like that," she said softly. "Pretty dumb, huh?"

"I have a comfortable sofa in my living room," he said. He reached out and touched her face, ran his fingers across her forehead.

"Who do you think you're kidding?" she said. She reached up and captured the hand that was touching her face and held it against her cheek.

"All right, then," Bud said, "let him sleep on my sofa, and I'll sleep on your sofa."

"Five pounds," she said. "That was our deal."

He looked at her, at her short, plump body, her eager, offbeat face, her head still bristling with hot rollers, and wondered why the hell he was so turned on.

"How do you know I won't go find someone else?"

"Them's the risks," she said, and turned to go upstairs. He pulled her back, more roughly than he had intended. She lost her balance and fell against him. He tried to catch her, but they both went down.

She landed on top of him. She tried to get off, but he held her there, and slowly brought her face down to his and kissed her on the lips.

"Now, what information do you have for me?" he said.

"Oh, you cops."

She told him something he already knew. That Oliver Kelsey was running around with Gypsy Doniger. What he had to find out now was how and why.

They were sitting in his parked car in front of her apartment. She had taken her hair out of the hot rollers and put on another sad sack of a dress and red-and-black cowboy boots. He would talk to her about her wardrobe one day when they had more time.

"It's just such an incredibly small world," she said. "My typist—actually I never really use her—I mean, who can afford that? Only I had to when I had a broken

wrist a few years ago, and we've become sort of telephone friends since then. Anyway, she's very good and
fast and catches all her own typos which most of them
don't. . . ."

"Why are you rambling?" he asked her. She didn't say
anything for a moment. She looked away from him.

"Well, I guess it's because I sort of care for you, and
I'm afraid I'm going to screw up or something. How's
that?"

"You're doing just fine," he said, and, as he looked
over at her, he knew where he wanted to be. In bed with
her, not just to make love, but to talk and touch and
listen to her ramble on disjointedly. And what scared
him the most was that those feelings didn't scare him
that much.

"Anyway," she went on, "Jeanmarie called me a while
ago just to talk, and she mentioned very casually she'd
just typed her first X-rated movie script. She said it
wasn't bad, really, sort of touching in places, and that
she was embarrassed because she'd gotten very horny
while she was typing."

"Yeah, go on."

"She told me it was being written for someone named
Gypsy Doniger, sort of a new Marilyn Chambers type,
and just to make conversation I asked her who wrote the
script and she said it was a man named Orion Halsey."
She turned to him, waiting for a reaction, but he just
stared at her, waiting for her to go on.

"Who the hell is Orion Halsey?"

"Jesus, don't you know anything?" Ivy said, very
pleased with herself. "That's the name Oliver Kelsey
uses when he writes crap."

"You did good," Bud said, suddenly seeing the pieces
start to fall into place, or, if not into place, at least into
the same ball park.

"The description that Gilbert Ritner gave of the girl
in the camper in the driveway," Ivy said excitedly, "that
could have been Gypsy Doniger."

182

"How do you know what she looks like?"

"I just did an article a week or two ago, sort of a raunchy rundown of porno hopefuls, and I had a publicity still of her around somewhere."

"Get it," Bud said.

"Are you kidding? I threw it out the moment I got paid for the article. I kept the Harry Reems picture, though, if you're interested."

"If that was Oliver Kelsey and Gypsy Doniger parked in Koenig's driveway on Monday, what the hell were they doing there?" Bud took out Peter Lutz's message sheet. Oliver Kelsey had telephoned three times that morning, and twice in the afternoon.

"I'll bet I know what it is!" Ivy said. "I'll bet Peter told him Koenig was sick at home. He probably drove over there to check it out."

"Why didn't he phone instead?"

"Because big agents don't give little clients their home phone numbers."

"Your friend, the horny typist," Bud said. "I'd like to talk to her now."

"I doubt that can be arranged," Ivy said, a lascivious grin on her face. "She couldn't even finish talking to me because she said someone from her 'maintenance crew' was at the door."

"What the hell does that mean?"

"It's the way she happens to refer to the many people she has come to count on for impersonal, reliable service," Ivy said lightly.

"Do you have a maintenance crew?" Bud asked her. From where his voice was coming from, they both knew it was not a casual question.

"I have a weirdo aunt who used to tell me, practically when I was in kindergarten, that you should never, never have an affair with a man you wouldn't want to give a pedicure to," Ivy said. She leaned back and stared out the window. "It sure keeps you on the straight and narrow."

Bud smiled at her in the darkened car. He thought about all the women he'd been to bed with over the past year. He tried to imagine himself paring their toenails, softening their calluses. He shuddered involuntarily. He didn't mind entering their bodies, but the thought of intimately caring for their feet repelled him. Not a bad barometer at all, he decided.

He liked Ivy's aunt already.

Jeanmarie was thin and angular, with acne scars and a too-short haircut. She was pissed off with Ivy for bringing a cop over and didn't bother to disguise it. Given her looks and sour personality, Bud wondered how she had managed to get anybody to service her, let alone a whole crew.

"He's a nice, nice man," Jeanmarie said, her voice aggressively resentful, "and this whole thing makes me feel like a fink."

Bud asked politely to see the script, amused by the fact that a cop's duties would call for him to look at two scripts in one night. Only in Beverly Hills.

"He's okay," Ivy said. "If you have it, show it to him."

She didn't have a copy. She said that Orion Halsey had picked it up three or four days earlier. He had been upset and had told her there were a lot of changes, that the producer was having some problems with the script, that he'd get back to her as soon as possible with the new material.

"And did he?" Bud asked.

"No," Jeanmarie said, "but the next day there was a message on my answering machine from him. He said they'd hired another writer and that as soon as he got his money, he'd pay me for the typing."

"Imagine being fired off a dirty movie," Ivy said. Her voice was no more than a shocked whisper, the writer in her anguished for the rejection, the humiliation.

"What was the plot of the movie?" Bud asked.

"As dirty movies go," Jeanmarie said, "I thought it was pretty good. It was about a thirty-five-year-old millionaire rock star who couldn't get it up anymore. So he advertises that he'll buy people's sex fantasies, pay them lots of money to stage and act out their erotic dreams for him. And, let me tell you, he invented some pips!"

"How does it end?" Bud asked.

"Well, it was actually a very strange ending," Jeanmarie said in a troubled voice. "When the millionaire had gone through all the fantasies, and none of them turned him on, he decides to go home to his wife and just live with it. But when he gets home, he finds her in bed with his advance man . . ."

"What's an advance man?" Bud asked quickly.

"It's sort of an agent," Ivy said, "someone who manages your affairs, goes on the road and arranges things."

"And then what does he do?" Bud asked Jeanmarie.

"He climbs into bed with them, gets in between them, and finally gets it up. And then makes love to both of them."

Ivy and Bud turned and looked at each other. They said nothing. They both rose to their feet at the same moment. Ivy thanked Jeanmarie for her help, and they walked out to the street. He opened the car door for her and then climbed in behind the wheel.

He must know all about them, Bud thought to himself, about his wife and his agent and their earlier relationship. As he drove, he thought about Vera Kelsey. Perhaps she had been lying to him and had not kissed off her agent. Perhaps she had been having an affair with Koenig all this time, and Oliver Kelsey had walked in on them, discovered them together, and had returned to murder him.

It was all swimming, churning around in his brain. He was tired and he wanted to go to bed, to lie in the dark and sort it all out. But he still had Peter Lutz's script to

185

look at, plus whatever was in the trunk of Vera Kelsey's ruined car.

"If somebody fired you off a dirty movie?" Bud asked finally, "could it make you angry enough to kill?"

"You bet your ass," Ivy said quietly. "You bet your ass."

He dropped her off in front of her apartment. She got out of the car and walked around and put her head in his window.

"I want to thank you for the nice murder," she said. "I've really enjoyed it."

"I wouldn't have missed it for the world either."

"Since all of this started," she asked him, "have you bothered to go back in time and figure out exactly what was happening in his life while you were out there being little Buddy Bacall?"

"Too busy for that crap," Bud said, but, in fact, it had occurred to him when he was taking notes in Vera Kelsey's hospital room. He had discovered that those last anguished days of Koenig's relationship with Vera, their break-up, her quick marriage to Oliver Kelsey, coincided with the last movie he had made in the blistering Utah desert.

Had it been a combination of pain, rejection, impotence, round-the-clock grieving that had caused D. P. Koenig to jump into a studio car and give deadly pursuit? If Vera Lakin had chosen to marry the agent instead of the writer, Bud wondered suddenly, would his father be alive today?

"I know all about you back then," Ivy said softly. "Maybe we could talk about it one day."

"Oh, you have a manila envelope on me, too?" Bud had intended to sound nasty, but not that nasty. She looked up at him quickly.

"I didn't want to hurt," she said. "I wanted to help."

"When I want help I'll goddamn well ask for it," he said, his voice angry, shaking. She tried to put her hand on his arm, but he pulled away and started the car engine, racing it as noisily as he could.

"Where are you going now?" she asked him. He didn't answer her. He raced the engine a few more times, then drove off down the street, leaving her standing at the curb in her ugly dress, her heavy boots.

While he was driving, he took out his note pad. He checked the dates Vera had given him. She and Oliver Kelsey were married on October second. D. P. Koenig came to Utah, subdued, distracted, on October sixth. His father died on October fourteenth.

He pulled his car over to the side of the road because he was suddenly having trouble focusing, inhaling, exhaling, steering; things like that.

There were five movies back to back. Screen-magazine photographers followed little Buddy Bacall around day and night. Crates of fan mail were dropped off at his home from the studio every week.

His sixth movie was called *The Little Renegade*. It was his biggest part. He remembered D. P. Koenig squatting down in front of him.

"Kid," Koenig said to him, "I got you a lot of money. Now it's all up to you."

"Will you be there?" Buddy had asked nervously. He felt better when Koenig was around, as if nothing bad could happen to him. It made him feel terrific when he heard Koenig telling people, "That's my boy there. That's my kid."

"Naw, you don't need me around." Buddy had thrown his arms around the agent, had knocked him off balance, and the two of them had gone down laughing, rolling over and over. He never played that way with his father. His own father was not the kind of man you played with like that.

They were going to be on location in Kanab, Utah, for six weeks. Buddy wanted his mother to come there with him, had begged tearfully, but his father had said no. She had to stay and run the grocery store. The more he begged and cried, the colder and more adamant his father became. There was no way his mother was going with them.

Just before they packed and went to Utah, Buddy remembered some trouble, some ugliness. Gordon Flemming, the director, did not want Buddy's father around, tried to have him barred from the location, from the state of Utah.

He remembered the humiliation when his father called the Los Angeles *Times*, the Hollywood trade papers. With Buddy held firmly on his lap, Frank Bacola complained noisily to the reporters that he was being barred from the set because they wanted his son to do dangerous stunts, that he would not permit his son to be in the movie, any movie, if he were not allowed to watch over his son, as any good, concerned father would insist on doing.

Frank Bacola won. He and his famous son went to Kanab together.

The southwest corner of Utah is stark and blisteringly hot at the end of June. Within a radius of a few miles there are shimmering sand dunes, rugged, eroded mountains, brick-red in the punishing sunlight. There is little that is green and there is no place to hide from the heat until long after sundown.

Kanab is a small town just across the Arizona border. The location site was thirty miles away over narrow, gritty desert roads. The cast and crew had rooms in two motels. Buddy and his father shared the best suite in the best motel. They had been assigned a smaller suite, but Frank Bacola had complained noisily until Gordon Flemming, through clenched teeth, offered to switch with them.

Everyone traveled to and from the location site by studio limousine or bus. Everyone but Buddy and his father. Frank Bacola had demanded his own wheels, wanted to be able to be alone with his son without having people pulling, tugging at him, clamoring for him every moment.

Buddy may have been D. P. Koenig's kid, but Frank Bacola was definitely not D. P. Koenig's anything. The two men hated each other and barely spoke. Even to a young boy their hostility was apparent. It troubled and confused him.

"Why are you so mad at him?" Buddy would ask his father after one of their gruff, minimal conversations.

"He is a terrible man," his father would say, always enunciating very carefully, "if it weren't for me, he'd eat you alive." Buddy didn't actually believe that the agent would eat him alive, but the phrase, repeated often by his father, remained with him for many years to come.

Koenig had said goodbye to Buddy the day he left for Utah.

"See you next month, kid," he had said. "Make me proud of you."

The first two days in Utah were a nightmare for everyone. The heat, the sand, the script, the food. And Frank Bacola. He was in everyone's hair from sunup to sundown, making demands, causing discord wherever he went.

On the third day of shooting, D. P. Koenig showed up. Buddy, who had not expected to see him until his return to Los Angeles, let out a noisy whoop, ruining a take, and ran excitedly to greet him.

The only people who seemed to be surprised by his arrival were Buddy and his father. Everyone else seemed to know he was coming, seemed almost to be waiting for him.

Buddy noticed immediately there was something different about him. He seemed quieter, more distracted, almost unapproachable.

"How come you're here?" Buddy asked him.

"They just sort of . . . sent for me, kid," the agent said. He kept turning away, staring out into the desert.

"Is there anything wrong?"

"Just grown-up stuff," the agent said quickly. "Don't give it a second thought." He straightened up and walked away without looking back.

From that moment on, everything on the set changed. Buddy saw his father and D. P. Koenig disappear into one of the air-conditioned trailers. When his father came out, he had a large drinking glass in his hand, although it was just after breakfast. He was laughing good-naturedly. Buddy watched as the agent filled his father's drinking glass again and again.

When Buddy came into his dressing room that afternoon, he found his father stretched out on the bed, sweating and snoring noisily. He turned around and tiptoed out. He had enjoyed the morning without his father's usual interruptions and outbursts.

Frank Bacola drank and slept through the next few days. There were jokes that Buddy didn't completely understand.

But the spell of noisy good humor and daytime sleeping was short-lived. Buddy could hear his father bellowing off camera once again, his voice thick, his words slurred. He would see D. P. Koenig walking with his father, talking earnestly, continually pouring, filling his glass to the brim as quickly as it was emptied.

And then the actress came. She was flown in five days after they started shooting. It was a small part that had not been in the original script. She was pretty and very blond and always wore shorts that were too small for her. When she sat down she would spread her knees wide and Buddy remembered staring at the wiry, reddish hairs that slipped around the edge of her shorts. Her legs were long and incredibly smooth and she wore black toenail polish. And little Buddy Bacall could not take his eyes off her.

From the first day of her arrival, Buddy was aware of Gordon Flemming's face whenever the actress was around. It was angry, brooding, his eyes eternally searching for her, responding uneasily to the sound of her distant laughter.

Often, if she was not there, he would send the second assistant director to find her, to bring her back so she could watch, and, as he put it cruelly, discover the key to her own small part.

She would come obediently and sit near the camera, occasionally bringing one bare foot up under her. She would then methodically pick at one after the other of her black-lacquered toenails until D. P. Koenig would come and lead her away, despite Gordon Flemming's dark and threatening glances.

The agent made a big point of introducing her to Buddy's father. From that moment on she seldom strayed from Frank Bacola's side. She would laugh at his jokes, urge him to talk about himself, her hands always touching, caressing, as she walked with him.

While he was in front of the camera, Buddy would often hear the actress's high, shrill laughter, hear his father's loud voice echoing from one mesa to another.

Buddy began to enjoy himself. His father was never around, no longer embarrassed him. Buddy never wondered what his father and the actress were doing half the day, locked in one of the trailers, did not question the fact that this ever-present man was now absent. He did not question the fact that every evening the actress, not his father, would now slip behind the wheel of their rented car, and drive while his father would sleep or sip something out of a large plastic cup.

One afternoon, between takes, without saying anything to anyone, Buddy walked away to explore the nearby hills and sand dunes. When he had rounded the first hill, he heard his father laughing. There was a brutish, unfamiliar quality to the laughter that fright-

191

ened him. He wanted to turn and run back, but he kept walking, kept peering around the large desert rocks until he saw his father, saw that he was kissing the actress. She was taller than his father, but his father's arms were locked around her, his hands on her ass, pulling her hard against him.

Buddy blinked, turned silently and walked back to where the movie was being shot. When the director, the cameraman, asked him why he was crying, he said it was nothing, that he got sand in his eyes, but the doctor on the set could find no trace of it.

A week later was Frank Bacola's forty-fourth birthday. When the motel operator woke them up, Buddy climbed out of bed and walked into the bathroom without even looking at his father, without saying a word.

"Aren't you going to wish me happy birthday?" Frank Bacola called out to him. Buddy heard, but he did not answer. He turned on the water and started brushing his teeth.

Frank Bacola climbed out of bed, stretched noisily, and then followed his son into the bathroom.

"We're going on a picnic for lunch," Frank Bacola said. "Just you and me. For my birthday." Buddy kept brushing his teeth as if his father had not spoken.

"Hey, what's wrong with you?" Frank Bacola asked.

"Nothing," Buddy said, his back still turned, his mouth full of toothpaste.

"Don't tell me, nothing," Frank Bacola said angrily. He grabbed Buddy by the chin and turned him around, forcing his son to look him directly in the eye.

"Nothing," Buddy insisted stonily. He pulled away, turned around and spat a mouthful of toothpaste into the sink. "There's nothing wrong."

But he was lying. Something had happened the night before, something that he couldn't remember, that his brain fought against, that made him want to strike out savagely at his father.

But he could not remember what it was and ultimately came to believe that his safety, possibly even his own life, might depend on his not remembering it.

That morning D. P. Koenig came over to Buddy just as he was about to start the first scene of the day. He got down on his haunches in front of Buddy and told him very solemnly that he was not to go anywhere with his father, not to get in a car with his father, not to move from the set unless he, D. P. Koenig, told him it was okay. Although he didn't understand it, there was something in the agent's eyes that made him know it was important that he obey.

Buddy's father was waiting just behind the camera when the last shot of the morning was printed and the lunch break was called. He saw his father come over to him, a drink sloshing over the side of a large plastic cup. His voice was loud, his words slurred, almost unintelligible.

"Okay, kid," his father called noisily, "it's picnic time." His father had never called him "kid" before. It was D. P. Koenig's name for him. Nobody else's. It sounded strange, somehow unsettling, coming from his father.

Frank Bacola put his hand on his son's shoulder and guided him on a zigzag course through the camera equipment, around the heavy cables that snaked across the scorching desert sand. When Buddy saw where they were going, he turned uneasily to his father.

"I'm not allowed to go anywhere," Buddy said nervously.

"I give the orders around here!"

"Mr. Koenig said I wasn't supposed to." Buddy tried unsuccessfully to pull away from his father's grasp.

"Fuck Mr. Koenig."

Buddy had never heard his father use that word before. It shocked him, frightened him. He wanted to run away and hide.

He remembered his father's fingers digging into his shoulder, he remembered being led to the Oldsmobile convertible. A young assistant director tried to separate Buddy from his father, tried to take the car keys. He heard his father cursing, then felt an icy spray as his father hurled the rest of his drink in the assistant director's face.

Then it was all right. They were driving with the top down along the winding desert road. His father was singing noisily, pointing out the scenic wonders of Utah. Buddy remembered the way the car was weaving from one side of the narrow road to the other.

He saw his father look into the rearview mirror, then turn quickly and look over his shoulder. Buddy looked too and saw a studio limousine closing the distance between them. Then he felt the car surge forward so suddenly that it threw him backward against the seat.

"Maybe they want me back," Buddy said quietly, remembering the agent's last words to him, his warning about not leaving with his father.

"If they want you, they've got to come catch you first," his father shouted happily, his tooled-leather boot bearing down hard on the gas pedal. Buddy turned around again and saw a second studio car passing the limousine, with one long, frantic honk.

"Maybe we'd better stop, Daddy," Buddy said. "Now there are two cars."

Frank Bacola turned around and looked at the studio car, which, despite the fact that he was flooring it, was rapidly gaining on them.

"That son'bitch, Koenig," his father said.

"Stop, Daddy, I'm scared."

"He can kiss my ass!" Frank Bacola shouted into the hot desert afternoon. "Kiss my ass, agent!"

Buddy looked up at his father and said something. His father did not hear him at first, so he put his hand on his father's knee and repeated what he had said, coldly enunciating each word.

Suddenly Frank Bacola stopped shouting. He looked down at his son, his eyes frightened, unfocusing. He put his foot on the brake, decelerated for a moment, then he hit the gas pedal again. Hard.

In the rearview mirror, Buddy could see the second studio car speeding up closer and closer behind them. He recognized the driver, a large, friendly man with red hair and freckles. Sitting next to him was D. P. Koenig. He was turned toward the driver and he seemed to be shouting at him.

Then Buddy saw D. P. Koenig reach across the driver and put his hand on the horn. There was one loud, continuous blare. Buddy felt the Oldsmobile surge forward, felt himself pressed back against the seat. The sound of the horn grew louder. He looked up and saw his father's face, now distorted by velocity and anger, saw his dark, thick hair blown straight back, the cheeks flattened, the eyes blinking against the gritty desert wind.

The studio car with Koenig in the front seat sped relentlessly after them. Less than a minute later, its speedometer jammed at ninety-four miles an hour, Frank Bacola's car left the road and slammed into a sandy embankment. Both he and his son were thrown clear. Little Buddy Bacall ended up with a total of seven broken bones. His father had only one broken bone, but it happened to be his neck. He died instantly.

Buddy was flown to the Children's Orthopedic Hospital in Hollywood. He was written out of the rest of the picture, and, when he couldn't be written out, his stand-in was photographed at a distance or with an over-the-shoulder shot.

The studio got a hell of a lot of publicity out of it, and it helped the picture at the box office.

Buddy was in a body cast for the next three months. Each day his mother came to the hospital with his meals.

There were casseroles with pasta and cheeses and heavy, rich sauces. She came with boxes of candy and pastries. She sat by his bed and fed him because both of his arms were in casts.

"How did it happen?" she asked him, the day after they took him off medication.

"I don't remember," Buddy said, shrinking back into his cast, away from her, away from everything.

"In the car, did you talk? Did he say anything? Did you say anything?"

"No," Buddy answered nervously. "Nobody talked."

When she kept asking questions, he began to cry. This frightened her so much that she never asked him another question, never brought the subject up again. She would just sit there by his small hospital bed, smiling supportively, shoveling carbohydrates into his opened mouth.

Koenig came to the hospital to see Buddy several times. Once he brought a clown covered with brightly wrapped candies. Another time he brought a hundred-dollar gift certificate to a Beverly Hills toy shop. Buddy would not look at him. He would turn away, straining painfully against his cast.

"I only did it for you," Koenig said to him. "I did it for you."

When Buddy came out of the cast, he was fourteen pounds heavier. His face was pale and bloated and he had the beginnings of a pot belly. Even his fingers and toes were fat and pudgy. A Hollywood columnist who had covered little Buddy Bacall's return home from the hospital had cruelly dubbed him Mr. Three-by-Three.

For the next couple of weeks his time was divided evenly between physical therapy and hard-core eating. He regained the full use of his broken bones and joints and he put on another thirteen pounds, a gross, distorted nine-year-old boy. The studio doctor examined him and put him on a strict diet. He cheated and put on three more pounds.

Then Koenig gave him a bottle of medicine. *One swig in the morning, kiddo, and you won't be hungry all day.* It was a thick, murky mixture of equal parts of Pentiplex, a vitamin compound, and a then little known or understood drug called Dexedrine.

Within a week Buddy lost seven pounds. He also threw a baseball bat at his mother and smashed his new bicycle beyond repair with a tire iron. The second week he lost five more pounds, but he was still fat, and his part in a new motion picture was taken by another discovery of D. P. Koenig's. This boy was blond and blue-eyed with an impish smile. And he was thin.

During the third week of his diet, and just after he was told that he had been replaced in the movie, Buddy stuck the garden hose in the living-room window and flooded the house.

His mother did not spank him or punish him. She walked into the kitchen over the ruined carpets and took the bottle that Koenig had given her son and poured it down the sink.

Then she telephoned a real estate company and asked them to come over immediately and appraise her house. Then she gathered up all her towels and started to mop up the water damage.

She accepted the first offer she got for the house, which was low but not unreasonable, and they moved to Fountain Valley, a small community an hour's drive south of Los Angeles, because she liked the way it sounded.

In Fountain Valley, she took a two-bedroom garden apartment, and despite the fact that her son had a lot of money in his own right, she opened an Italian delicatessen, the first and only one around at that time. Both mother and son ran the store and continued to grow fatter and more withdrawn as the years went by.

When he was sixteen, Buddy rediscovered Dexedrine in the form of Dexamyls. Within four months he had lost enough weight to put him back into the normal range.

He also went a little crazy. A friend whose father was a doctor had sold him the Dexamyls, but when the father discovered what the kid was up to, he sent him off to military school.

It wasn't until then, until his source had dried up, that Buddy knew that he was hooked. A speed freak, but they didn't call it that in the early sixties because they didn't know then what bad news the drug really was.

He began chasing around Fountain Valley looking for a new supplier. Even without the drug he had no appetite and he was losing weight. What he needed it for now was energy. Without the Dexamyls, it was hard for him to get out of bed in the mornings, to climb on his bike and ride to school. He couldn't concentrate on his studies. His brain kept going to sleep on him.

Then he found another supplier. The daughter of a pharmacist. She gave him thirty days' worth in return for his doing all her homework for that month. Now, with the drug again in his system, he could do her homework and his own and still be charged with energy, his brain once again snapping and crackling. There wasn't anything he felt he couldn't do. And he was thin and wiry and he didn't want to think about his pupils that were always dilated or about his hands that were starting to shake full time.

One day when he came home from school, he found his mother sitting in the living room with her younger brother, Ralph. They both greeted him solemnly and then he noticed his luggage packed and waiting by the front door. His mother said nothing, but held up his bottle of Dexamyls. The bottle was empty so he knew she had thrown away the remaining pills.

Ralph got up and put his hand on Buddy's shoulder, nodded for Buddy to pick up his suitcases, and then ushered him out the front door to where his car was parked. Mrs. Bacola stood in the doorway and watched her son climb into the front seat. He looked at her, but she did not acknowledge him, did not even wave. Then she turned and walked back into the house and closed the door behind her.

They went to a small cabin somewhere high in the Sierras. They did not see anyone else the entire time they were there. Six weeks later Buddy was brought back home. He had gained seven pounds, but his system was clean. His mother kissed him and helped him unpack. Neither of them ever discussed it or mentioned it. But Buddy knew that his room was searched at least once a day for a long time after that. She never found anything. There was never anything to find.

From that time on he was clean. Clean and eternally obsessed with the fear of gaining weight.

11

When Bud pulled up in front of his apartment house, he saw a Beverly Hills squad car slowing down. He parked in the underground garage, then walked over to the police car as George Dibbey got out and handed Bud an expensive-looking Gucci attaché case.

"This was in the trunk of Vera Kelsey's car. It's already been fingerprinted," George Dibbey said. "There was some other stuff there, a beach back rest, a few empty nursery flats, but this was all that looked like it was worth taking."

Bud looked down at the case and studied the fine monogram near the fine leather handle. G. D. Gypsy Doniger. Bud wondered what the hell a porno queen was doing with a Gucci attaché case? He took the elevator up to his apartment trying to sort it all out.

Vera Kelsey had told him that she had taken something from Koenig's house, something that belonged to, as she put it, the "cunt." But what was the connection?

Bud wondered suddenly if Koenig himself had been involved in the making of a dirty movie.

He ran his finger over the fine beige leather, studied the monogram. G. D. Gypsy Doniger. Then it hit him. G. D. also stood for Glenda Deering.

Bud started to smile. He didn't stop smiling until he was sitting down on his understuffed sofa. Partly he was smiling at his own denseness in taking so long to figure out the G. D. connection, and partly because he was so eager to see what was inside.

He slipped a kitchen knife around the brass lock, but the lock wouldn't give. He even tried hitting it with a hammer wrapped in a hand towel, but no dice. Those Italian craftsmen really knew their business when it came to attaché-case locks.

He picked up the telephone and called Glenda Deering.

"I think something of yours has come into my possession," Bud said. There was a long pause.

"Yes?" Her voice was tense, but noncommittal.

"If you would care to describe it," Bud said, but she stopped him.

"I already have the item we were talking about earlier."

"All right, then," Bud said quietly. "I'll describe the item to you. A beige leather Gucci attaché case with . . ."

"Damn," she said.

"That's what I thought."

"Where are you?" she asked finally.

Bud gave her his address and she said she'd be right there.

"Have you opened it?" she asked finally.

"No. Bring the goddamn key."

He dialed Oliver Kelsey's number again. There was still no answer. He went into the kitchen, opened the refrigerator. There was a bottle of liquid protein sitting right next to a crock of port cheese. He was torn for a moment, then took a few half-hearted pulls on the protein and lost his appetite immediately. Maybe it did work after all.

When the phone rang, he jumped as if the bell had been wired to the base of his skull. The bottle slipped out of his hand and bounced noisily on the floor, but did not break. He was almost sorry it hadn't.

"Hi, sport." It was Chuck, sounding like his old self, no longer zonked or even nasal.

"That's some speedy recovery."

"I yanked the packings out myself a few minutes ago. It hurt like bloody hell."

"You're not supposed to do that, are you?"

"So, instead of looking like Robert Redford, I'll look like Ernest Borgnine. At least I can breathe."

There was a long time when neither of them spoke. That was when Bud realized that his partner had not called up just to talk about his nose or shoot the breeze.

"What's up?" Bud asked finally.

"I've been getting a few calls about you."

"From where?"

"From Upstairs," Chuck said. "They're wondering if they ought to kick your ass off the case."

"Why?" Bud asked. As if he didn't already know. He felt things starting to churn in his head.

"They think you're screwing up, leaving a lot of holes, taking on more than you can handle," Chuck said uneasily. "Like that."

"They can give the case to six other detectives if they want," Bud said, "but just tell them to keep away from *my* suspects."

"*Your* suspects," Chuck picked up on it instantly. "Buddy, you've got it all wrong. *We* have suspects. The *B.H.P.D.* has suspects. The *State of California* has suspects. *You* don't have suspects."

"Can you keep them off my back for twenty-four hours?" Bud asked finally.

"Drive to Santa Barbara with us tomorrow," Chuck said. It was his loony-handling voice again and it would have started a monumental fight between them, but they were saved by the doorbell.

"That's one of *my* very own suspects right now," Bud said lightly. "See you around." He hung up before Chuck had a chance to say anything more.

Glenda Deering was standing at his front door twenty-two minutes after their phone conversation. He could tell that she had been crying and drinking and her breath, even from a few feet away, stank from a combination of bourbon and Binaca. He felt very sorry for her. She looked ten years older than when he had first seen her, and she hadn't looked too hot then.

"Where is it?" she asked, pushing past him, looking nervously around the apartment. She spotted the attaché case on the sofa and ran to it. She picked it up and held it to her chest with both arms. There was something childlike about the way she did it that touched him. When she started to walk to the front door, he stopped her.

"The key," he said, holding out his hand to her.

"It has nothing to do with anything," she said. "Just get out of my way."

"Lady, I've got to see what's in there, so be a good guy or I'll have to take you and the bag down to headquarters, and we'll open it there before a cast of thousands."

Suddenly she swung the leather case at his head with all her strength. It took him off guard, but he managed to deflect the blow so that it only grazed his cheek. Instantly he grabbed her free arm and twisted her around to where she could do him no more damage. He felt the anger, the strength, go out of her. She even let him take the case away from her without a struggle.

"Must you?" she asked in a choked voice.

"Yeah, I really must," he said gently. "You want a

203

drink?" She shook her head and sat down on the edge of his sofa. She fished around in the pocket of her black velvet slacks and handed Bud a pair of fine small keys.

"Would you like to hear my story first?" she asked without looking at him. "My side of it?"

He didn't want to hear anything. He wanted to open the damn case and see what was inside, what had caused all the hysteria and telephone calls.

"You talk and I'll open," Bud said, but she came and put her hand over his and begged him just to listen, to hear her story before he looked inside. He stopped what he was doing and looked up at her.

"Start talking," Bud said.

Glenda Deering and D. P. Koenig had a highly unusual arrangement, even by Hollywood standards. After one reading for a small part in a motion picture, Koenig took Glenda aside and told her as kindly as he could that she was possibly the worst, most wooden actress he had ever seen.

"But, despite that, I could still make you the toast of Beverly Hills, the queen of Hollywood society," Koenig said, smiling reassuringly at her.

"Yeah," Glenda said in the flat midwestern voice that had first drawn him to her. "What's it going to cost me?"

"Oh, just . . . everything." He led her out of the producer's office, his hand on her elbow, guiding her gallantly away from her first and last theatrical reading.

"You are a sow's ear," he told her. "It would amuse me to try to turn you into a silk purse."

He suggested she turn her entire bank account over to him. She was not, from that moment on, to buy so much as a tea towel without his approval. He would rent a house for her, oversee its furnishing, select her wardrobe, her friends, her lovers. He would turn her into Hollywood's leading party-thrower, party-goer, the undisputed social leader of Southern California.

"What's in it for you?" she asked warily.

"Just enjoyment and satisfaction," he told her. "My first test-tube hostess."

"All right, then, what's in it for me, except for a lot of bullshit and going broke in a hurry?"

"My dear," he said, "I guarantee, absolutely guarantee, that I will find you a suitable, well-heeled husband long before your money runs out."

"So why don't you find me one now?"

"Because right now you are nothing, you are no one. Oh, I might be able to scare up a Harry Karl for you, a loser on his way down. But, if you just put yourself in my hands, I promise I will deliver to you a studio head, an Iranian oil exporter, someone of substance."

"But what if I run through all my money and you still haven't found me anyone?" she asked shrewdly.

"You do what I say and you will be well married before you go broke. But if you're not, I will see that at the end of, say, two years, you are no worse off financially than you would have been if you'd led the sort of grubby life you were cut out for if you hadn't met me."

She thought about it, thought about her other alternatives, thought about the possibility of the Deerings ending up with the money, then solemnly opened her purse and handed D. P. Koenig her bankbook.

Koenig involved himself totally in her life, her image. He found a beautifully furnished house for her, a two-year sublease from a man who had been deported to Sardinia. He bought her clothing, planned the menus for her parties, supplied her with the right caterers, the right books to read, often underlining the important parts, subjects that would be useful for dinner conversations, make her appear brighter, more curious than she was.

He hired Jeremy Salters, who made sure her name appeared in the trade papers, the gossip columns, almost on a daily basis. Within the first six months of their arrangement, she threw twelve large important parties, sixteen small but elegant dinners, and innumerable luncheons and brunches. The eleventh large party put her over the top. Her guests included the Paul Newmans, the Frank Sinatras, David Bowie, Sue Mengers, and, in a way, Neil Diamond, who accepted even though he did not show up.

And she was asked to all the parties. She was always seated next to important single men whom she dated and went to bed with, always keeping a nervous eye on her rapidly dwindling resources. There would be two or three dates and the eligible men would be off for the Cannes Film Festival, a high-level OPEC meeting, the haberdashery show in New York, and she would never hear from them again.

"What are you doing wrong?" Koenig asked her once when she came by his office to look over some bills. "You're an attractive woman, and you're not a complete idiot, so I just don't know why you're not doing better than you are."

"Because I'm out of my league," she said unhappily. "For all your plots and plans, I'm still a sow's ear."

"This town is filled with sow's ears who are doing a hell of a lot better than you are," he said accurately, if not too tactfully. He sent her home after giving her a halfhearted pep talk. They both knew that he was bored with her, tired of the arrangement. They also both knew that her money was going faster than either of them had believed possible.

On the way home, she stopped at the Bel-Air Market. She had no parties to give, no parties to go to, no dates, and she had seen all the movies in the greater Los Angeles area. She missed Ohio, missed her children, who were spending more and more time with her mother. She was depressed and frightened.

When she came out of the market into the parking lot, she saw a small, well-dressed man slip a piece of paper under her windshield wiper. She saw him look around several times, then start to climb into a dark green Corniche parked directly across the narrow aisle from her own Mercedes.

She removed the slip of paper, but before she could read it he was standing by her side. He had backed into her car accidentally, had done some minimal damage, and wanted to pay her cash, not go through his insurance company.

She recognized him immediately. He was Richard Maxwell, he was a big producer, he was a party-goer. She had seen him, sat at the same table with him. He was always with lovely, long-legged, very young girls who used bad language. She had only seen him sitting down before and was startled at how short he was, and how intense his eyes were. Blue and without humor.

"I know you," he said, leaning against her car. "You're the lady with the forced smile at all the parties."

"It shows, huh?" She was pleased that he had noticed her, even if it was because she looked perpetually pained in social situations.

"You know when I'm really happy?" he said. "When I have a whole week stretching out ahead of me with no cocktail parties, no intimate dinners upstairs at the Bistro staring me in the face."

"If you don't like them," she asked, "why do you keep going?"

"I guess because they're there." He grinned at her. She hoped he wouldn't ask her why she went to parties, why she threw parties herself. She was afraid that if he did ask, she might tell him it was in order to meet people like him.

But he didn't ask. He tipped the edge of her grocery bag down and looked inside.

"Your stuff looks better than my stuff," he said. "Let's go to your place." She hesitated for a moment. Mona, the maid hired for her by D. P. Koenig, was off and she hadn't straightened up yet.

"Fine," he said lightly. "Bring your stuff and follow

me back to my house." He ran his finger professionally over the dent in her rear bumper. Then he took out his wallet and peeled off five one-hundred-dollar bills, folded them and stuffed them in her purse.

"If it comes to more, let me know." He turned and climbed into his car. She followed him through traffic, almost losing him once or twice at red lights, but she would find him each time a block ahead, double-parked, waiting for her.

He had a beautiful home in the Palisades overlooking the Pacific Ocean. His butler, a courtly black man with the improbable name of Pineapple, made them a pitcher of frosty margaritas and they got drunk together in the late afternoon sun. He asked her questions about herself, and listened carefully to her answers. He lent her a bathing suit and they sat in his Jacuzzi, the margarita pitcher close at hand, until it was dark outside.

He asked to see pictures of her children and suggested that when they came back from Ohio she bring them to the studio for lunch to watch a movie being made.

He lent her a terry cloth robe and took her on a tour of the house. He had decorated it himself, had selected the fabrics, the colors, the furniture. Glenda thought it was a little vulgar, but said all the appropriate things. He was a house-plant freak and knowledgeable about all the greenery, calling each tree, each plant, by its botanical name, but he was so earnest that she was prepared to forgive him for it.

After a light dinner, served on the terrace overlooking the Pacific, he led her upstairs to his bedroom. They sat close together on the edge of his massive bed talking quietly, enjoying the reflection of the moon on the ocean.

Then, with four of his finest Brooks Brothers neckties, he trussed her limbs to his bedposts and made savage but inadequate love to her. She had cooperated because she was confused and embarrassed and not just a little frightened. She got up immediately afterward, got dressed, and drove home. She took a long, hot shower and thought about what had just happened to her. She was no innocent, of course, but she had been exposed primarily to men of little sexual imagination, men who practiced mainly what her late husband had referred to as "straight-up-and-down-Vermont."

The phone was ringing as she stepped out of the shower. She sat on the edge of the bed and stared at it until it stopped ringing. She climbed under the covers and cried for the first time since she had moved to Los Angeles.

Richard Maxwell called her again early the next morning and invited her to his house for dinner. She thanked him politely and told him she was busy. He asked her to an opening the following night. She did not accept.

"Is anything wrong?" he asked finally.

"Why should anything be wrong?"

"Just thought I'd ask," he said lightly. After he hung up, he called a florist and had them send her six dozen long-stemmed roses, but she still wouldn't go out with him.

The following day he sent her a large and lavish basket of cheeses and pâtés from Vendome. D. P. Koenig appeared at her front door at the same time as the delivery boy from Vendome. Before she answered the door, Koenig had slipped the small card out of its envelope.

"Hey, you can't do that," the boy said nervously, trying to grab the card.

"It's all right," Koenig said. "I own her." He returned the card and they stood silently side by side at the door until Glenda opened it.

"Since when is Richard Maxwell sending you nourishment?" Koenig asked as he sat across the breakfast table from her, spreading her bills fanlike before her.

She did not want to tell him, but he persisted and

finally she got across to him that there had been some "funny stuff." She said she thought he was attractive, but he frightened her.

"My dear," Koenig said, pushing the fanned-out bills closer to her, "stop being a fool. Your money is running out, the tops of your legs are starting to go, and your personality was never that much to begin with."

"I wish I'd never met you," Glenda muttered under her breath.

"You will have a small dinner party tomorrow night. You will serve cold poached salmon with cucumber sauce. And you will invite Richard Maxwell." He stood up and without another word, without even looking at her, he walked out of her house.

Richard Maxwell was busy and could not come to her small dinner, but he asked her over to his house for dinner for the following night. She accepted and then telephoned the two other couples she had invited and canceled the dinner.

He seemed genuinely happy, almost relieved, that she had accepted his invitation, that she was once again in his house. He kept asking her if she were too warm, too cold. He could not do enough for her.

After dinner, when they were in bed, he was tender and caring. He spoke reassuringly of their future together and she believed that she might be falling in love with him. They were together every evening for the next week and a half. Sometimes they made love. Sometimes they watched old movies on television.

On their twelfth consecutive night in bed together, he opened the drawer of his country French nightstand and took out a large black rubber dildo and suggested that he use it on her. She started to cry and rose quickly from the bed and got dressed. She was not so much upset by the dildo itself as by the fact that she was sure it was the *house* dildo, used no doubt on half of Hollywood before her. He reassured her that it had been boiled recently, which hurt and angered her even more.

210

She was not amused by the large bunch of bananas he sent her the following day, or by Koenig's attitude when she came to him and told him the whole sordid story. Koenig smiled patronizingly and vowed to her that Maxwell was not, as she now believed, a hopeless pervert, but merely an adventurous and enterprising lover, and once she overcame her provincialism she might one day see the endless possibilities for joy and variety he was offering her. Then he showed her her bank statement, which was dangerously close to rock bottom.

That afternoon Koenig drove her to Gucci's and helped her select a large leather attaché case. It had been reduced from $900 to $650 because there was a small, barely visible scratch along one side. He insisted they wait while her initials were embossed in Old English script. She was confused and upset by the extravagant purchase, kept demanding to know what it was for, but Koenig refused to tell her. He would smile and say only that what he was doing would insure her a happy and prosperous future.

He drove her next to the International Passion Boutique on Hollywood Boulevard. She had never been inside a shop like this before. What she saw in the windows alone shocked and outraged her. And from where she stood, her heels dug into the street outside, refusing to go a step farther, she could see through the open door a life-size plastic woman lying on her back, knees up and spread, waiting to receive she did not even want to imagine what or whom.

"I'm not setting foot in that place," Glenda said and started to walk back to Koenig's parked car.

"You are not only going in there, you are also going to stroll up and down the aisles by my side, and we are going to fill up your Gucci case with many marvels." He took her arm and led her firmly through the doorway, past the spread-eagled plastic body on the floor, past a case of multiracial dildos, to a stack of shopping baskets. Koenig reached down and picked up a basket, slipping it over one arm as if he were at the supermarket. He kept her close by his side with his other arm to keep her from fleeing.

They were not the only shoppers there. Up and down the aisles Glenda could see other customers, some with shopping baskets, some without. They were not sleazy-looking degenerates, she observed with some surprise. There was one man in a fine three-piece business suit standing in a section designated for Leather Lovers. He had a leather riding crop in one hand and a studded Ping-Pong paddle in the other. He was studying each of them, weighing their respective merits as if he were Ralph Nader.

Across the aisle from the well-dressed man were two seemingly normal-looking young men in French blue jeans and flannel shirts. One of them was trying on a black leather executioner's hood with a heavy, punishing zipper across the mouth. There were no eye holes, no ear holes. The man not wearing the mask was studying the man wearing the mask. He walked around him very slowly. Once he reached up and experimentally pulled the zipper open and closed.

"Well?" Glenda heard the man in the leather mask ask in a muffled voice.

"Sixty dollars is a lot of money," the man not wearing the mask said finally. The other man took off the mask and studied it.

"What the hell," he said, "you're only thirty once."

Glenda was digging her fingernails into Koenig's arm, but he was not paying attention. He reached down and dropped a small box into his shopping basket. Glenda picked it up and studied it. At that moment, she didn't even know what a bondage collar was. The illustration helped, informing her that the collar itself was adjustable, that the two metal rings were for "attachments."

"What attachments might those be?" Glenda asked Koenig uneasily.

"For a leash," he said casually, and leaned down to pick up a medium-weight chain to add to her collection.

When she got over being appalled, shocked, she began to think it was funny, even giggled as she observed the serious, dedicated way the shoppers were examining, testing the obscenities for sale. The one thing she was not was turned on.

"I want to get out of here," Glenda whispered to Koenig, but he continued holding her fast, leading her down an aisle of assorted female forms in lifelike plastic, complete with tits and soft, flexible vaginas. A complete woman named Linda was a hundred dollars. Next to Linda was Venus, for the financially strapped. Venus was exactly the same as Linda, but minus head, arms, and legs. Venus was twenty-five dollars less. Glenda tried to imagine who would want to make love to an armless, legless, headless hunk of plastic.

She did not have to wonder long because a nervous-looking man with ragged cuticles was moving along the aisle, picking up one form after another. Glenda fully expected him to whip out his cock and try each of the plastic ladies on for size.

"Glenda," Koenig said, tugging her arm, "in here we do not stare with our mouths open." He had made many other selections. A fur love glove, thumb cuffs that looked like little doll handcuffs, a deck of bondage playing cards, crème de menthe-flavored orgy butter, a tube of Jamaican Rum vice cream, and a container of something called "Hap-penis" just because he thought the pun was amusing.

She looked down into the shopping basket at the assortment of vile obscenities he had chosen for her, then she looked up into his face. He smiled impersonally at her and tapped his finger on his lapel directly over her bankbook. He leaned over and picked up a studded leather one-size-fits-all garter belt and dropped it on top of the other purchases.

They walked past a section for Rubber Lovers, through the Erotic Novelty department, which was featuring a hot-water bottle with breasts and a squirt gun in the shape of a penis.

There was a gray-haired woman wearing a baggy cardigan sweater behind the counter. She had a lined face and wore thick-lensed glasses. Somebody's mother, somebody's grandmother, Glenda thought, and there the woman stood, unembarrassed, unshocked, idly picking up one dildo after another, wiping each one thoroughly with a damp rag, then moving on to the next.

"Can I help you?" the old woman said to them, as if this were the linen department at the May Company. Glenda was outraged by the old woman's calm indifference to her surroundings.

"Do your children know what you're doing?" Glenda asked.

"It's my son's store," the old woman said and there was a note of unmistakable pride in her voice as she said it.

Glenda had always thought of herself as a normally passionate woman. She enjoyed sex, but did not often have orgasms, and the ones she did have, she admitted secretly to herself, were pretty tame, almost unidentifiable. She tended to believe multiple, earth-shaking female orgasms were part hype, part wishful thinking. But that was all before her trip to the International Passion Boutique.

From that afternoon on she would show up at Richard Maxwell's front door with her fine leather attaché case, like a visiting nurse. Sometimes Maxwell would come to the door himself, often wearing only an expensive silk robe. Other times, Pineapple would open the door, greet her formally, and lead her upstairs to the master bedroom.

Richard Maxwell assured her he was delighted with

her wantonness. Each evening he was available they would sit together on the edge of his bed. She would take out her tiny brass key and open up the Gucci case to show him what she had found in her rounds of all the adult bookstores. They would examine, read the directions of her new purchase, and end up in bed or on the floor or in the stall shower, wherever their fantasies took them. She discovered quickly that multiple and earth-shaking orgasms were a reality after all.

Over the next three months, she tried and had tried on her every sexual invention the town had to sell. She could not remember what straight-up-and-down-Vermont was like anymore. She came to need, totally depend on for her gratification, items that throbbed, pulsated, gyrated, pumped, twisted, twirled—things that were festooned with plastic, encrusted with studs, powered by 4-D batteries.

Maxwell told her over and over again that she was the most gifted lover in the world and that he would cherish her always. But while she was driving home from the opening of a new porno shop in Granada Hills, she heard on the radio that Richard Maxwell had just gotten married in Lake Tahoe. The bride's name was Thea Chappel. She was a professional photographer.

Glenda had never heard of her before, did not know of her existence. She had believed herself to be Maxwell's one and only. It was that security, that sense of dependence and trust that had allowed her to start leaving her Gucci case in Maxwell's hall closet instead of carrying it portal to portal. She kept the keys herself.

She pulled over to the side of the road and cried noisily for close to half an hour. Then she drove to Koenig's office.

He was jogging in place in his office, up to seven minutes, and he was still not sweating. She raced in and told him hysterically about her own true love's elopement.

He did not react, so she assumed he already knew about it. He reached out and patted her arm reassuringly.

"You're lucky to be out of it," he said, moving up and down. "The man's a terrible pervert."

Then, without breaking rhythm, he jogged to his desk and showed her her file, her bank statement.

"I thought surely you'd have latched onto an appropriate male by this time," he told her. "There's obviously something wrong with you that I didn't perceive when we made this arrangement."

She began to berate him noisily for the extravagance and fruitlessness of the life he had forced her to lead. The press agent, the parties, the clothes, and ultimately the kinkiness encouraged and abetted by him that had become an essential part of her life.

"You are my only failure," he told her, and he turned and walked out of his office, closing the door behind him, leaving her with the ruins of her life.

Over the next few days she made repeated efforts to get through to Richard Maxwell only to find his home number had been changed. When she called his office at the studio, his secretary would say impersonally that he was unavailable and would assure her that her call would be returned. It wasn't.

On the fourth day his secretary tried to dust her off again.

"Give him this message, please," Glenda said, enunciating each word carefully. "Tell him my fun-filled Gucci bag is in his guest closet. I would like to have the bag returned to me and the contents of the bag donated to his bride."

Three minutes later, Richard Maxwell called her back. He was on location in Nevada. His voice was cold and punishing. He said he would send her a check for the bag and its contents, but that he did not wish to see her, to speak to her, to have his wife see or speak to her.

"I want my Gucci bag back right now," Glenda told

him, "and if it isn't in my possession by five tonight, I'm coming to your house to take it up with the little woman."

"I'll kick your lips off." His voice was quiet, menacing, and she believed him.

"I'll have D. P. Koenig come to your house and pick it up," she said. There was a long pause.

"Jesus Christ," Maxwell said, "does he know?"

"Everything!"

"If my wife finds out, you're both dead," he said, and then he hung up the phone. If she had not been so hurt, so bewildered, she might even have enjoyed the knowledge that she really had him going over this. She was sorry she didn't have the Gucci bag in her possession at that moment because she knew that the gold-plated Ben-Wa Vibra-Tone Balls would have relaxed her, made her feel better.

She telephoned Koenig and he agreed to pick up the Gucci case at Richard Maxwell's house. His voice was impatient, irritable, and she knew unquestionably that he was through with her, would no longer manage her finances, guide her life. She had failed him by not landing a rich husband in the allotted time.

She waited at home all that day, telephoning Koenig's office at least once an hour to find out about her Gucci case. Finally, at six in the evening, Koenig accepted her call and told her that he had picked up her property without event, that he had even met the new Mrs. Maxwell, whom he reported to be a pale, washed-out young woman with a pinched mouth.

"I would never have thrown you over for her," Koenig said smoothly, if not too sincerely; then he suggested that she come by his house that night or the following day to pick up her Gucci bag. If he was not at home, his couple would know where it was.

When she got off the telephone, she decided she would have a glass of sherry to calm her nerves, possibly cheer her up. She sipped as she changed her clothes for the drive to Koenig's house. She had a second glass because the first one had been so soothing. Then she finished the entire bottle trying to insure the restfulness, the surcease of pain that the second drink had given her.

She spent the rest of the night vomiting into the toilet, and when she was too weak to leave her bed, she used the costly Lucite wastebasket that D. P. Koenig had selected for her.

The following morning a massive hangover coupled with intense depression kept her in her bedroom the entire day and that night.

She still felt terrible the next morning and spent the day lounging around the house. She thought several times of throwing herself together for the ride to Koenig's house, but she was afraid the nice Guatemalan couple would somehow know what was in her bag and would snicker as they handed it over to her. She felt too unstable to face that bonus humiliation. She washed her hair and gave herself a pedicure.

In the mail that day she found a catalogue in a plain brown envelope with no return address. It was from the Pleasure Chest in West Hollywood. There were seventy-four pages of raunchiness for sale, and there wasn't an item there that didn't excite her, turn her on. And the man who had done this to her, had turned her into a hopeless pervert, was now safely married to a pale, pinched photographer.

She felt outrage, anguish, fury. She closed her eyes and imagined Richard Maxwell stepping off a curb with his new bride, imagined herself at the wheel of her car turning the corner, felt herself floor it, saw the quick moment of recognition and terror on his face as she crashed into him. She saw his limp body fly into the air and then land on one fender of her car, his pale bride on the other fender. Glenda Deering's trophies.

She woke up Wednesday morning feeling almost human. She planned to break her lease, sell her furniture, let them repossess her car. She would return immediately to Ohio and throw herself on the mercy of the Deerings.

She hummed to herself in the shower as she thought about leaving Hollywood. The town, the people had all been too much for her simple midwestern brain. She smiled as she soaped her body, which she knew was still firm and appealing, at least by Ohio standards.

She turned on the radio in the kitchen as she prepared her coffee and learned that D. P. Koenig had been murdered in his Beverly Hills home. Stunned, she got in her car and drove through five red lights, cursing herself, cursing Richard Maxwell, cursing the late agent who she believed was responsible for everything terrible that had happened to her over the past two years.

Bud stared down at the top of Glenda Deering's head, saw the dark roots at the part in her red hair. He thought she was either crying or pretending to be crying. He thought she was an idiot, a weak, shallow woman, but he felt sorry for her because she had come up lame on possibly the fastest track in the world.

"You know that you were provided for in his will, don't you?" Bud asked.

"His lawyer called me and told me that," Glenda said, her head still down.

"Were you surprised?"

"I thought he was just cutting me loose, that he'd gotten bored with the arrangement and was going to dump me." Glenda looked up at him. There were no tears, no red blotches, so Bud assumed she'd been faking the tears, stalling for time. "So, yes, I was surprised."

"He never mentioned to you that he was leaving you any money?"

"He said that at the end of it all I'd be no worse off

than I would have been without him, but that's pretty vague, don't you think?"

"He obviously wasn't going to help you any more while he was alive," Bud said, "so his death could have been more useful to you than to most."

"His death could have been useful to half of Hollywood," Glenda said bitterly. "And, if not useful, at least enjoyable." Bud smiled. He wouldn't disagree with her there.

He started to fit the fine brass key into the fine brass lock when he heard a light rap on the front door. Glenda started nervously and Bud smiled to reassure her that he would not expose her bag of tricks in front of strangers. He crossed to the door and opened it.

"Yes?" Bud said, studying the man standing before him. It was someone he had never seen before. He was tall, pale, possibly an albino. He was wearing a beige felt hat, sunglasses, and a heavy, soiled raincoat. *On a hot August night in Southern California!*

Bud tried to slam the door, but the man threw his weight against it, and in the same motion drew a Smith & Wesson out of his pocket. As Bud lunged for the hand with the gun, he felt the top of his head smashing in and he knew that he had been hit by something from behind.

Goddamnit, he thought, as he felt himself lose consciousness, I'm going to die hungry.

12

What was worse than the pain in his head was the sure knowledge that he would be ribbed mercilessly about this foul-up for the rest of his life, which he suspected, from the intensity of the throbbing, might not be too long.

He sat up slowly and felt the back of his head. There was blood, not too much, and it had already started to congeal. He looked at his wristwatch, having some difficulty with his focusing mechanism, and calculated that he had probably been unconscious for no more than a minute.

No wonder she had looked so nervous when she heard the knock on the door, Bud thought, as he climbed unsteadily to his feet. He walked slowly into the kitchen and drank a glass of water. He took the kitchen sponge, moistened it, and put it to the back of his head. He didn't even bother to look around for the Gucci case because he knew it wouldn't be there.

Now he realized why she had told him the story, sparing none of the sordid details. She had been waiting for the appearance of the tall pale man in the soiled raincoat. But how had he gotten there so quickly? Until the moment Bud called Glenda Deering, ostensibly no one knew the whereabouts of the Gucci bag. Had the man in the raincoat been sitting by a telephone waiting for the call? And who had called him? He did not believe Glenda Deering had such contacts. So that left one person. Richard Maxwell, who Bud assumed would have such contacts. Plenty of them.

Bud could not believe his own stupidity in not having looked into the bag, for having permitted her to stall him, trick him. Suddenly he wondered if the stakes might be higher than he had originally believed. You can't go to jail for possession of a dildo or a rubber sheet, but you could get a long lock-up for possession of narcotics. He wondered grimly if he had let a load of coke slip through his fingers. Most people, he believed, would have to get high to use the gadgets she had described to him.

He knew he had never screwed up a case so badly before. The big question was why.

He got in his car and drove to the place he least wanted to be. The Beverly Hills Police Department. The lump on his head was approaching the size of a jumbo egg. If anybody started to kid him about it, he was sure he'd take a swing at them, but he managed to get by the night crew without notice.

He went directly to the mug file. The man in the raincoat was not there. He requested an A.P.B. on him and gave orders to have Glenda Deering picked up and brought to headquarters. He stopped at his desk and saw two messages from Gilbert Ritner and one more from Oliver Kelsey.

He dialed Oliver Kelsey's number, but there was still no answer. He sat down at his desk and wrote a full report of the evening's screw-up, taking full blame for the loss of the Gucci case. However, he did not mention

couch in his shirtsleeves, taking a long drag on a joint. Bud was so pissed off he put his finger on the bell and didn't take it off until the door was opened.

"Smoke on your own goddamn time," Bud said angrily as he walked past Peter into the living room.

"I don't know what you're talking about," Peter said lightly, as he waved his hand through the dense marijuana fumes.

"Aren't you afraid I'm going to run you in?" Bud asked, amused at his blatancy.

"Run me in? You've got to be kidding, Bacola," Peter grinned. "We're practically engaged."

"Yeah, yeah, right," Bud said impatiently.

"Where's the manuscript?" He saw Peter zero in on his head.

"Who got you?" Peter said. He reached up to touch the lump. Bud pushed his hand aside in the same motion.

"Glenda Deering and a hood," Bud said. "Know anything about it?"

"Christ, no," Peter said. He sounded genuinely shocked. "Are you sure?"

"The guy was tall and thin, maybe an albino," Bud said. "Have any idea who it is?"

"I don't know any albinos," Peter said, moving around Bud to get a better look at his wound. "What'd he hit you with?"

"*He* had a gun, but I got zapped from behind by *her* and her goddamn Gucci case."

"You're a regular Class A screw-up, aren't you?" Peter said. "What happened to the Gucci case?"

"Just give me the manuscript," Bud said irritably. He sat down on the couch. It had just the right amount of down in it. Not too much. Not too little. If you're ordering upholstered furniture, Bud thought, it probably didn't hurt to be gay.

"So she split with the case," Peter said, his voice

smug, almost triumphant. "Bacola, you are really something, aren't you?"

Peter walked into the kitchen and brought out a bottle
of good French wine and a Dansk tray with a wedge of
ripe Brie surrounded by neatly sliced sourdough bread.

"Oh, Christ," Bud said, "get that out of here. I don't
even want to look at it."

"You have a real thing about weight, don't you?" Peter
said. He sat down next to Bud and spread some Brie on
a slice of bread.

"Just get me the script, huh?"

"I can tell by the way you always suck your gut in that
you think you're too heavy," Peter said. He offered Bud
the bread and cheese.

"I should have run you in days ago," Bud said. He got
up and paced around the room. He knew if he made eye
contact with the food he was lost.

"You're too hung up," Peter said, starting to polish off
the bread and cheese himself. "Actually, you're just
about right."

"Where's the script?"

"I want you to come into the bedroom with me," Peter
said.

Bud shot him a quick, wary look.

"You're gorgeous," Peter said over his shoulder as he
opened the door leading into the back of the apartment,
"but you're not that gorgeous."

Bud could hear a television set, the volume turned
very low, could see a bluish light coming from under the
closed bedroom door.

Peter knocked on the door and opened it in the same
motion. Bud saw a gray-haired man sitting on the edge
of the bed. Behind him on the bed was an extraordinar-
ily pretty girl stretched out watching a black-and-white
movie on television. She had frosted blond hair and a
small, upturned nose that was so perfect Bud suspected
that it might not be her own. She looked familiar and he

226

wondered if he might have met her, seen her some-where before.

She was wearing a pink linen sundress and Bud could see the pale pink edges of a pair of generous breasts trying hard to fall out of the halter top. She was barefoot and her knees were raised and separated enough so that from where Bud stood, he could see a lot of thigh and startlingly black pubic hair.

She did not move or adjust her skirt as he approached the bed. She kept her eyes focused on the television screen and he kept his eyes focused on her crotch. Fair was fair.

"This is *the* Oliver Kelsey," Peter said. "And this is *the* Buddy Bacall, a.k.a. Bud Bacola, one of Beverly Hills' finest."

"Gypsy Doniger," Oliver Kelsey said, reaching around, placing a possessive hand on Gypsy's bare knee. He left his hand there although it appeared to be an uncomfortable position for him.

"Hi," Gypsy said, looking at Bud for a moment through her separated knees, then returned her full at-tention to the movie. It was a western with Jimmy Stew-art. The female lead was a pretty girl whose face Bud did not recognize, a Hollywood hopeful who had made it far enough to have a lead opposite one of the all-time big movie stars, but for one reason or another couldn't keep it afloat.

But he recognized the location, all right. Suddenly he felt his flesh shrink along his bones. He felt with an icy certainty that he had been there, had run across those same shifting sand dunes. He was sure he remembered those same eroded desert monuments, the hot, blinding sun.

Bud tried not to watch the movie, tried to pull his attention from the desert background that had suddenly become familiar to him, like something out of an old and troubling dream. As he watched Jimmy Stewart's horse stretching out over the arid scrub land, he began to believe unshakably that he could predict what was on the far side of each mesa, each twist or turn in the dusty desert road.

Bud stepped up to the set and turned it off. Gypsy Doniger was up and off the bed in one swift, angry motion. She gave Bud a dark, almost feral look, then turned the set on again, and settled back on the bed and continued watching.

"I think we've been missing each other," Oliver Kelsey said.

Bud looked down at him, noted that the hand on Gypsy Doniger's knee was unsteady. His face was lean and ashen, with tremors and tics running along the surface of his skin like a horse trying to shake off flies.

He was a good-looking man, Bud thought, despite the shakes, eternally thin, probably nothing that a good night's sleep and a good haberdasher couldn't take care of.

He was a miserable dresser. Possibly more fashionable clothes were still in his closet in the Bel-Air house, but Bud doubted it. In Hollywood there are two kinds of casual wear. One is imported blue jeans, heavy denim work shirts, white sweat socks and Gucci loafers or dirty Adidas. That look is okay, in, classy. What Oliver Kelsey was wearing was about as unclassy as you can get on the West Coast. Shiny brown synthetic slacks, a Robert Bruce two-tone knit sport shirt with matching aquamarine socks and black business shoes. Bud felt like running him in for his wardrobe alone.

"Listen, guy," Kelsey said in a voice that was as shaky as his hands, "I don't know how to tell you this, but I destroyed the manuscript." Before Bud could respond, Kelsey added, "It was mine. I wrote it, not Koenig."

"Why the hell did you tell him about it before I had a chance to look at it?" Bud said, turning angrily to Peter.

"I didn't know he was coming over. It was sitting in

the living room waiting for you. He saw it and tore it up."

"Lutz, you're starting to get on my nerves," Bud said, but secretly he was relieved. He hadn't wanted to read the script, knew none of it could be used in a court of law. All he had hoped for would have been a clue, a tip-off of feelings of love or hate that might have helped him locate a murderer.

"Mr. Kelsey," Bud said, "could I speak to you in the living room? Alone, please?" Bud turned and started to walk out of the bedroom.

"I have no secrets from her," Kelsey said.

"I'm sure that's very enriching for both of you," Bud said politely, "but I don't do joint interrogations."

"Go on," Gypsy whispered, squeezing Kelsey's leg reassuringly. He remained where he was, on the edge of the bed. Then Gypsy leaned over and whispered something in his ear, her eyes never leaving the TV screen. Bud could see her tongue flick out for a moment, disappear deep into his semicircular canal. Either her words or her tongue worked, because Oliver Kelsey stood up and followed Bud into the living room.

"You know, of course, that your wife is in the hospital," Bud said.

"Yes," Kelsey said guardedly, "I'm aware of that."

"There was a time when you and your wife were considered to be extremely happily married," Bud said, pacing around the tastefully furnished room, fingering the lump on his head. "Something seems to have changed that."

"What do you want to know, Bacola? I mean, let's cut through the crap here. I'm tired. I've got the shakes."

"Okay, then," Bud said. "Did you murder D. P. Koenig?"

"No," Kelsey said, a bemused smile on his face, "but I won't deny that it was on my list of things to do for that day."

"Do you have any idea who did murder him?"

"Yes."

"And who might that be?" Bud asked. He felt a surge of blood rush through his throbbing head.

"I think there's every possibility that it was my wife," Kelsey said. He looked up into Bud's face with impassive eyes.

"That's interesting," Bud said, moving away from him. "She seems to think it was you."

"She's quite crazy," Kelsey said. "You must have picked that up when you talked to her."

"Were you and Miss Doniger parked in Koenig's driveway in a camper last Monday afternoon?" Bud asked quickly, hoping to take him off guard.

"Monday?" Kelsey said slowly. "Yes, I believe we were."

"What were you doing there?"

"We'd been at the beach swimming. I kept telephoning Koenig from a phone booth on the Venice pier, and every time that little queer in there would tell me Koenig was at the doctor, was out sick, was getting mouth-to-mouth resuscitation."

"Did you try calling Koenig at home to check?"

"I haven't had his home phone number since at least two changes ago," Kelsey said bitterly.

"Why were you trying to reach him?" Bud asked.

"I was always trying to reach him." Bud could hear the anger, the impotence, rising in his voice. "And the keeper of the keys in there was always coming up with some cockamamie reason why Koenig couldn't talk to me, wouldn't return my calls. I mean, Christ, he was inventive, truly creative, with his charitable explanations."

"Tell me about Monday," Bud said. He was too tired, too drained for any more Hollywood digressions.

"Anyway, Monday I got more paranoid than usual and we left right from the beach and drove to Koenig's house so I could see for myself if he was, in fact, at home."

"And he wasn't?"

"He usually left his car in the driveway," Kelsey said, starting to get worked up as he relived the rejection, the humiliation. "But when I didn't see it, I still thought that maybe he was there. Maybe he'd put his car in the garage, so I rang the bell for about five minutes, and then I even went around to look in the garage, but his car wasn't there either."

"What if he had been there?" Bud asked gently. "What did you have in mind?"

"Quite simply, I was going to murder him."

"Why?"

"For not answering my phone calls," Kelsey said in a quiet, reasonable voice. "I would have choked him with my bare hands for that alone."

"Any other reason?"

"He's been fucking my wife for the past twenty-two years." Bud looked at Kelsey, studied his face closely, was amused that the pain and anger were so much more visible when he had spoken of the unreturned phone calls.

"Are you sure of that?" Bud asked.

"You mean, do I have photographs?" Kelsey asked. "No. It's just a fact of our lives."

"When did you first begin to believe she was having an affair with Koenig?" Bud asked. He kept thinking of Vera Kelsey lying broken, swollen in a hospital bed because she had driven too carelessly in pursuit of her faithless husband and his porno-queen girlfriend.

"It was going on long before I met her," Kelsey said, shifting his weight nervously. "She's always been a cunt."

"And it took you twenty-two years to get around to doing something about it?"

"She comes on like Mrs. American Pie," Kelsey said.

231

He stood up and walked to the front window and stared out into the street. "The all-I-want-in-life-is-my-husband-and-my-garden bit, but she's one of the world's leading ball-breakers."

"Where does Gypsy Doniger fit into all this?" Bud asked. Kelsey turned around quickly and gave Bud a long, warning look.

"She's a wonderful, bright, troubled lady, and she has nothing to do with any of this," Kelsey said, looking toward the bedroom, his eyes smoldering with late-life passion.

"Why were you trying to reach me?" Bud asked. "I've got a pocketful of messages from you. What was it you wanted to talk to me about?"

"I just wanted to get you before you got me," he said. "The woman next door, down in Venice, said you were nosing around. I hate that kind of crap."

"You do your work, I do mine," Bud said.

"He was an evil man," Kelsey said, then added pointedly, "but then I don't have to tell *you* that."

Bud wondered if there was anybody in town who didn't know who he was, or who he used to be. It annoyed him, made him edgy, but he had to admit to himself that there was some secret part of him that was pleased, the old hambone in him, that he was not thought of as just another cop.

"Where were you Tuesday night, the night your agent was murdered?" Bud asked, fixing his gaze on Oliver Kelsey's gray, upturned face.

"I was in the sack with Gypsy Doniger," he said, a trace of something between belligerence and male pride in his voice.

"Will you both be prepared to testify to that in a court of law?" Bud asked.

"If it comes to that, yes."

"Do you know anything about your wife's whereabouts that night?"

"She was probably thinking up new ways to destroy me, bring me down, pulverize my ego," he said, a tight, joyless smile on his face.

"Is it true that you were just fired off a filthy flick?" Bud asked bluntly, hoping to pry something loose with this bluntness. "That your script wasn't even up to porno standards?"

Bud got the reaction he was looking for. Kelsey leaped out of his chair, his face ashen, then suddenly blood-maroon. He stood toe to toe with Bud, his horse-flesh face quivering.

"That's a goddamn lie," Kelsey shouted. "It was politics, and jealousy and a cretin of a fucking Arab producer who was hung up on Gypsy who didn't understand intelligent dialogue. He wanted her for himself."

He sat down again, then began to cry noisily, large, fat tears raining down off his cheeks onto his terrible, tasteless shirt.

"Hey," Bud said gently. "We've all been there." But the writer continued to sit there crying unashamedly, the tears splashing unchecked from his eyes.

"I mean, Christ, it was just a dirty movie," Bud said.

Maybe it was the throbbing lump on his head, but Bud felt a sudden need to sit down next to the writer, to touch him, reassure him that they were all hit-and-run victims, sideswiped over the years by a lethal and uncaring driver named D. P. Koenig.

Why do I keep self-destructing? Bud asked himself as he stood over the weeping writer. He fingered the lump on the back of his head and thought for a moment of Glenda Deering and her late-arriving hood, of the now forever lost Gucci case with its treasure trove of filth and Christ knew what else.

"Hey, look," Bud said finally. "Can you pull yourself together long enough for me to ask a few more questions?"

Oliver Kelsey shook his head, too emotional to speak,

then got up and walked back through the open door into the bedroom. Gypsy was still stretched out on the bed, her legs still parted, watching television.

Bud started to follow the writer, but Peter emerged from the bedroom and put a restraining hand on his arm.

"You can give him a few minutes to pull himself together, can't you?"

"Pulled-together people don't reveal as much as unpulled-together people," Bud said, but he turned around, walked back into the living room with Peter, who flopped down on his perfectly stuffed couch and patted the cushion next to him.

"No thanks," Bud said, pacing around the room, giving Peter a wide berth.

"What's the problem?" Peter asked, grinning at him. "Am I starting to look good to you?"

"Yeah, you're beautiful," Bud said lightly. He liked the end tables and the lamps, would like to have known where Peter found them, but didn't want to start talking interior decorating with a fruit.

"How come there are only losers on my list?" Bud asked suddenly. "Didn't Koenig handle any winners?"

"Sure, but why would someone on the top of the heap want to kill him? Murder is a loser's game. For the impotent only."

Bud knew he was right, but he was becoming impatient with the downtrodden, embittered leftovers of Hollywood. He would like to have stood on Charlton Heston's doorstep, badge in hand, be invited into his home. Or Barbra Streisand or Goldie Hawn. Someone interesting, someone who had forgotten how to whine or bitch or weep.

The door to the bedroom was still open. Bud could see Oliver Kelsey sitting on the edge of the bed, could see Gypsy Doniger now kneeling behind him, massaging his shoulder, the base of his neck. Even from where he was standing, it looked good to Bud.

234

He felt like sitting down next to the writer to wait his turn, to get some of that relaxing, therapeutic action from the porno queen who was stroking, rubbing, never taking her eyes from the television screen.

Bud looked at Gypsy Doniger's empty, impassive face as she worked over the now almost comatose writer. It was a small, pinched face with fine dark planes under the eyes that glittered, almost without blinking, as she watched the Jimmy Stewart movie that had probably been filmed in the same gritty desert where years before his own acting career had come to an end.

"We've got alibis, Bacola," the writer said sleepily, without raising his head. "I think even my wife would tell you where we were on Tuesday night."

"What does that mean?" Bud asked quickly.

"I think she was snooping around our place in Venice that night."

"What time?"

"I don't wear a watch when I make love."

Bud suddenly remembered the mattress with the not-so-white sheets nestled in among the lint balls on the bare wood floor. He imagined Vera Kelsey, potting soil still under her broken fingernails, tiptoeing through the hollyhocks, peering over the edge of the window at the heartbreaking tableau of her husband effectively plunging into Gypsy Doniger's small, perfect body.

He would go back to the hospital tomorrow morning to talk to Vera Kelsey. But first he needed some sleep.

13

The telephone tore him out of the middle of a troubling dream. He was in a motel room. It was dark and the air conditioner was rattling in his ear, sending shafts of icy air across his bed. There were not enough blankets. He was shivering and cold and frightened and he kept calling out, but nobody answered.

"Yeah?" he mumbled into the phone. He checked his wristwatch. It was twelve past seven. He reached up and touched the lump on his head. The constant throbbing of the night before had now diminished to a dull ache and the swelling was down.

"You want a progress report, Buddy-boy?" It was Tom Edwards sounding very pleased with himself.

"Go ahead," Bud said, swinging into a sitting position, trying to push the dream away from him. He felt slightly sick to his stomach, almost hung over, even though he had had nothing to drink the night before.

"We haven't turned up any albinos, and Glenda Deering's Mercedes is parked near the TWA terminal at LAX."

"Great," Bud said. He was sure now that she had driven directly from his apartment to the airport, had hopped a plane to God only knew where. Well, that was that. The day's first bad news, and he hadn't even brushed his teeth yet.

"Anything else?"

"Yeah, Kenny Bartlett wants you to call him, and that fat Ritner kid has been driving me nuts. Will you for Chrissake call him back?"

"Keep in touch," Bud said minimally. He dialed Gilbert's number. The maid who *no habla Inglés* answered the phone.

"Geelbart *no está en casa esta mañana*," she said. Her voice was soft and musical. He left his name, trying to remember the letters in Spanish, but the effort was too much, so he hung up.

You could never reach anybody in this town before ten o'clock in the morning.

When he got to Ivy's apartment, the morose-eyed Northern Californian had split, but Gilbert Ritner was sitting at the glass-topped table in the dining alcove. He was spooning down cold cereal and talking a mile a minute.

Ivy was wearing blue jeans and an Indian gauze shirt. No makeup. She looked about twelve years old and incredibly clean. Bud gazed down at her bare feet. They were baby's feet. Small, pink. No corns, no calluses. Maybe wearing the big ugly boots wasn't so dumb after all. If pressed, he thought for a moment, he could see himself giving her a pedicure.

"Hi," she said. She slipped her arm around his waist, impersonally, as if he were a relative or an old friend. Then she leaned in and brushed a kiss across his shoulder. He felt the warmth of her lips through his shirt. He put his arm around her waist and pulled her in close.

"It's like Grand Central Station around here," he said to her.

"All this time you were a movie star and you didn't say a word," Gilbert said, his hand moving rhythmically from bowl to mouth.

"What have you got for me?" Bud asked, cutting him off quickly. He came and sat down across the table from Gilbert. He looked disapprovingly at the big bowl of cereal.

"Don't sweat it," Gilbert said. "It's Special K and skimmed milk."

"First breakfast or second?"

"Do you want to know what I have or not?" Gilbert said impatiently.

"Go ahead," Bud said. Ivy came and stood behind Bud's chair. She did something casually intimate with her hands at the base of his neck that felt restorative and absolutely essential. It was not so much a massage as a reassurance, and when she bent over and kissed what was left of the lump on his head, he felt a fast sting of tears come to his eyes which both confused and alarmed him at the same time.

"It was either the night he got scragged or the night before," Gilbert said, the dripping spoon poised midair, "I heard him talking to someone at the front door."

"Go on," Bud said skeptically.

"I only heard his voice, no one else's, but he was kind of apologizing to someone."

"What did he say?"

"He kept saying things like 'You must believe me, I didn't know' and 'I swear to you, I had no idea.' "

"What time was it?" Bud asked, almost to be polite, because he strongly suspected the kid was starting to improvise to keep himself involved.

"It was late. I was already asleep so it had to be around midnight."

"And you don't have any idea if it was a man or a woman?"

"I only heard Koenig's voice."

"Why didn't you tell me about this before?" Bud asked irritably.

"I put myself under hypnosis yesterday and that's what I came up with," he said reproachfully. "If you'd answer your phone messages, I'd have told you that last night."

"That's it?" Bud asked. "That's all you could dredge up?"

"I'm practically solving this whole case for you," Gilbert said, returning to his cereal. "And I don't like your attitude."

Bud felt Ivy's fingers press minimally deeper into the flesh at the base of his neck. It was subtle, like a signal to a finely trained horse to stop what he was currently doing or to do something else.

"I don't like my attitude either," Bud said finally. He felt Ivy's fingers relax again.

"I went out and bought a book on self-hypnosis yesterday, just so I could help crack this case for you," Gilbert said. "I'm good at it too. I can put myself under in no time flat."

"I want you to burn the goddamn book," Bud said quickly. He was starting to get uneasy feelings. Maybe it wasn't bullshit after all. Maybe the kid actually heard something, yanked it out of his unconscious, or imagined he did. Any which way, it was a dangerous game and all Bud needed was to have headquarters find out he was working on the biggest case of the year with his new partner, who happened to be twelve years old.

"Quit fooling around, Gilbert," Bud said sharply. "That's an order."

"I'm not breaking any laws," Gilbert said haughtily.

"Maybe you're not, but I am," Bud whispered, almost to himself. He leaned back against Ivy. She bent down and rested her chin on his shoulder. He felt her hair against his cheek. He could not remember the last time he had touched or been touched by anyone where immediate sex was not a factor. Obviously there was something wrong in the way he had been conducting his life. He reached up with his right hand and touched her face to let her know that what she was doing was okay with him. More than okay.

"Gilbert," Ivy said. Bud's fingers could feel a soft smile start as she spoke to him. "How'd you like to take a walk for yourself?"

"Are you kidding?" Gilbert bleated. "There's work to be done."

"How'd you get over here?" Bud asked.

"By cab," Gilbert said. "I mean, I've spent bags of money running around for you."

"Keep a list of your expenses and I'll see you get reimbursed," Bud told him. He would pay it out of his own pocket and tell the kid it was from the Beverly Hills Police Department. It would be easier than explaining it to them.

"Great," Gilbert said. He stood up, then leaned over for one more spoonful of Special K. "But first I want you to tell me about your days of fame and stardom."

Bud looked up quickly to see if the kid was putting him on, being a smart-ass, but Gilbert was smiling at him, his eyes wide and almost respectful.

"Did you tell him?" Bud asked Ivy, running his finger along her lower lip. He did not want to make her think he was sore at her, did not want her to pull away from him.

"My Dad told me," Gilbert said, wiping his mouth carefully with a paper napkin. "I spoke to him in Italy and told him how I was like solving the case for you, and when I told him your name, he said he remembered you, that he'd been a third assistant director or something like that on an old movie of yours."

"Yeah, well, that was a million years ago," Bud said quickly.

"He said something terrible happened and that I shouldn't even talk to you about it, but what the hell?"

240

"Hate to do this to you," Ivy said, "but I'm kicking you out." She walked around the table and took Gilbert's hand, pulling him gently but firmly from the table.

"I'm very pivotal to this case," Gilbert said, trying to hunker down in his chair. "I mean, once I uncork my brain, I can make you a real hero."

"He's a hero right now," Ivy said, leading him to the front door. "Keep in touch." She kissed him quickly on the cheek and tried to close the door, but he stood his ground.

"Isn't it horrible for you," Gilbert said over Ivy's shoulder to Bud, "I mean, being just a policeman in the same town where you were famous?"

His voice was filled with so much genuine feeling that Bud just smiled at him and kept nodding his head up and down.

"Some of the time, kid, some of the time."

Ivy closed the door firmly on Gilbert and a moment later Bud could see the top of his head through the slats in the venetian blinds. He turned and waved through the window to Bud. Bud waved back then got up and walked to where Ivy was standing. He put his arms around her.

He had the weird, shaky feeling that he was about to cry as he stood there holding her in the middle of her living room. He felt he was coming apart, was afraid to speak because he did not trust his voice.

"Something's happening to you, isn't it?" she said softly. When he did not answer her, she stepped away from him and studied his face. He thought of turning away, but he just stood there and let her look at him.

"If you wanted to cry," she said finally, "I could live with that."

"I don't know," he said. "But I think I'm gettin' there."

"I want to make you feel better," she said. "You want some bacon and a cheese omelet, some Acapulco Gold, an ice bag for the lump on your head, however it came to be there?"

"Would you lie down with me?" he asked, his voice as unsteady as he ever remembered it.

She hesitated for a moment, tried to read his eyes, his heart, in that one quick glance. Then she took his hand and led him into her bedroom. She eased him down onto her already made bed and lay down beside him. He felt the comforting warmth of her body along the entire length of his own. He knew, if he wanted to, that he could make love to her, but she was giving him now all that he needed, all that he could possibly handle.

"I'm screwing up," he said quietly. "Badly. This whole case."

"Who says?"

He told her about the lump on his head, how it came to be there, how he deserved it, about Glenda Deering's car abandoned at the airport. Her only response was to tighten her grip on him, to kiss him just above where his collar met his throat.

What he wanted to do was just continue to lie there with her warmth against him, to empty his brain of all the jangling, nagging thoughts. He knew that with very little effort he could become aroused, could force her under him, knew unquestionably that she would not protest because she had assessed his needs.

He looked at his watch. It was just after eight. He was tempted to stay there, maybe even go to sleep, blot everything out. Even fifteen minutes sounded good, but it was a luxury he couldn't afford. He eased himself away from her and sat on the edge of the bed.

"How much do you actually know?" she asked him. She had rolled over onto her back and her blouse had worked its way up so that he could see part of her mid-section. Her stomach was white and smooth and he reached over and ran his fingers gently along the exposed flesh.

"About Koenig's murder? Not as much as I should."

"No, about you," she said. "About Buddy Bacall."

"Oh, that," Bud said uneasily. He got up from the bed and crossed to the window. "Not all that much, I guess."

"Would you like to know more?"

"Do I have a choice?" he asked. Both of them were startled at the quick, icy edge in his voice.

"I have a list of people who were in Utah with you," she said. Her voice was quiet but unrelenting.

"So?" It came out cold, nasty, guarded. Just the way he felt, but he could see she would not be intimidated by it.

"So, I think it's time you found out a few facts."

"I've managed very well all these years on the facts I do have."

"Very well?" she asked.

"God damn well enough," he answered. He walked out of the bedroom and through the living room. She caught up with him at the front door.

"Koenig may have been a cold, unfeeling man," Ivy said quietly, "but I think your perceptions and memories of your father, of what happened in Utah, need some major overhauling."

"I don't want to discuss my father with you or with anyone," Bud said, his voice cold and savage. "He never went past the Italian equivalent of the eighth grade, but he was a decent, loving man with a sense of his own dignity, and D. P. Koenig was as responsible for his death as if he'd put a bullet in his head."

"Why did you feel it necessary to memorize that speech?" Ivy asked. Bud did not trust himself to respond. He opened the front door, but she slipped in the way, quickly barring him from leaving, from running away.

"Go to hell," he said because he did not trust himself to say any more.

243

"What is it you're afraid of?" she asked him, never taking her eyes from his face. "Of finding out that all this time you might have been mixing up the heroes and the heavies?"

"You don't know what you're talking about," Bud said, trying to turn away from her steady, uncompromising gaze.

"Call somebody," Ivy said. "Talk to somebody who was up there with you when it happened and get rid of the demons once and for all."

"I almost called someone who was on that movie with me," Bud said finally, "a couple of years ago, but he died before I got around to talking to him. I thought maybe it was an omen."

"There were over a hundred people there in Utah. Statistically some of them were bound to die over the last twenty years."

"What's it to you?" Bud asked angrily. "Why are you pushing it so hard?"

"Because I have this thing about being hung up on under-achievers," she said.

He stared at her without saying a word. He had thought for a moment that he might strike her. Then he pushed her aside roughly and left. He knew she was standing at the top of the stairs looking down at him, but he did not turn around. He walked around the aluminum-webbed loungers, around the corrugated plastic wall, and slipped under the wheel of his car. He put the key in the ignition. Then he leaned back and waited for the heaviness to lift from him.

He thought about what she had just said. *Under-achiever.* Who the hell did she think she was? Soothing him, reassuring him, building him up, then—zap. Laying something like that on him when she had to know he least could handle it.

No one had ever accused him of that before. His father had run a grocery store. To his mother, to his family,

244

being a detective in Beverly Hills was a hell of a lot higher up the ladder than that. The other thing, the few famous years, were never mentioned, never talked about, never thrown up to him.

And yet, as he sat there in his car on that hot August morning, he had to admit to himself that at parties, when he met people, there was that moment's hesitation when they asked him what he did for a living. Even the way he would tell people what he did was derisive, theatrical, apologetic.

"Just a cop," he'd say, accompanied by a quick embarrassed grin intended to preclude any further questions.

And it wasn't like he hadn't given the acting thing another shot. He had. He was nineteen then, and it was the second brutal lesson that D. P. Koenig had taught him.

When you're hot, you're hot, and when you're not, you stink like rotting fish.

On the day he graduated from Fountain Valley High, in the upper 5 percent of his class, his mother gave him a check for five thousand dollars. When he tried to thank her for it, she told him that it was his anyway, that he had earned it, that she had merely held onto it until she believed he was ready to assume some responsibility for his life. She hinted obliquely that there might even be more where that came from.

He bought a used Pontiac convertible for five hundred dollars, packed everything he owned into the trunk and headed back to Los Angeles.

He rented a bright, airy bedroom in a house in Westwood, and went to the beach at the foot of Venice Boulevard every day for the next three months, surfing, blistering and peeling, idly wondering what he was going to do with the rest of his life.

Still undecided in September, he enrolled at Santa Monica City College and rented a less bright, less airy, less costly bedroom in a house a few blocks from the campus.

In his first year he took courses in psychology, English, history and business administration. In his second year he quit kidding around and took as many acting classes as his schedule would permit. Some of the students remembered who he was and were mystified at why he was starting at the bottom. He was a little mystified himself, but he hung in there, studying, rehearsing scenes, reading for parts in school productions as if he had never acted, never been in front of a camera before, never been a household name.

One day, after his drama coach had told him he'd done extremely well on a scene from *Death of a Salesman*, Bud decided he would call D. P. Koenig. It had been over ten years since they had last spoken, since the agent had turned him onto Dexedrine and had then cut him loose forever.

Bud had fantasized the scene over and over again in his years in Fountain Valley, had imagined the emotion, the relief he would hear in the agent's voice at finally being reunited with his boy, D. P. Koenig's kid, now a man, now ready to enter the arena again.

His hands were shaking when he telephoned Koenig's office. A woman with a cold, stern voice answered. Even before she heard his name, she seemed to resent his having made her pick up the phone.

"Could you tell him that Buddy Bacall is on the phone?" he asked, angry with himself for the raw pleading tone he heard in his own voice. As he said it, the name seemed strange, alien to his ear. Since his first day in Fountain Valley, his mother had told him that he was now just plain Bud Bacola. There was no more Buddy Bacall.

"Could you tell me what this is in reference to?" she asked.

"He knows who I am," Bud said.

"One moment please." After a series of clicks, he heard her voice again.

"Mr. Koenig is out of the office right now," she said. "If you'll leave your number I'll have him return the call."

Bud left his number that morning, and five mornings after that, cutting classes for the long and agonizing vigil. D. P. Koenig did not return any of his calls, did not even bother to have his secretary return any of the calls.

Bud could not believe that the man who had discovered him, transformed him into a famous child star, then into a semi-orphan, and finally into a full-time nobody, could turn away from him so totally. He thought perhaps the agent might be sick, comatose, hospitalized, out of town, even an amnesiac. Anything was easier, less painful to accept, than the hard, cruel fact that D. P. Koenig had refused to acknowledge his existence.

Bud wrote several letters marked personal, clinging to the belief that possibly Koenig's secretary, angered by his persistence, had chosen independently not to bother the agent with his string of messages.

D. P. Koenig did not answer the letters, so he followed this up with a new barrage of telephone calls. He became obsessed with the idea of getting through to the agent. He no longer had any hope that Koenig would help him. Now all he wanted, or believed he wanted, was to reach him, tell him what a bastard he was, and then hang up.

On the fifth morning, more for nuisance value than anything else, he telephoned Koenig from a booth in a supermarket in Hollywood. Bud was stunned to hear, not the secretary's impersonal voice, but D. P. Koenig himself.

"Hello, Kenny," the agent said. He'd obviously screwed up, picked up the wrong phone.

"No," Bud said quietly, barely able to speak, "this is Buddy Bacall. Do you remember me?"

"Oh, Christ, kid," Koenig said quickly. "I'm sorry. My secretary is out sick and I've got six calls backed up. Give me your number and I'll get right back to you."

"I'm in a booth," Bud said eagerly and gave him the number, enunciating carefully so there could be no errors, no slip-ups.

"Hang in there," the agent said. "I'll get right back to you."

Bud hung in there for the next three hours, riding shotgun on the phone booth, threatening all would-be phoners, ready to take on in mortal combat anyone who would try to come between him and D. P. Koenig. As the hours wore on, he would dart away long enough to buy a package of Fritos or a sugar-glazed doughnut to ease the growing anguish of his rejection.

On his nineteenth birthday, Bud received another five thousand dollar check from his mother. He moved into a small apartment in North Hollywood and joined a little theater group. After a series of small, unimportant parts, he ended up with the lead in a revival of *Golden Boy*.

Deciding not to let pride get in his way, he sent a letter to D. P. Koenig suggesting that he might like to catch his ex-boy actor eleven years later. He enclosed two front-row seats with the suggestion that if he could not make it opening night, he call and have them exchanged for any other night of the limited run.

Koenig never called for new tickets, never showed up. On opening night, when Bud peered out at the seats he had sent Koenig, he saw an uneasy-looking black couple. The man was wearing a chauffeur's uniform. Bud could only assume that Koenig had either thrown the tickets in the trash and they were spotted by his eagle-eyed help or that he had given the tickets outright to his domestics. Nothing to raise his hopes either way.

Bud got one okay review and two that were not so hot, both critics calling him attractive, an interesting type, but self-conscious, uptight. One of the trade papers cruelly suggested that all ex-kid performers take a cue from Shirley Temple—marry well and go into another line of work.

When he wasn't going to school or rehearsing, Bud began to hang around Schwab's drugstore on Sunset Boulevard where he could drink endless coffee and shoot the breeze with other show business hopefuls. He became friendly with a tall, thin Southern boy, who, had he been half as bright as he was aggressive, would have known that his virulent and still eruptive acne would keep him from stardom, possibly even from work as an extra.

His name was Tom Cantwell. Bud was intrigued by his methodical and dogged pursuit of agents, producers, casting directors. He would make the rounds each morning, every network, every studio, the trade papers tucked under his arm, a hopeful and engaging smile on his badly pitted face.

Each afternoon he would return to Schwab's, deflated but good-natured. He would flop down in a booth and noisily outline the day's failures and rejections to anyone who cared to listen.

"What do I need this shit for?" he would say. Bud loved the sound of his soft Southern voice, his unique ability to turn shit into a three-syllabled word.

Tom was staying with his Uncle Mitchell, a thin and thoughtful man who was a sergeant with the Beverly Hills Police Department. He had come up through the ranks and was now at a desk, out of harm's way, giving orders, pushing papers.

Occasionally, on their way to an audition, Tom would bring Bud by headquarters. They would have a cup of coffee while Uncle Mitchell lectured them on the foolishness and futility of ever believing they'd make it in show business. Bud listened carefully. Tom did not.

"See," Tom would say, pointing proudly to his uncle,

249

"he doesn't have to take nothin' off'a nobody." Then they would drive off to an endless round of demoralizing rejections and failures.

A couple of times, on his way to Schwab's, Bud dropped by to see Uncle Mitchell on his own. With great interest he watched the detectives at their desks, their jackets off, their gun holsters in place. He watched them as they filled out endless reports, talked earnestly over the telephone, occasionally jumping up and racing out the door in pursuit of a criminal who had invaded the sanctity of Beverly Hills.

A few days after the less than spectacular run of *Golden Boy*, which yielded Bud exactly zilch in the way of acting opportunities, there was a murder in Bud's apartment building. Following a day of rude and bewildering turndowns, Bud returned home to flashing red lights, swarms of policemen running up and down the stairs.

The murder had taken place on the second floor in the apartment directly below him. The victim was an old man who had moved in only the week before. Bud remembered him as quiet, nervous, afraid to make eye contact.

As Bud walked up the stairs to his apartment, he saw the coroner bending over the body. The man appeared to have been strangled with a dark paisley tie which was still looped around his neck.

But more than at the murdered man, Bud found himself staring at the detective in charge of the case. He was silver-haired with a young, lean face and an air of unmistakable authority about him. He was questioning some of the tenants on the same floor, and Bud could sense the fear, respect, almost awe, that they felt for this well-organized, unsmiling and theatrical man.

Bud suspected that this man's telephone calls were always returned, and if they were not, it in no way affected his sense of himself. There seemed to be a shape, a form, a purpose to his life. He looked like a man who didn't have to take "nothin' off a nobody."

Bud decided at that moment, over the body of a murdered stranger, that he would be a cop, that he would put an end forever to the punishing, soul-crunching business of trying to become an actor.

And he did not want to be just a cop anywhere. He wanted the Beverly Hills beat. One more time.

He drove out Hollywood Boulevard to the Cahuenga Pass. He felt lightheaded, almost irresponsible. He wondered if he were about to snap, if possibly he had already snapped. Either way, he felt surprisingly detached about the whole thing.

At La Brea, he watched a radiantly beautiful girl dart into the street mid-block, stopping traffic as she jaywalked to her Fiat parked in a tow-away zone on the other side of the boulevard. At any other time in his life, Bud would have stopped her, flirted with her, possibly even gotten her telephone number. Now he was just appreciating her from a distance, secure in the knowledge that he lived in a part of the world where everyone was beautiful. Or nearly beautiful.

Wherever you looked, there they were: package wrappers in department stores, parking-lot attendants, firemen. Pretty, hopeful people from all over the country had migrated to Hollywood in the twenties and thirties to seek their fortune in the motion-picture business. They had hounded the casting agents, and when they no longer had hope, they settled in the outlying communities, in Pomona and Pasadena, in Laguna and Simi Valley. They found other beautiful, failed people, married them, shared their disappointments, and ultimately gave birth to a generation of super-pretty children, some of whom tried to get into motion pictures, but most of whom settled for what their parents had settled for— construction work, orange growing, stenography. Then they, too, selected pretty mates and had even prettier children who were all sunbronzed, chlorine-bleached and largely responsible for bringing down the state reading averages.

As he slipped uneasily across the eight lanes of the Hollywood Freeway, he thought about Ivy, about her unwavering determination to make him face his past. He knew that she had been willing to risk his walking out and never coming back. It was the kind of weirdo strength and confidence that up until that morning he had believed only gorgeous women possessed.

He wanted to hate her, to dismiss her forever, for daring to push him in a direction he had steadfastly and successfully avoided for the better part of his life, but he also wanted to rush back to her, to lie down by her side and have her touch him, reassure him, keep the world at bay.

What in Buddy Bacall's days had been known as Warner Brothers was now called Burbank Studios. He had some trouble at the gate—an officious red-necked guard told him he didn't have a drive-on pass. Wearily Bud shifted his weight and pulled his wallet out of his back pocket and showed the guard his badge.

"Sorry," the guard said, obviously enjoying pulling rank, "but nobody comes on the lot unless somebody has telephoned here with a drive-on."

"Would you get Mr. Maxwell's office on the phone and tell them to okay Detective Bacola," Bud said patiently. He had learned over his years on the police force that you go out of your way to avoid confrontations with petty tyrants. In the long run they can't stop you from doing what you want to do, but they sure as hell can slow you down.

He watched the guard make a leisurely phone call. From the disappointed expression on his face, Bud knew that authority had been given for him to drive onto the lot.

"Don't park in a slot with a name on it or in front of a fire hydrant or blocking a driveway," the guard said irritably, slipping a card under his windshield wiper. "And leave your keys in the car."

"Thanks, pal," Bud said and drove through the narrow streets to a building that said Maxwell Enterprises.

The receptionist was a knockout. Big tits and a slow, phony smile that must have soothed countless men who were kept waiting for long periods of time in the expensive leather chairs in the outer office.

"Detective Bacola to see Mr. Maxwell," Bud said, showing her his badge, and looking down the front of her dress at the same time.

"You must be very important," she said, her voice a study in throaty sexiness, "because I was told to show you right in."

Richard Maxwell's office was large and elegant and beige. Everything was beige—floor, ceiling, drapes, desk, chairs. Even Richard Maxwell's complexion was beige. Yellow, almost, a waning suntan or perhaps a low-grade infection.

He looked to be in his late thirties. He was losing hair, not unattractively, in two V's on each side of his head. His remaining hair was dark and glossy, and he may have been the last man in Hollywood, if not the world, who used greasy kid stuff.

He was good-looking, well-built, not an extra ounce on him, but even from behind the beige desk, Bud could see that he was probably no more than five-two or five-three. About normal for a studio executive.

"Let's get this over with fast, okay?" Maxwell said. He had a pouting mouth that drooped at the corners, and Bud decided he neither liked him nor trusted him.

"I ran *Little Renegade* the other night," Maxwell said.

"What is the nature of your relationship with Glenda Deering?" Bud asked quickly, as if he had not heard, but he had heard it all right.

"Friends," Maxwell said easily, then added, "now."

"And before?"

"Prior to my marriage, we had a small impermanent sort of thing." Bud saw Maxwell studying him, trying to assess how much he already knew.

"Can you tell me something about the albino?" Bud said, shifting quickly to try to catch him off guard.

"Is that a new book?" Maxwell stared blankly at him.

"No," Bud said, "it's an old hood who showed up on my doorstep last night."

"I'm a busy man, Mr. Bacola," Maxwell said, starting to shift papers industriously on his beige desk top to prove his point. "Would you please get to the point?"

"Somebody felt strongly enough about Miss Deering's Gucci bag to send some muscle over to retrieve it. Could you possibly throw some light on that?"

The intercom buzzed. Maxwell flipped the switch and told his secretary to hold all calls.

"The albino," Bud prodded.

"You were damn good, you know that?" Maxwell said. "A natural."

"I'm a better cop," Bud said. "And the work's steadier."

"I don't know any albinos, and if I did, I wouldn't hire them for muscle. They're a little too traceable for me."

"On such short notice, maybe you have to take what's available."

"Look, she's a kinky lady. She had a bag of tricks that I didn't necessarily want my bride to discover. She was going to make some trouble for me, so I had Koenig pick the bag up from my house, and that's the last I know of it."

"She said there were a couple of ounces of cocaine in the bag," Bud lied easily. "That's the big leagues, Mr. Maxwell."

"Bullshit," Maxwell said, jumping up, his eyes blaz-

254

ing with possibly genuine indignation. "I don't drink tap water, Bacola. I won't even let the cook steam my vegetables with tap water. You think I'm going to snort coke or inject anything into my veins?"

"I can only repeat what Miss Deering told me." Bud heard the sincerity in his own voice and it amused him. He knew he sounded as if he were telling the truth, the whole truth and nothing but the truth. Maybe Maxwell was right. Maybe he was a natural after all.

"I don't even know what you want, what you're doing here," Maxwell said. He started pacing around his desk, occasionally stopping to pull a brown leaf off a ficus tree in front of the window. "I can't imagine you think I'm involved in Koenig's murder. So what do you want?"

"Where were you Tuesday night?"

"Working on a movie in projection room J on this lot."

"Who was with you?"

"Nobody. I was doing some post-production work all by myself."

"May I please have the name of the projectionist?" Bud took out his pad and pencil.

"Who the hell knows? Who the hell cares?" Maxwell sat back down and put his Bally loafers back up on the desk. "I'm putting together a movie about the peacetime navy," Maxwell said. "There's a small but very strong part in it for someone like you. You want to read for it?"

"The name of the projectionist, Mr. Maxwell?"

"I mean, shit, I'm not handing it to you," Maxwell said irritably. "You'd have to read along with everyone else."

"I was in town a week ago. Nobody made me any offers then."

"The projectionist's name is Greeley, Jonathan Greeley." Maxwell pushed the telephone across the desk to Bud. "It's extension 1040. If he's not there try 1213." Bud made no move for the telephone, but he jotted down the name and numbers Maxwell gave him.

"I was sitting in Glenda Deering's den when you telephoned her two days ago," Bud said. "What was the nature of that call?"

"Just to say hello," Maxwell lied casually. "I got married very suddenly and I knew she was . . ." He stopped mid-sentence, then went on in a flat, almost nasal voice, "I wanted to know if she had the fucking Gucci case."

"And she didn't . . . *then.*"

"It could have been mildly embarrassing," Maxwell said. "That was all, believe me. Just mildly embarrassing."

"How well did you know D. P. Koenig?"

"Lunches, meetings. I'd run into him at parties, openings, and screenings, but that was about it."

"And what was Glenda Deering's relationship with him?"

"Weird. I don't think they were ever lovers, but he was kind of her protector. Maybe even her procurer. I never really understood what was going on there."

"She says he came to your house and picked up the Gucci bag."

"Yeah, that's right."

"I'm surprised you'd let someone you know so casually come into possession of something as intimate as that."

"I'm a married man, Bacola, I was a thousand miles away at the time. What choice did I have?"

"When did you find out that the Gucci case had fallen into the wrong hands?"

"I could care less who had it as long as it was out of my house."

"I'm having a little trouble with that, Mr. Maxwell," Bud said quietly. "I mean, none of us wants to have our sexual preferences or alternatives too widely publicized."

Bud thought for a moment that Maxwell was going to

take a swing at him. Instead he leaned in close, so close that Bud could smell Binaca on his breath.

"That was hers," Maxwell said, his voice choked with anger, "all hers. She was like the Fuller Brush lady of filth. It was a new number for me. I mean, man, she was unbelievable."

"How did you get the albino over to me so fast," Bud asked, moving slightly to one side to avoid the Binaca fumes.

"You're starting to bore me, Bacola," Maxwell said. He yawned convincingly, then looked at his watch. "When you have something concrete to pin on me, give me a call."

"Do you know where Glenda Deering is now?" Bud asked. "Her car is at LAX."

"I'm sure she went back to Ohio to wow them with her wardrobe of crotchless underwear," Maxwell said. He smiled and shook his head. He was trying out a macho man-to-man number. Bud could wait. "She was unbelievable. Cut nipple holes in everything she owned, used to show up at the front door in a mink coat with maybe three sequins on underneath."

"That ought to go over very big in Canton."

Maxwell suddenly pushed a script across the beige desk, turned it around so that Bud could read the title. It was called "Anchors." Bud did not recognize the writer's name.

"The part of Mannie," the producer said. "You want to cold read for me right now?" Bud picked up the script and flipped through the pages, saw the name over a lot of good-sized speeches. Anyone else, Maxwell would have pushed cash across the beige lacquer desk top. To this cop, the bribe was an acting part.

Bud knew he should not even have touched the script, should not have indicated even curiosity. He was startled to see small damp spots where his fingers had rested on the paper. Maybe he wasn't untouchable after all.

"No thanks," Bud said slowly, hoping that the producer would not see his nervous fingerprints on the pale blue paper.

"What are you afraid of?" Maxwell said quietly. "Success, failure, rejection?"

"You want to try corruption?" Bud said. He got to his feet, wiped his damp, sweating hands on his gray trousers.

"Look," Maxwell said, casually leafing through the pages of the script, "you get all your police work out of the way, solve the crime, get your commendation for the brilliant way you're handling this case, and then come back and read for me."

Maxwell was smiling now—it was an infuriating top-dog smile to let Bud know that he knew there had been a screw-up with the missing Gucci case. He had offered Bud a bribe so clever, so subtle, that no court of law in the land could convict him for it.

And the worst part of it was that Bud had felt a quick surge of elation, potent and jarring enough to let him know that some of the old craziness still remained.

"I'll get back to you," Bud said. He headed quickly across the beige carpeting to the beige door.

"You were damn good," Maxwell called out to him. Bud stopped at the door and turned to see if the producer had the same top-dog grin, but Maxwell was looking at him impassively, a mixture of curiosity and compassion on his sallow face.

"Glenda Deering said nothing about drugs," Bud said. "An old police trick you've used in a dozen movies." He could give him that much.

"If I weren't just a simple country boy, you'd have really had me going."

"You're not out of the woods yet, Mr. Maxwell," Bud said.

"You can call me Dick," Maxwell said, the top-dog smile taking over his face once more.

Bud walked out of the office. It was one of the worst interrogations he'd ever conducted, on the defensive most of the time, outsmarted, outmaneuvered at every turn.

He thought about the script, about the part of Mannie, about the movies. He'd been offered money before, bags of it, clothing, cars, vacations, in exchange for merely looking the other way. He'd had no problem turning any of it down. Instantly, emphatically. He never ran anyone in for offering, but he had never been on the take for so much as an apple. But this time he knew he had kept the door open, or, if not open, at least ajar.

He stopped at a pay phone. As he was starting to dial, a boyish, bearded actor in a cowboy outfit opened the door of the booth.

"Hey, man, give me a break," he said amiably. "I gotta call my agent."

Bud was not even sure why, but he stopped dialing, hung up and stepped out of the booth. On a studio lot it seemed only fitting for a cop in pursuit of a murderer to step aside for an actor in pursuit of an agent.

The actor thanked him, dialed a number from memory, and waited, his face darkening as the minutes went by. Bud flipped through his notes, making new ones, crossing out old ones. A few moments later the actor stepped out of the booth.

"Son of a bitch," the actor muttered as he strode angrily down the studio street toward a distant sound stage. Bud watched him as he drew a gun from each holster, twirled them professionally, and then aimed with both weapons at a spot which Bud assumed to be precisely the altitude of an agent's heart.

Bud stepped back into the phone booth. He dialed the Balboa Medical Center.

"Vera Kelsey's room, please," Bud said distractedly, his eyes following a pair of actresses in white bikini bathing suits, vermilion Candies on their feet, and their hair set on what appeared to be jumbo-sized frozen-orange-juice cans. That's Hollywood for you.

"We do not have a Vera Kelsey here," the operator said crisply.

"But that's not possible," Bud said. "On the third floor. She was very badly hurt. Check again, please."

"I'll connect you with the nurses' station on that floor." The third floor picked up the phone on the first ring.

"Vera Kelsey," Bud said quickly. "When did she leave, who discharged her, and who is her physician?"

"Who is calling please?"

"Beverly Hills Police Department," Bud said. "Detective Bacola."

"She was not officially discharged," the nurse said guardedly. "She left on her own sometime between six and seven this morning."

"What was her condition at her last medical check?"

"Poor."

"Who is her physician?"

"I can try to reach him for you," the nurse said. A few moments later, Dr. Brix was on the line.

"All I know is that she was out of here when I came to make my rounds at seven," Dr. Brix said. He sounded tired, already on the defensive.

"How sick was she?" Bud asked. When he had last seen her, she'd appeared close to death, quite incapable of the effort that would be involved in getting dressed, slipping out of a hospital.

"Are we talking physically or mentally?"

"Both."

"Physically, aside from a few broken bones, contusions, abrasions, and a possible concussion, I'd say escape wouldn't have presented too much of a problem for someone with her strength and determination." Suddenly Bud remembered the ease with which she hoisted the heavy tree in her garden the day he had first met her.

"Okay, what about mentally, emotionally?"

"Quite frankly, I'd arranged for her to talk to a psychotherapist today," Dr. Brix said.

"Why?" Bud asked quickly.

"She seemed to be under a bit of a strain."

"Are you her family physician?"

"No, Dr. Seitz is in Europe, and I'm covering for him."

A bit of a strain, Bud thought. Some medical diagnosis. He wondered if Dr. Brix were deliberately withholding information or if he just had his head up his ass.

"Are you aware of the fact that Mrs. Kelsey is a prime suspect in a recent murder?" Bud asked. There was a long pause. Dr. Brix started to say something several times, then cleared his throat instead.

"No, I am not aware of that," Dr. Brix said finally.

"Is there anything you are aware of that you'd care to discuss?" Bud asked with more patience than he felt.

"I don't think so."

"Would Mrs. Kelsey be physically able to drive a car at this time?"

"Yes, I believe so."

"Would she be physically able to commit murder?" There was another long pause, another throat clearing.

"You cannot seriously expect me to answer a question like that," Dr. Brix said.

"If you hear from her or hear of her, please contact me at the Beverly Hills Police Department," Bud said.

Dr. Brix coughed again. "I think it might not be . . . inadvisable to let Mr. Kelsey know that Mrs. Kelsey is no longer hospitalized," the doctor said uneasily.

"Is that all you want to say?" Bud asked quickly.

"It's even more than I had intended to," Brix said, then hung up.

Bud knew he had to find Vera Kelsey and find her fast. He figured that she had probably walked away from the hospital and then had phoned a cab from a few blocks away. Then, if she wanted wheels, since her own car had been totaled, she would have to rent one. He thought of her swollen face, her bruised, bandaged body, and wondered if anyone would rent a car to someone in that condition.

He called headquarters and asked for an A.P.B. on Vera Kelsey, asked that a description of her be telephoned to every cab company, every car-rental agency in the west valley. When he asked for his messages, he was told to hold on, that Tom Edwards wanted to talk to him. It was urgent.

"Just give me my messages," Bud said impatiently. "I'll get back to him."

"He says he's got a hot flash for you, he's been trying to reach you all over town." Bud waited uneasily, fishing in his pocket for more coins. A young actress dressed as a nurse came and stood directly in front of him and pantomimed that she'd like to use the telephone. Bud smiled and shook his head. She held out her hands in a pleading gesture. He shrugged and turned away from her.

He heard the door to the phone booth open. He turned quickly.

"I am a nurse and this happens to be an emergency," she said, her eyes narrowing to indicate she meant business.

"Yeah, well I'm a cop, and this happens to be an emergency, too."

"Don't bullshit me," she said angrily. "You're just an actor, too."

Bud pulled out his wallet and showed her his badge.

"So, it was worth a try," she said, grinning at him, and closed the door to the booth.

"That you, Buddy-boy?" Tom said.

"Okay, what is it?" Bud asked impatiently.

"You're not big man on the case anymore is what it is," Tom said, obviously enjoying himself.

"On whose authority?"

"Right from the top."

"Any reason why?"

"Shall we call it a little conflict of interest?"

"Stop diddling me, Edwards," Bud said savagely. "I want to know what's going on."

"Just pick up your marbles and come on back," Tom Edwards said, his voice turning almost human. "You're in a lot of trouble."

"Give me my messages and I'll be back as soon as I can."

"First, about Gypsy Doniger. Nothing. Couldn't turn up a thing. No police record, nothing in the newspaper morgue. She doesn't have a credit card or driver's license. It's like she dropped out of the sky yesterday."

"It's probably a made-up name, then."

"Yeah, I guess there aren't too many Gypsys around."

"She's got the lead in a new porno flick."

"Why didn't you tell me?" Tom Edwards said eagerly. "I'd have tried harder."

Bud thought about Gypsy Doniger, stretched out on the bed, her eyes riveted to the television screen, her long, smooth legs slightly separated. He recalled her perfect features, the nose so perfect, in fact, that now Bud was certain the nose was new, freshly shaped and chiseled to hasten her on the raunchy road to fame.

He thought about the name G. Dunn that the Rose Avenue telephone was listed under. Another made-up name, Bud thought, using her own first initials. But who was Gypsy Doniger and where had she come from with no record, no driver's license, no credit cards?

"Now, the messages," Bud asked again, putting Gypsy's name on his note pad. He would have to do some more checking around on the porno queen.

"Another call from Kenny Bartlett. The fat kid's called about four times. And Ivy Greenwald has been by twice and called twice, says she has to talk to you."

"Is that it?"

"What is it, Buddy-boy?" Tom Edwards needled him. "You working as a team with half the citizens of Beverly Hills?"

"With backup like you, what's left for me?" Bud said, his voice a lot lighter than his current mood. He needed Tom Edwards. When I no longer need him, Bud promised himself, I will punch him out.

"Peter Lutz says call him at his office." Then Tom Edwards laid the real zinger on him. "By popular request, your partner's on his way back here from Santa Barbara. He's taking over for you, and if you're smart, you'll get the hell out of town yourself." His laughter enraged Bud.

"When he gets here, it's all his, but he's not here yet," Bud said. He hung up quickly, fished in his pocket for a dime, then called Ivy's apartment.

She was not home. He smiled as he listened to the message she had left on her machine. It was terse, businesslike, almost unfriendly, a refreshing departure from the cloying cuteness of most Hollywood messages that made you hang up just to punish them.

At the sound of her no-nonsense voice, despite his recent anger he felt something warm and pleasant surge through him and was willing to entertain the possibility that it might even be love. He left his name, told her to keep trying to reach him. He thought of saying something nice, something intimate and promising, after the way he had stormed out of the apartment, but the machine clicked off. It was the story of his life.

He called Gilbert Ritner's house. The kid was not there. The maid admitted guiltily that she had not seen him since the night before, that he had left before she woke up and had not come home for his guitar lesson, and that he had never missed a guitar lesson before. From the emotional broken English, he knew she was approaching hysteria.

There was no answer at Oliver Kelsey's Bel-Air number, nor in Venice. He had to find out if the writer had anything to do with his wife's unauthorized departure from the hospital, or, failing that, he had to warn Oliver Kelsey that she was on the loose, and possibly stalking him or Gypsy Doniger or both of them.

He called Peter Lutz with his last dime. He saw the actress in the nurse's costume approach him again, now with a grim expression. She had obviously had no better luck at other pay phones and was now prepared to sweat him out. He knew there was no way he'd be able to get her to change a dollar bill for him to make any more calls.

"Christ," Peter said impatiently, "you'd make a fantastic agent, Bacola. You never answer your phone calls." It was Kenny Bartlett. Why he had called Peter Lutz to complain about Bud was something of a mystery to both of them. Bud figured that he'd probably complained to headquarters, too, which may have had something to do with Tom Edwards' hot flash.

The actress-nurse kept moving around to maintain hostile eye contact with Bud, and was now additionally giving him the finger. It seemed more than appropriate.

"I don't know what he wants," Peter said. "Just get him off my back."

"If you hear from Oliver Kelsey, tell him his wife is out of the hospital and unaccounted for," Bud said. "And to lock his doors."

"Another screw-up, Bacola?" Peter said lightly.

"Yeah, right," Bud said quickly. "And I'm trying to reach Ivy Greenwald . . ."

"She's looking for you, too. It's about the kid next door to Koenig. He's got something for you and she's very uneasy about it."

"Where is she now?"

"Moving around. Trying to find you," Peter said. "When she called you at the police department, they

265

told her you were on vacation, that the case was being handled by a Detective Coleman. Who's that?"

"He's my partner," Bud said. "A good man. Really."

"Funny," Peter said quietly. "All this time I thought you were a good man, too."

"Anything else?"

"Yeah, as a matter of fact, I think I got Gordon Flemming a job," Peter said, something between amusement and pride in his voice. "A real honest-to-God directing job. Just a replacement for a director who got smashed up in a car last night, but it's work, and it's sure more than the corpse did for him lately."

"Is he at home now?" Bud asked. He thought that Flemming might be able to give him some information on Vera Kelsey and her relationship with D. P. Koenig. He also thought he might now take the director up on his offer of the scrapbook of *The Little Renegade*.

"He's not home now," Peter said, "but he's due out at Universal at four this afternoon. Borden Sprague's office. If you want to catch up with him, you can bet your ass he'll be there."

Borden Sprague was one of the young hotshot producers in the industry. He was aggressive, intelligent, and he was also gay, which was probably how he had come to Peter Lutz in his time of need. Being a homosexual in Hollywood sure didn't seem to hurt anybody.

Bud got into his car and drove to a gas station on Cahuenga Boulevard. He filled his tank and got three dollars worth of dimes. He called Ivy's number again, listened to her message, and this time left one of his own.

"For whatever it's worth, an under-achiever cares."

He called Gilbert Ritner, who still had not returned home. The maid cried noisily into the phone. No more broken English for her—just a nonstop stream of hysterical Spanish. From what Bud could interpret, her terror stemmed from the missed guitar lesson, but he was starting to get uneasy feelings about the kid himself.

He returned Kenny Bartlett's phone call. He was asked to hang on. After four minutes, Kenny Bartlett picked up the phone.

"Why the hell didn't you tell me who you were?" Bartlett shouted into the phone. "I mean, you got some pair of balls being on this case."

"It seems I'm no longer on this case," Bud said quietly, wondering if Bartlett might have been responsible for his removal.

"Christ, kid," Bartlett said, "I was with Koenig during the whole thing. I mean, you put him away. It was the only thing in his whole life that ever touched him."

Bud felt a surge of hot rage rush through him. Then numbness, nothing, except that the phone in his hand suddenly felt so heavy that he had difficulty holding it up to his ear. It was a lie, Bud told himself. It had to be a lie. D. P. Koenig had never cared, not at the beginning, and certainly not at the end.

"May I come and talk with you, sir?" Bud asked quietly.

"Are you sure you're off the case?"

"That's what I hear."

"Okay, be here at three," Kenny Bartlett said and hung up the phone.

Bud looked at his watch. It was not quite noon. He drove out Sunset Boulevard to Beverly Hills. He ran two red lights and almost rear-ended another Porsche. Until he got the word directly from the Chief that he was off the case, he wasn't going to walk away from it.

He turned right on Bedford Drive and stopped in front of D. P. Koenig's house. As he gazed in through the shuttered windows, he felt a pain so acute that he believed he could not endure it. He had been all right, or almost all right, until he had spoken to Kenny Bartlett.

He kept telling himself it was a lie. It had to be a lie. If little Buddy Bacall had touched D. P. Koenig so deeply, why had the agent chosen to ignore him, totally deny his existence, ten years later? It would have cost him nothing to accept one phone call, say a few encouraging words, but even that small act of charity was more than he had been prepared to make.

Bud rang Gilbert Ritner's doorbell. He didn't know what the kid was up to, but whatever it was, he'd better cut it out. The maid answered the door. She was a solidly built Mexican with a once pretty face. Rings of nervous sweat darkened her powder-blue uniform. Gilbert was still not home, she told him, her voice rising emotionally. He could not understand much else of what she said except that she was going to call the police.

"I am the police," Bud told her in his best Fountain Valley High first-person, present-tense Spanish. "When Gilbert gets home, keep him here."

He drove back down Bedford to the police station. Without knowing exactly why, he kept driving around the block. He turned on the news, moving quickly from station to station. On his seventh lap around the block, he saw Ivy's car pull up in front of the post office.

At the same moment, he caught the tail end of a news bulletin. An actress named Gypsy Doniger had been stabbed by an unknown assailant as she watched television in her home in Venice Beach. She was in critical condition at St. John's Hospital.

Dazed, Bud got out of his car and slid into the front seat of Ivy's VW. From the expression on her face, he knew she had been listening to the same news bulletin. She looked at him, then, without a word, put her arms around him and held him close. It didn't help.

"It's got to be Vera Kelsey, then," he said tonelessly. "She left the hospital early this morning. I guess she got Koenig, too."

"You're off the case," she said quietly. "What happened?"

"I thought I could handle it," Bud said. "You know, stay above it. I didn't do too good, did I?"

"It's not your fault." They both knew it was a lie.

"Where's Gilbert?"

"He's been trying to reach you and he finally got me," Ivy said, her voice troubled. "He was doing the hypnosis thing with a friend and he said he'd dredged up something very big, but he wouldn't tell me what it was."

"That kid is starting to scare me."

"He said when he was through cracking this case for you, he was going to take himself right back to the womb."

"Sounds great," Bud said lightly. "Maybe I'll join him there."

"You might even beat him there." She reached out for him as she said it, tried to rest her hand on his shoulder, but he pulled away.

"I was making a joke," Bud said icily.

"I wasn't." She slipped her hand across the distance between them and covered his hand very gently with her own.

"Richard Maxwell tried to bribe me," Bud said finally.

"So? That's never happened to you before?"

"He offered me a part in a movie."

"Smart," she said. "Very smart."

"I was tempted."

"Then you're smart, too."

"Do me a favor?" Bud asked, fishing in his pocket for a dime. "Call headquarters and ask to talk to Chuck Coleman and tell him I'm out here, a little on the comatose side, and to come talk to me."

Ivy picked up his left hand, kissed the back of it, then placed it gently back on his knee. He watched her as she hurried over to the pay phone in front of the post office. She looked back at him and smiled. Suddenly he had the feeling that he had known her, had counted on her, for a very long time. It didn't even scare him anymore.

She came back quickly and reported that Chuck had just arrived and that he'd be down in a few minutes.

"Shall I split?" she asked.

"Don't even consider it," Bud said. He took her hand and held it hard against his thigh. He knew he should be thinking, sorting out the facts, but all he could do was hold onto her cool, slightly chapped hand, which he now believed was the only thing that stood between him and total disintegration.

He saw Chuck shuffling toward him. There was a T-shaped bandage over his nose, his eyes bruised, almost swollen shut, but the concern, the emotion, was clear from half a block away. Bud knew that the polyp-removal cover had been blown and he felt a quick spasm of regret.

"You look like shit, Buddy," Chuck said, leaning down, sticking his head in the car window.

Without knowing he was going to do it, Bud reached up and locked Chuck's face next to his own and held it there. Chuck put his hand on top of Bud's head and stroked his hair, patted his head. They were both bewildered and immeasurably moved by the intensity of the feeling they had for each other.

"This is Ivy Greenwald," Bud said in a tight, choked voice, "who'll be around for a while."

Chuck studied Ivy with a pleased, warm smile on his face. It was a look that let her know she was not anything like any of the others, that he was glad she was not like any of the others.

"What's with Gypsy Doniger?" Bud asked.

"She's unconscious, but the hospital says she'll live."

"Did she identify anyone?"

"No, she was out of it when they got to her."

"What about Oliver Kelsey?"

"No sign of him."

"What about Vera Kelsey?"

"She disappeared off the face of the earth," Chuck said. "She didn't take a cab, didn't rent a car. You think she scragged Koenig?"

"I don't want to, but it sure as hell fits," Bud said. "She came to Koenig, her lover from her single days, to ask him to get her husband a job. And he did, a real plum, on a dirty movie with Gypsy Doniger, so Kelsey, whose ego was zilch by then, latches onto her, abandons his wife, moves in with her, and Vera Kelsey goes crazy with jealousy and who does she blame?"

"Very good," Chuck said. "Have you ever thought about being a cop?"

"What do they have on me upstairs?" Bud asked.

"You mean, over and above the fact that Koenig practically murdered your old man?" Chuck said roughly. "Christ, Buddy, I thought he was just an agent who gave you a bad time."

"That's all he was," Bud said quietly.

"Who are you kidding?" Chuck shouted at him. "You've been waiting for this. All this time. All those detours to Bedford Drive. All those corpses you've dragged me to. It was him. You were looking for *him!*"

"You're out of your mind," Bud said without much conviction. His partner was right, of course. Whenever there had been a report of an unidentified man found dead on the streets of Beverly Hills, at the wheel of an expensive car, struck down as a hit-and-run, no matter whose case it was, Bud was usually the first one there, turning the body over, studying the moribund face.

He had never been quite sure what his feelings were when he found that the body, the face, belonged to a stranger. Was it relief or was it disappointment? But whatever it was, Bud realized now that it had kept him searching all those years.

"Now that he's dead," Chuck asked quietly, "what are you going to do for fun?"

"It's a good question," Bud said. He got out of the car and stood on the sidewalk next to Chuck. He looked across the newly cut grass to the police station. It suddenly appeared to be very far away.

"From here on in, consider yourself a consultant," Chuck said, "a consultant with clipped wings. And that's an order from upstairs. You're to do nothing, but keep me supplied with pertinent information."

"Yeah, sure," Bud said. They'd been together long enough for Chuck to know that this meant Bud was having no part of it.

"They'll have your ass."

"Big deal," Bud said. "They already have it."

"You know what really finished you," Chuck said, as he was starting to leave. "Eight million requests by reporters from all over the world for personal interviews with you. Big story. You're a star. And we know how big that goes over Upstairs."

"Funny, huh?" Bud whispered. "Maybe I ought to find myself an agent."

"Just . . . go home," Chuck said. He put his arms around Bud and gave him a quick clumsy bear hug, then trotted back across the grass to the police station.

"I'm sorry about the nose," Bud called, but he was too far away to hear it.

When Bud got back into the car, Ivy slid her hand up along the inside of his left thigh, a few inches above his knee, and just held it there. It was a gesture, both tender and possessive, with distinct maternal overtones that at any other time in his life would have enraged him. Now he was grateful that he had found himself a toucher, a layer-on of hands.

"Up until about three days ago, I was not a half-bad cop," Bud said. "Aggressive, thorough, effective . . ."

"What kind of a part was it?" Ivy asked suddenly. "Maxwell's bribe?"

"It looked like a big part," Bud said slowly. "A lot of speeches."

"But who's counting?" Ivy said, smiling at him.

He turned the radio on, moving from one station to another, to pick up some last-minute news. He was sure in the darkest area of his heart that he would learn that Vera Kelsey had been found dead in a motel room, washed up on the beach, a suicide, with a murder and an attempted murder under her belt.

Had she lied to him about everything? Bud wondered idly. Had she over the years of her marriage slipped casually in and out of D. P. Koenig's bed, as she had before her marriage. If this were true, Bud believed that pleasure alone must have motivated her. If she had done it to further her husband's career, surely he would have been in better shape professionally.

Bud tried to imagine this tree-hoisting earth mother, this alleged ball-breaker, lying naked and panting, her thick, pale body underneath Koenig's thin, pale body. The mental picture upset him profoundly. He was not at all sure why.

Bud thought about the story line of Oliver Kelsey's now shredded manuscript. Was it paranoia, the creation of a man with too much time on his hands, something invented to distract him from the harsh reality of his own failure? Or was it nonfiction? The Writer, the Actress, and the Agent. He remembered the phrase Peter quoted as the Agent delivered the final eulogy over the Writer's coffin.

Those whom the Gods wish to destroy, they first stop returning their phone calls.

"Where will you be, say, at six tonight?" Bud asked Ivy.

"Where do you want me to be?"

"If I give you the key to my place, will you wait there for me?"

"I could maybe follow you around in my car," Ivy said. She looked at him and smiled, but he knew she was concerned about him, afraid that he'd get into more trouble than he was already in, which they both knew was a distinct possibility.

He shifted his weight minimally so as not to dislodge

her hand on his leg. He pulled his keys out and slipped his front-door key off the ring and put it on top of the dashboard.

"Be there, huh?" he said.

She picked up the key and studied it with a troubled smile on her face.

"Hey," she said, "are you still going to be madly in love with me when you're out of crisis?"

"I gave you my front-door key, didn't I?" he said. He leaned over and kissed her on the corner of her mouth, then, almost involuntarily, he let his fingers slip down inside her dress, under her brassiere, until he reached her left nipple. He felt it grow hard between his second and third fingers. She said nothing, but her hand on his thigh moved upward about as unmaternally as you can get.

He got into his car and drove back to Gilbert Ritner's house. He was starting to get an uneasy gnawing feeling about the kid and his bouts of self-hypnosis. He would order him to knock it off, along with the frantic phone messages to headquarters.

The maid opened the door before he hit the first step on the terra-cotta-tiled front porch. She was now completely out of control, crying and using the backs of her chunky wrists to wipe the tears away.

Gilbert still had not come home and had missed both his guitar lesson and a beach date with a school friend.

Bud picked up the phone and started to dial headquarters to see if there were any further word from the kid. While he was dialing, the other phone rang. It was Gilbert, calling casually to pick up his own messages. Bud turned to the sobbing maid and indicated it was Gilbert on the phone.

She rushed into the kitchen, picked up an extension and shouted in bare-bones English for Gilbert to come to his *casa*, dire threats of exposure to his parents, his grandparents, all his living relatives, and most of hers. Then she gave the phone to Bud.

274

"You've got to come in from the cold, Gilbert," Bud said. "The case is closed. Where are you? I'll come get you."

"The night he was murdered," Gilbert said excitedly, "I heard his voice. I heard him say, and it was almost kind of a pleading voice, but kind of snotty, too, and he said, 'I can still be useful to you.' He said it over and over, maybe three times."

I can still be useful to you.

That phrase, those exact same words. I've heard them before, Bud thought. Somewhere. He felt a coldness pass through him, settle deep within him.

"I want you to quit horsing around," Bud said. "I want you to get back here and stay here."

"His front door is right under my bedroom window," Gilbert insisted noisily. "I know he was talking to someone. I can hear his voice right now."

Bud could hear his voice too, could hear those same words float back to him through a fog of fear and uncertainty. I heard him say that, Bud thought. I heard him say those same words. But when? And why? And to whom?

I can still be useful to you. His hands were starting to shake so badly he could hardly hold the phone to his ear.

"Tell me where you are, and I'll come get you," Bud said finally.

"I'm a couple of blocks away, at a friend's house," Gilbert said. "He's helping me with the hypnosis. You know, dangling a medallion in front of my eyes. It really works."

"For Christ's sake, Gilbert," Bud said, "knock that off right now!"

"I'll see you later," Gilbert said. "And tell Maria I'll be home for dinner and she shouldn't worry. She worries."

"I worry, too, kid," Bud said, but the phone went dead before he was able to finish.

He knew he should go home, go to bed, sleep, fly to Acapulco. He should do anything but continue pursuing D. P. Koenig's murderer. And now the person who had attempted to murder Gypsy Doniger as she sat in front of her television set in Venice Beach. He wondered what she had been watching. He strongly suspected it was not the morning news.

He followed the sounds of Latin hysteria into the kitchen. Maria was standing sniffling noisily at the kitchen stove, putting additional sweat rings on her uniform. She was flipping a tortilla expertly from side to side over a low burner. When it was hot, charred on the edges, she spread butter on one side, poured *salsa verde* in the middle, then rolled it, tipping the edges up so nothing would spill out of the ends.

She looked up and saw Bud staring at her. She smiled shyly and held out the rolled-up tortilla to him. Without a word he took it and finished it in two mouthfuls.

There was something in her smile, her uneasy sadness, perhaps even in the quick, automatic way she handed him the tortilla that she had prepared for herself that made him think of his mother.

For the first time he thought about how immeasurably his mother's life had been altered by D. P. Koenig. Up until that moment, he had always selfishly believed that everything that happened had affected only his life, that it was *his* tragedy.

As soon as this was over, he vowed he would go and see her, spend time with her, possibly even take Ivy with him. He had given out his front-door key once or twice before, but he had never brought anyone home to meet his mother.

14

Kenny Bartlett was in his bedroom doing a steady thirty miles an hour on his exercycle. He was wearing a navy-blue sweatsuit and had a thick white towel around his neck. He looked young and vigorous.

"You're early, kid, and you look like hell," he said, and he waved Bud over to him. "I've got fifty miles to go, but we can talk if you don't mind the hard breathing."

Bud walked across the dazzling white carpet and was startled when Kenny Bartlett reached out and grabbed him, kissing him noisily on the cheek without breaking rhythm.

"Thank you for seeing me," Bud said. He could not help looking over Bartlett's shoulder, out the window to the garden below. Both the girl and the cat were gone.

"First, you want to know who's responsible for getting your ass kicked off this case?" Bartlett demanded. "I am."

"You weren't wrong," Bud said quietly.

"Christ, kid, if I knew who you were that first day . . ."

"I am Detective Bud Bacola with the Beverly Hills Police Department," Bud said, enunciating each word carefully. "That's who I was three days ago. That's who I am now."

"Don't lay that crap on me," Bartlett said, grinning over the handlebars. "I remember you. I remember everything. I mean, Koenig came by my place right from the hospital, the day he visited you after the accident. And you'd better believe me, he was really down."

One man dead, one child nearly dead, Bud thought, and the great D. P. Koenig was *really down*.

"He managed to get over it," Bud said finally.

"Yeah, he got over it. He got over everything," Bartlett said, his navy-blue knees pumping up and down. "It was the secret of his success. It probably also got him killed."

"Do you think Vera Kelsey could have done it?" Bud asked.

"Are you on this case or aren't you?"

"I'm off it," Bud said, "but I'm not out of it."

"She dumped Koenig for Kelsey just before he went out to Utah," Bartlett said. "That fat-assed bitch really had him going. She was the only one who ever did."

"But he managed to get over that, too, right?" Bud said with a bitterness that startled both of them.

"Christ, you really hated him, didn't you?" Bartlett said quietly. He stopped pedaling and looked up at Bud. "Still have a real thing against him. Even now."

"Shouldn't I?" Bud asked, his voice rising, suddenly distorted, as if he had just taken a deep breath of helium.

"Koenig was a first-class shit and your old man was a great guy," Bartlett said roughly. "Is that what you were brought up on?"

"Something like that."

"The truth is," Bartlett said bluntly, "your father was a pain in the ass and a major troublemaker."

"He was a simple man who never went past the eighth grade. . . ."

"He was the joke of the goddamn industry," Bartlett said, starting to pedal angrily. "They hired Koenig, paid him a frigging fortune, to come out to Utah just to keep your old man out of everybody's hair so they could make a movie."

"He was my agent," Bud said uneasily. "That's why he was there."

"Oh, bullshit," Bartlett said impatiently. "Was anybody else's agent out there in that Christforsaken hole?"

"I don't know," Bud said. "I don't remember. I don't remember anything." It was only partially true. Things, dark, troubling things, were starting to boil up in his brain and he was having a hard time keeping the lid down.

"It was the last thing in the world he wanted to do then, go to Utah in the summer, but he got the word from *Above* and so he went."

"You mean, he was just following orders?" Bud asked derisively.

"No matter what happened, he loved you," Bartlett said angrily. "Don't you remember? You were D. P. Koenig's kid."

"If he loved me so much," Bud came back instantly, not knowing a moment before that he was going to say it, that he was even thinking it, "why did he stiff me when I called him back ten years later?"

Kenny Bartlett stopped pedaling and looked up at Bud, studied his face with the beginnings of a terrible smile.

"So that's it?" Bartlett said.

"I called him. I wrote him. I waited in a phone booth for three hours once because he said he'd get right back to me," Bud said. He could not stop himself. Suddenly, even to his own ears, he sounded like Oliver Kelsey, like Gordon Flemming. Even like Glenda Deering. The old Hollywood whimper.

"I never said he was Jesus Christ," Bartlett said. "He was just an agent with a short attention span."

"Why wouldn't he talk to me?" Bud asked. "All I wanted was—"

"Yeah, tell me about it. You wanted what they all wanted. His love, his attention, his time."

"He nearly destroyed me and he wouldn't even answer my goddamn phone calls," Bud said, hating the self-pity in his voice, unable to do anything about it.

"You made him uncomfortable," Bartlett said. "He brooded about you for a while, then he put you out of his mind completely. Forever. That's who he was. He hated . . . unpleasantness, confrontations. That's why he still had that stable of losers."

Bartlett climbed off the exercycle and began pacing around the bedroom. Bud could see the emotion on his face, perhaps D. P. Koenig's only mourner.

"Actually, the only thing he did that I wouldn't have done was the hooker," Kenny Bartlett said. He started to climb back on the exercycle, then changed his mind and flopped down on the bed. He was breathing very hard.

"The hooker?" Bud said. He was completely confused. He had no recollection of a hooker in Utah, of a hooker anywhere.

"He told me afterward that it was necessary, but he felt kind of shitty about it."

"What hooker? What are you talking about?"

"They pretended she was an actress," Bartlett said. "They brought her out there and wrote a part for her, but her only purpose there was to keep your old man off the set, keep him otherwise occupied."

"No," Bud said, his voice dazed, "she was an actress. I remember her now. She was an actress. I knew she was an actress."

"Kid, how old were you then?" Bartlett asked, his

voice gentler than Bud had ever heard it. "Eight, nine? What did you know from hookers?"

"A hooker," Bud said again. "She was a hooker?" He felt a hot wave of rage surge through his head. Suddenly he remembered her, remembered her shiny black toe-nails, her too-small white shorts, her pubic hair. And finally he remembered his father socking it into her in the shimmering desert heat.

"A hooker," he whispered to himself. Christ, how low, how vile could you get? The son of a bitch had imported a prostitute to distract a married man, a father, had even masqueraded her as an actress in case the old guy had a few scruples left himself.

The casual amorality of it was just one more reason for him to hate D. P. Koenig. He felt a stab of guilt for his father, unquestionably a pain in the ass and a trouble-maker, but a naive innocent caught up and destroyed in a cold, efficient plot to ease the tensions of making a motion picture.

But there was more. He was starting to remember more. His mind kept trying to switch channels, to pull him away from the hard center of his thoughts.

"There are worse things than having had an old man with a wandering eye," Bartlett said in his best soothing voice.

"He killed my father," Bud heard himself mumble. "That bastard killed my father."

The walls of the bedroom were starting to ripple. Bud felt that if he did not run, they would fall in on him, crush him.

"Are you okay, kid?" Bartlett said. Bud picked up the concern in his voice, but he was already out the bed-room door.

I can still be useful to you. Bud heard the voice. It might even have been his own, but he was not sure. He was not sure of anything anymore.

"What's the big deal, kid?" It was Kenny Bartlett. He

was trying to open the door of Bud's car, to get in beside him, but Bud was already backing up. "That was twenty years ago!"

Bud headed down the steep grade of Loma Vista. He tried not to think about Utah, about the hooker hired by D. P. Koenig to keep his father out of everybody's hair.

It didn't work. He pulled over to the side of the road and remembered.

Buddy Bacall woke up in the motel room in Utah. It was dark and icy cold because his father had turned the air conditioner up too high. The day's heat and the excitement had tired him so much that he had fallen asleep at the dinner table while it was still light out, had been carried upstairs and put to bed without waking up. But now he was wide awake, and cold, and he could not fall back asleep.

He pulled the blanket up over his head, but the noisy whine of the air conditioner kept after him, and his throat was beginning to feel scratchy. He got out of bed in the dark to turn the air conditioner off, but he got lost and ended up walking into a closet.

"Daddy," he called out, "I don't know where I am." There was no answer, no response. Buddy felt around for a light switch. Then he called out again. There was still no answer.

He bumped into a standing lamp and it crashed to the ground. He could hear the light bulb shatter. The noise frightened him, and the cold dry darkness. He dropped to his hands and knees and crawled slowly to his father's bed because he was afraid of stepping on the broken glass in his bare feet. He would slip into bed next to him until the fear went away.

The sheets were smooth and cold to his touch. The bed had not been slept in. Buddy fumbled for the light on the nightstand.

It was almost two o'clock. He stared at his father's

empty bed and listened to the whine of the air conditioner for a long time. He crawled back into his own bed and tried to go back to sleep, but the noise and the cold and the realization that he was all alone kept him awake.

Finally he slipped out of bed and opened the door to the dim, lemony light of the hallway. The moment he opened the door he heard the voices, shouting angry voices and somebody banging on a door.

Buddy walked down the hallway to the staircase. The voices were coming from the floor above. He tiptoed up toward the noise, in the direction of the anger. He knew he was doing something wrong. His father had warned him never to leave the motel room at night, but he was cold and frightened and he didn't know how to turn off the air conditioner.

At the top of the stairs, he peered down the long corridor. At the end he could see D. P. Koenig and Gordon Flemming. The director was banging on a door over and over again. His fist would hit the same spot three or four times, then he would rattle the doorknob, then return to banging with the end of his fist on the exact same spot.

Gordon Flemming was wearing a short, dark robe. As Buddy slipped quietly down the hallway, he could see that the director's legs were thin and hairless, and his bare feet were so pale they were almost green.

"Open the fucking door," he kept saying. "Open the fucking door." D. P. Koenig was trying to pull the director away from the door, but each time Gordon Flemming would shake him off, angrily cast the soothing hand from his shoulder. Then he would continue knocking, continue begging morosely for somebody inside to open the fucking door.

"If I had known you were *acquainted* with her, I would have sent for somebody else. Anybody else," Koenig said. "You must believe me."

"She's a baby," Flemming said, between knocks and rattles. "She's just a baby."

"She's a baby with a set hourly price," Koenig said, enunciating each syllable cruelly, "and worth every penny of it for the job she's doing."

Buddy felt a cold shiver go through his body. He knew he should slip back downstairs and crawl into his bed, but he kept moving closer and closer, drawn inexorably to the ugliness.

"Open the door," Flemming shouted. "You want me to kick the goddamn door in?"

"She's nobody," Koenig said, once again trying to pull the director down the hallway. "She's not worthy of you. You're an important man in this industry and you're too good to waste yourself. I mean, Christ, man, what you're doing is degrading."

With the fist still clenched from knocking on the door, Flemming pivoted on his pale feet and caught D. P. Koenig somewhere between his chin and his shoulder. He went down instantly with a look of surprise on his face.

"I'm going to kill you, Koenig," Flemming said, standing over the agent, who was already starting to climb to his feet. Buddy remembered D. P. Koenig's face as he rose from the floor. There was no anger, just a taut, icy smile.

"You're not going to kill me, Gordon," Koenig said, absently rubbing his right elbow with his left hand, "because you know that *I can still be useful to you.*"

The door that the director had been pounding on opened suddenly. Buddy could see the actress through the crack in the door, could see the name of the hotel stitched in red on the edge of the towel she was holding up in front of herself, in front of her nakedness.

And beyond her, beyond the white towel with the red stitching, beyond the sunburned shoulders and swelling breasts of the actress, little Buddy Bacall could see his father's short, naked body as he sat on the edge of an unmade bed patiently waiting for the actress to close the door again and return to him.

Buddy slipped back down the hallway, down the stairs. He walked slowly across the living room of the suite his father had hassled away from Gordon Flemming, walked through the broken glass in the bedroom and crawled into his bed. He pulled the covers up over his head, but he could not stop shivering.

Buddy got up the next morning and without even looking at his father walked into the bathroom.

"Aren't you going to wish me happy birthday?" Frank Bacola called out. Seven hours later he was dead.

Bud only realized how tense he was when he reached out to turn on the car radio and found that his hand was shaking so violently that he had to steady it with his other hand. Even then he had trouble reaching the knob.

He eased his Porsche out into the middle of Loma Vista and headed down through the deepening layers of smog to Sunset Boulevard. He knew he should drive directly to the Beverly Hills Police Department, lay everything on them, let them take over. He also knew that he was not going to do it. Not yet.

He checked his watch. It was just three-twenty. He was sure that Gordon Flemming would not be at home, would be on his way to Universal Studios for a four o'clock appointment that might bring him work and dignity.

The director's face suddenly appeared before his eyes. Bud could still see him in the dim yellow light of the motel corridor, pounding on a door behind which were a hooker and Frank Bacola.

I can still be useful to you. Possibly it was no more than a handy phrase D. P. Koenig used on all his clients at one time or another. It would hardly stand up in a court of law, a boy's shaky memory of some long-forgotten words, but it was all he had to go on now.

It was not difficult to figure out why Gordon Flemming, his mind warped by years of rejection and imagined betrayal, would single out D. P. Koenig as the instrument of his failure and murder him. But where and how did Gypsy Doniger fit in?

There was no indication from anyone that the director knew her or had any connection with her. The only one with an undeniable link to both the agent and the actress was Vera Kelsey, or perhaps Oliver Kelsey, both of whom were still missing.

As he turned left on Sunset Boulevard, it came to him, settled almost serenely into his brain. I know everything now, he thought calmly. I know it all. My father and the hooker. D. P. Koenig and the hooker and my father. All the ugliness I ran from, I couldn't face, and now I've faced it and I'm still here, still in one piece.

There are worse things than having had an old man with a wandering eye, Kenny Bartlett had said to him. Suddenly Bud thought about his mother, a good woman, he knew, but certainly drab and uninteresting and probably always had been. His father, at least, had had some zest and passion before D. P. Koenig had snuffed out his life on his forty-fourth birthday.

As he turned right on Doheny, he probed the last dark corners; he made himself think about the final ride through the desert with his father. He remembered it all with a sharp clarity now, remembered the feel of the car as it scraped and shimmied on the gritty road.

He remembered looking up at his father and saying something, then repeating it. But he still could not focus on what it was he had said, or why he was having so much difficulty dredging this up when everything else had already come tumbling out.

He pulled up in front of Gordon Flemming's house. The mailbox was still on the ground by the curb. He knew before he got to the front door that there was no one inside. He knocked on the door until his knuckles ached. There was no response, no sign of life inside, not even the cats stirred. He went quickly from window to window, pressing his face against the dusty glass to peer into the empty, untidy rooms.

The laundry-room window was not latched. Bud eased the window up and slipped inside. He walked through the spotless kitchen, through the hallway into the dank-smelling den. He knew he had no official business there, knew that he could be fired, even prosecuted, for what he was doing. He no longer cared.

He went directly to the pile of scrapbooks. The one he was looking for was still on top. He picked it up and tucked it under his arm. Might as well add theft to illegal entry, he thought as he started to leave. Then he stopped, bent down and tipped the moist grit from the cat box out onto the carpet so that he could look at the photograph that lined the bottom of the box. He did not even know why he was doing it.

He picked up the damp, distorted picture of Sabrina LaFever. Holding his breath, he held the photograph to the light, turned it very slowly from side to side. As he studied the face, he wondered why he felt with such certainty that he knew her, had met her before, why she was so elusively familiar.

Then he put his thumb over her slightly too large, too angular nose.

Everything suddenly fell together. He let the picture float to the floor and dialed Peter Lutz. An operator told him that the line was busy and two calls were waiting.

"I'm a cop," Bud said quickly. "Put me through." It worked. There was a series of clicks and he heard Peter's voice. It was no longer a secretary's voice. It was an executive's voice and it irritated Bud immeasurably.

"Peter Lutz here," the voice said crisply.

"I want you to call Borden Sprague and tell him not to let Gordon Flemming out of his office until I get there."

"Oh, it's you," Peter said uneasily. "I thought you were off the case."

"Just do what I say."

"Are you kidding?" Peter protested. "They'll throw the book at me for that. Let me call the police department and tell them."

"If you do that," Bud said icily, "I'll blow the whistle on your school board, husband-and-father, pillar-of-the-community boyfriend so fast . . ."

"Shit, you know who it is then?" Peter said, sounding more like a secretary again.

"You bet your ass," Bud lied convincingly.

"Gordon Flemming will be waiting for you if Borden Sprague has to bugger him to keep him there," Peter said quietly, then hung up the phone.

Bud picked up the scrapbook again and headed for his car. He put the book on the seat next to him and backed out the driveway, narrowly missing a Japanese gardener in a pith helmet who turned and aimed a hose in the car window, dousing him liberally as he barreled out into the street. It was that kind of a day.

He turned on the radio, twisting the dial impatiently from one station to another in hope of catching some late news. He knew there was no way he was going to be able to get it through regular channels anymore. Finally he heard a newscaster mention the name Vera Kelsey.

Bud was convinced that he would now learn of her death, her suicide, but he could not have been more wrong. It turned out that Vera Kelsey was alive and well and enjoying a second honeymoon in Northern California with her recently estranged screenwriter husband, Oliver Kelsey. Due to positive identification by Western Airline personnel, the newscaster continued, both the writer and his ex-actress wife had been cleared of any suspicion in the attempted murder of a porno queen in Venice Beach.

Attempted murder, Bud thought, relieved. That meant that Gypsy Doniger was still alive, still hanging in there. He looked at his watch. It was almost four o'clock.

He was stuck on a long left-turn lane on Highland

Boulevard. If he had been in a police car, he would have turned on the siren and the revolving lights and floored it all the way to Universal, but he was in his Porsche and didn't need any official attention drawn to his mission.

He opened the scrapbook to the first page. It was the early trade-paper announcements of *The Little Renegade*. He saw his name three times in the first article. The short, happy life of little Buddy Bacall.

The honking started and Bud looked up, made a left turn just as the arrow turned amber. He was the last one to get through before the light turned red.

He flashed his badge at the guard at the east gate of Universal Studios. The guard studied it for a moment, then nodded his assent.

"Borden Sprague's office?" Bud asked. The guard waved his hand in the general direction.

"They're filming some exterior stuff on the next building," the guard called out to him as he started to drive through, "so you'll have to park in the north lot."

When Bud saw a stunt man free-falling off the roof of a four-story building into a giant airbag, he knew that he was in the right place.

He parked illegally and crossed behind the movie crew. The director was wearing army fatigues and had a dark, untended beard. He appeared to be still in his teens, but he was probably in his early twenties. He was shouting directions to two more stunt men still on the roof.

"Are you Detective Bacola?" the young male secretary whispered to Bud as he walked into Borden Sprague's outer office.

"Is Mr. Flemming still in there?" Bud asked, showing his badge, very possibly, he thought, for the last time.

"Mr. Sprague has requested that he be permitted to leave the office before you go in," the secretary said, "so I'll just give him a buzz, then you can do what you have to."

The secretary sniffed disapprovingly at Bud, then buzzed twice on the intercom. A moment later Borden Sprague walked through the outer office without even looking at Bud. He was slight, balding, with a deep suntan, and he wore a costly three-piece suit.

"He's all yours," Borden Sprague said in a high-pitched, hostile voice, as he plunged out the door into the hallway.

Bud stared after him for a moment, then walked into Borden Sprague's office. Gordon Flemming was standing at the opened window, watching the stunt men go off the roof.

"There are only two or three people in this town who know how to direct stunts," Flemming said easily. "And that little turd down there sure isn't one of them."

"Hello, Mr. Flemming," Bud said quietly. The director turned around slowly and looked at Bud.

"Jesus Christ," Gordon Flemming said. Suddenly all the color left his face. For one moment, he took a step forward, as if he wanted to make a run for it, but when he saw Bud firmly planted between him and the open doorway, he relaxed.

"Was this whole thing a fucking trap?" Flemming asked. "Just tell me that." There was a resigned, almost heroic sadness in the director's voice, and it touched Bud profoundly.

"Absolutely not true," Bud assured him quickly. "Borden Sprague specifically asked for you. He thinks you're remarkably talented."

"Ironic, isn't it?"

"You could say that."

"Now what?" Gordon Flemming said. He turned and looked out the window, studied one of the stunt men as he went over the side of the building directly across from them.

"We talk for a while, I take you in, and you get yourself the best lawyer money can buy."

290

"That nineteen-year-old bearded creep of a director down there doesn't know shit from shinola about stunts," Flemming said bitterly, "and he probably hasn't been out of work a day since he was toilet trained."

"How long have you known that Sabrina LaFever and Gypsy Doniger were the same person?" Bud asked. The question caught the director off guard. He turned slowly and stared at Bud, unable to speak for a moment.

"The whole thing blew wide open about five days ago when a *well-wisher*," he enunciated the word savagely, "sent me a nude eight-by-ten glossy of Gypsy Doniger as she was to appear in a Shamid Hakim production of some raunchy fuck movie."

"And you recognized Sabrina?"

"Just her twat," Flemming said gloomily. "I'd have known it anywhere."

"And you believe that Koenig was responsible for that?"

"She was his protégé, that Arab greaseball was his client."

"Is that why you killed him?"

"You always were a smart little shit," Flemming said, turning back to the window, to the stunt men free-falling off the distant roof. "You knew your lines faster than anyone else, didn't lip off. You were the only kid star I didn't actively want to poison."

"Maybe you should have."

"I don't suppose you'd consider letting me walk out of here," Flemming said without too much conviction, "for old times' sake?"

"It's crossed my mind," Bud said, and it was true, but they both knew beyond question that it would never happen.

"Sabrina was incredibly beautiful," Flemming said wistfully, then added, his voice filled with loathing, as if he were speaking of someone entirely different, "but Gypsy. God, what a mess they made of her with that little pig's nose and those distended tits, and she seemed so happy with her new vile self."

"From all the information I have, Koenig didn't know anything about any of that," Bud said quietly.

"So he claimed," the director said. A private, distracted smile flickered across his face, "So he claimed."

"Why did you kill him?" Bud asked, shocked by the urgency in his own voice, knowing that he was asking it not as a detective, but as a human being who desperately needed to know the answer. "What was it about him, about D. P. Koenig, that was important enough for you to risk blowing away everything by killing him?"

"How sharper than a serpent's tooth it is to have an indifferent agent," Flemming said finally, paraphrasing Shakespeare in a sad, distracted voice, as he stared once again out the window.

"You murdered him for . . . indifference? Because he was indifferent?" Bud asked.

"He was a dangerous man, the worst kind, because he made you think he cared intensely about you—personally just you, and, as a sensitive, creative person, you needed it, craved it, fed on it. But then, if you fell short anywhere, didn't quite live up to the picture he had of you in his mind, he would just cut you loose. Not *off*, which you could live with, but just . . . *loose. Semi-loose*, actually. And you'd hang there, filled with hope that things could be as they once were, that *Daddy* would love you again."

"But, my God," Bud said, "is that enough reason to murder someone?"

"He made me feel lower than whale shit," Flemming said in a chillingly calm and reasonable voice, "and that's as good a reason to kill someone as I can think of at the moment."

As Bud studied the director's face, now etched with defeat, he recalled his own dark and dangerous thoughts as, years before, he had waited by the pay phone at the

Hollywood Ranch Market for D. P. Koenig to return his telephone call. He remembered vowing to himself over and over again as he paced from the produce section to the bakery, *I will kill him. I will kill him.*

Perhaps, he conceded, there is in all of us the need to punish someone who has caused us to lose status, to abandon our sense of ourself. He wondered if a fine legal brain could convince a jury that an agent's indifference was, in fact, grounds for justifiable homicide.

"But what about Sabrina or Gypsy? Did you go to the house in Venice expressly to kill her?"

"No, no," Flemming said impatiently. "I went there just to see her, to talk to her. That was all."

"How did you know she'd be alone?"

"Because I was parked down the street and I saw Kelsey cut out with a duffel bag and his typewriter."

"What if he hadn't left?"

"I'd probably still be sitting in my car two houses down waiting for a glimpse of her," Flemming said grimly. "All I wanted was just to see her, to ask her why she was doing it, the dirty movie. The nose, the boobs. Everything. I had to know, so I stood outside the house and looked in the window and watched her watching a children's cartoon show.

"She would smile in all the right places, didn't miss a trick. Once or twice she'd even laugh out loud like some monumental cretin. And I realized, as I watched her responding so wholeheartedly to something aimed at a six-year-old brain, that I was still hopelessly in love with her. Yet at the same time she repelled me, appalled me, with her unworthiness."

"And that's why you tried to kill her?"

"Wouldn't you?" Flemming asked, his eyes incredulous, amazed that he might be questioned on this. "Wouldn't anyone? Especially if you had as little to lose as I did then."

"And you felt that D. P. Koenig was responsible . . ."

"Of course he was responsible!" Flemming shouted irrationally. "He was responsible for everything terrible that happened to me in the last twenty years!"

In his line of work, Bud had dealt with a lot of crazies before, had recognized the symptoms, the danger signals, instantly. Then why had it taken him so long to pick up on Gordon Flemming's madness? He was probably no further gone at this moment than he had been the first time Bud had come to question him.

Maybe they were right about him Upstairs. Maybe he should never have been allowed anywhere near this case. But then here he was, two days later, confronting the murderer, the murderer the second name on his list of suspects. He wondered if any one else at headquarters, even his own partner, could have zeroed in on Flemming that quickly, even with the advantage of their cool detachment.

Bud looked into Gordon Flemming's glittering, unfocused eyes and felt an oppressive sadness come over him for this once successful, respected film director who had once shared a joke with a president of the United States and would now probably languish for the rest of his life in a home for the criminally insane.

"How the hell did you put it all together so fast?" Flemming asked. "I mean, this town is crawling with people who hated him, and yet you've been on me since the morning after."

"First, it was the message sheet," Bud told him, now sitting on the edge of Borden Sprague's immaculate desk because he wasn't feeling all that steady on his feet. "All those unanswered phone calls. I mean, man, there's grounds enough right there."

"Christ," Flemming said. "I didn't expect that kind of sensitive thinking from a cop."

"I'm not just any cop," Bud said, smiling at him. "That's your big problem here."

"It had to be more than the unanswered phone calls," Flemming persisted.

"Then the kid next door overheard something Koenig said to you that night, and it put me away," Bud said. "Took me back twenty goddamn painful years."

"Something that probably wouldn't have meant a bloody thing to anybody else," Flemming said bitterly. "Just my luck."

"That ran out long before I came into the picture," Bud said gently.

"Look how he makes them fall," Flemming said peevishly, once again directing his attention to the action across the way. "You don't free-fall like that. You grab air, anything, your arms never stop. You struggle to get into a standing position. He doesn't know what the hell he's doing."

" 'I can still be useful to you,' " Bud said suddenly, his voice disembodied, intentionally dramatic. "Does that seem familiar, Mr. Flemming?" The director continued staring out the window, as if he had not heard. Finally he turned around and studied Bud's face with a look of compassion and sadness.

"You were there, then, that night in the motel in Utah?" Flemming said quietly. "That ugly scene with your father. I didn't know you were there."

"Neither did I," Bud said, "until today."

"Did you know that the 'actress' killed herself less than a year later? Drank a jumbo-sized container of liquid Drano?" Then he added, almost in the same breath, "Your father was a noisy, arrogant asshole."

"So I hear," Bud said. He felt no sudden rush of anger or resentment toward this man who had just insulted his dead father, as he had the day before. He wondered if this meant he was on the road to recovery or just hopelessly screwed up. He wasn't sure anymore.

"Being blunt, speaking your mind," the director said lightly, "is one of the fringe benefits of having absolutely nothing more to lose."

"Why did he do it?" Bud asked suddenly. The question startled him because he didn't know, even a moment before, that he was going to ask it. "Why did Koenig chase the car—back in Utah?"

"Because your father defied him, disobeyed him, cut his balls off in front of everybody."

"He chased me because he cared about me, because he loved me," Bud whispered. He could hear his own voice, pleading, pathetic, out of control.

"Oh, bullshit," Flemming said impatiently, "he did it because he always had to be right, had to be in charge, no matter who paid the price for it."

"Did he say anything to anybody? I mean, afterward? After the crash?"

"Yes, as a matter of fact. He came over to me and said, 'They just don't make Oldsmobiles the way they used to.' Then he got very drunk all by himself that night, and they shipped him back home the next morning."

"Mr. Flemming," Bud said, struggling to understand, "you've destroyed your whole life for him. Do you have any idea now why you did it?"

"Because it seemed to be the only thing that would allow me to feel better," the director said thoughtfully. "Because it made me feel as if I were back in control." Then he added lightly, "I stabbed him in the heart, directly in the center of his heart, right while he was denying he knew anything about Sabrina."

"Christ," Bud said softly, "you probably killed him for the one thing he didn't do."

"Then it all evens out, doesn't it?" Flemming went on in the same neutral voice. "He didn't bleed. He died almost instantly, but he didn't bleed. Like he didn't sweat. He was not a real person."

"Was it worth it?" Bud asked Flemming, who was now standing, a hand on either side of the window, watching two stunt men locked in mortal combat fifty feet away. He did not answer until both men had performed the stunt, had fallen off the building into the airbag below.

"Listen, you, whatever your name is," Flemming said angrily, still looking out the window, "he killed your father. If you'd had any class, you'd have done it yourself years ago and saved us all the trouble."

Bud felt the familiar, stabbing pain far back in his head. He closed his eyes. He tried to shut everything out, as he always had, only now it wasn't working. He suddenly saw with total clarity the desert road, the dazzling pink mesas of southern Utah, and he heard the words, heard them in his own young voice.

And it came to him, finally, at that moment, what he had said to his father as he sat beside him in the speeding Oldsmobile, the final words that he had never been able to face, words that had caused his father to stop shouting, to look down at him with stunned, frightened eyes that should have been focused on the road that twisted dangerously before them.

"I saw you naked with *her* last night." That was all he had said, but, more than the studio car with D. P. Koenig racing up behind them, those words had put his father on the final, fatal course.

Bud buried his face in his hands, and only when he felt how wet his fingers were did he know that he was crying, understood finally how passionately he had hated his father, had wished him dead, had accused, lacerated him while he was driving at ninety miles an hour because his hatred was so intense that he did not stop to think, no longer cared, that he, too, might be destroyed.

And he remembered then the love he felt for the agent, who was pursuing him like a knight on a white charger, come to rescue him, save him from his father, to make him forever D. P. Koenig's kid.

As the tears came, the pain in the back of his head eased up, almost stopped.

"I killed him," Bud said out loud. "I killed my father."

Gordon Flemming was still standing at the window.

Bud was grateful that his back was turned. He took out his handkerchief and took a couple of furtive swipes at his face. A crying cop doesn't carry a lot of weight.

"He doesn't know cameras," Gordon Flemming said, his voice detached, remote. "That little son of a bitch doesn't know what he's doing. Not with the stunt men, not with the cameraman, and he's working and I'm not."

Bud started to cross to him, started to put a reassuring hand on his shoulder, but, in a motion so fast, so deceptively agile, Gordon Flemming stepped out the window onto a narrow ledge, flattening himself against the building. Bud made a quick, reflexive grab for his leg, for anything, but he pulled away, inched along the ledge out of reach far above the ground, above the crew filming the motion picture below him.

"Christ, man, don't be a drag," Flemming said as he saw Bud start to climb out the window.

"You know I have to come get you," Bud said quietly. "You know I can't let you stay out there."

"Nobody can tell me anything anymore," Flemming sang out, almost joyously. "I am in control!"

"Just hang in there," Bud said, his voice professionally soothing. "I'm coming out on the ledge."

"Get the hell away from me," Flemming said, his body pulling away from the building wall, his four-fingered hand signaling Bud to stay back, to leave him be.

"Hey, you with the beard down there!" Gordon Flemming called out at the top of his lungs. Everyone down below stopped what they were doing and looked up. As Bud started to step out onto the ledge, he saw the young bearded director look up, then impatiently signal whoever was up there to get the hell away. There was work to be done.

"This is how it's done, asshole!" Gordon Flemming shouted. "This is how you do it!" At the same moment, just as Bud was near enough to try to grab him, the director let go. He fell outward, his arms flailing, as he

298

plummeted down, not into the soft, billowing folds of an airbag, but onto the ungiving asphalt below. He landed flat on his back and did not move again.

Bud could never be sure, not for the rest of his life, but he believed, or possibly wanted desperately to believe, that Gordon Flemming was smiling all the way down.

He climbed back into Borden Sprague's office and left Universal Studios without saying a word to anyone.

As he drove out Sunset Boulevard, through Beverly Hills, he realized finally that it was all bullshit. The lie of a lifetime. The noble son's burning and passionate rage against the man responsible for his father's death.

I hated my father, Bud understood finally. I wanted him to die, prayed for his death, not so much for the hooker as for the years of humiliation and embarrassment, for his Italian accent and his crudeness, for being the butt of overheard jokes.

I didn't want to be Frank Bacola's boy. I wanted to be D. P. Koenig's boy.

Gilbert Ritner answered the door himself. Bud could see the maid hurrying through the entrance hall. Gilbert turned to her and said something in Spanish and then she disappeared again into the back of the house.

"You all right, kid?" Bud asked finally.

"I've been listening to the radio. You're practically a wanted man and you risked everything to come here to see me?" Gilbert said, his voice filled with something between joy and amazement.

"I just want you to burn the cockamamie self-hypnosis book, okay?"

"Okay," Gilbert said eagerly. "But I helped, didn't I?"

"You only cracked the goddamn case for me, that's all."

"If you're going to go on the lam, I could maybe go

with you." Bud looked down at his plump, hopeful face. He was immeasurably touched.

"You're okay, Ritner," Bud said, no longer trusting his own voice. He turned quickly and headed back down the path to his car.

"Am I ever going to see you again?" Gilbert called out. Bud stopped and turned to him.

"If they don't clamp me in irons, you want to do the beach Sunday?" Bud waved and climbed into his car. As he was starting to pull away from the curb, he saw Gilbert's head poking in the window opposite him.

"Why did you let him do it?" Gilbert's voice was soft and troubled. "Why did you let him jump?"

"I didn't let him," Bud said quietly. "It just . . . happened." This is what he would say, would attest to under oath in a court of law, but he believed he would always wonder for the rest of his life why he reached out for the doomed director a moment too late.

"Hey, you know what?" Gilbert said. "I love you."

"Well, I kind of love you, too," Bud said quickly, choking on the words because he had never said them to anyone before in his life.

He drove to the Beverly Hills Police Station, walked in the door, laid his badge on the nearest desk and left before anyone could say anything to him. He knew they would come after him, land on him hard for having jerked them around, for having withheld information that would have kept him off the case in the first place, for having screwed up royally.

What he believed, and now reverently hoped they would do, was chew his ass out, keep him hanging for a while, then give him back his badge so that he could continue doing what he knew now that he did best.

He thought fleetingly of Richard Maxwell's bribe, the role of Mannie in his new motion picture, *Anchors*. I could read for it, he told himself. I might even get it. I'm not a half-bad actor. But then what? Hang around, waiting for the next part, waiting for my agent to return my phone calls. And then one day, years from now, I'll wake up with the taste of failure in my mouth, and I'll be Gordon Flemming or Oliver Kelsey.

No, he thought with sudden clarity. That's not who I am. I'm a detective, a cop, and I won't say it funny at cocktail parties anymore because I feel okay about it, almost proud of it. Hell. Proud of it.

He had to ring his own front door because he had given Ivy the key. He heard her footsteps hurrying to the door. She had on a real dress now with a cinched-in waistline and very high-heeled shoes. The dress was cut low in front and she was wearing eyeliner and green mascara.

"You're all right, aren't you?" she said, studying his face. She sounded surprised, as if it were the last thing in the world she expected.

"I've bottomed out, I think," Bud said slowly. "I just let a man jump to his death. . . ."

"It was on the radio."

"I've screwed up everything royally. I've broken about forty laws. I finally realize that I was kind of responsible for my father's death all by my goddamn self, and that my life from that time on has been a bucket of bullshit. And I'm *horny*. Do you think there's any hope for me as a meaningful human being?"

"You bet your ass," she whispered, a warm, eager smile on her face. She slipped her arms around his waist and rested her head in the curve of his neck.

"What happened to the boots and the terrible dresses?" he asked gently as he led her through the hallway into the bedroom.

"I threw 'em all out this morning," she said.

"No kidding?" he said, easing her back onto the pillows. "Gorgeous togs like that?"

"You think you're the only person who can undergo major changes overnight?"

301

"Ivy," he said, propped over her on one elbow, "I have this weirdo feeling that I may love you." His voice was still choked, but he found out it was a lot easier to say the second time.

"Some day, when you're off the critical list, tell me again, huh?"

He bent down and kissed her gently on the lips. She put her arms around his neck and brought him down on top of her, held him fast, not that he was putting up any kind of struggle.

They both started violently when they heard the loud knocking on the front door. Bud pulled himself into a sitting position. He heard his partner's worried voice calling his name over and over again.

"Now it begins," Bud said. He got up and started to walk out, then he stopped and turned to her. "Will you maybe still be here when I get back? Whenever that is?"

"I brought my typewriter," Ivy said softly. "I'm not going anywhere."

Christ, he thought guiltily as he walked through the hallway to the front door, I feel happy, wondering at the same time how he could feel happy after that day, after all those days. After his father, after D. P. Koenig, and Gordon Flemming.

"You really had me going there," Chuck said noisily as he bounded into the apartment. But neither the gruffness nor the swollen, crusty eyes could mask the intensity of his concern.

"I had me going there, too," Bud said finally, "but I'm not in half-bad shape now."

When they got downstairs, Bud offered to drive, but Chuck shook his head and climbed in behind the wheel. Bud sat down next to him and stared out the window as they sped up Rexford Drive toward the Beverly Hills Police Station.

"Are you going to put up a fight or just roll over and die?" Chuck asked, squinting over at him through his narrow eye slits.

"I'm going to put up the goddamndest fight you've ever seen," Bud said. "Do you think it'll do any good?"

"Yeah," Chuck said. "Be humble. Kiss a little ass and they'll get over it. I mean, you did find the guy a hell of a lot faster than any of us would have."

"Even if I did let him slip through my fingers," Bud said morosely.

"We've all had people slip through our fingers, Buddy," Chuck said quietly. They drove for another block or two, then he added, "Did you know him before, too? This Gordon Flemming guy?"

"Yeah, kind of," Bud said crisply. "I worked for him once, a long time ago."

"Do you think if he'd been a complete stranger that you might have been able to secure him before he jumped?"

"Do you mean, did I let him step off for old times' sake?"

"Something like that."

"Maybe. I don't know." Bud said, his voice troubled, uncertain, "I don't think so, but I'm not really sure."

"Okay," Chuck said simply.

"What does 'okay' mean?"

"It means, who the hell cares? You're my partner. I'm your partner. The only difference is now I'm better-looking than you are."

Bud glanced across at Chuck's bruised, swollen face, his oozing eyes, and smiled. He felt a surge, a massive spring thaw, moving outward from his heart. Suddenly there were people who loved him, people he could now permit himself to love, because he no longer assumed they would inevitably abandon him.

"You okay?" Chuck asked as they turned into the parking lot across the street from the police station. Bud thought about it as he climbed out of the car, thought about it as he gazed up at the Beverly Hills City Hall and noticed that while he had been racing around in pursuit of a murderer, in pursuit of his own illusive past, somebody had climbed up there and put a dazzling new coat of gold on the dome, had scrubbed down the teal blue-and-turquoise mosaic tiles so they sparkled in the afternoon sun. The building had never looked so beautiful to him before. He chose to take it as a good sign.

"I've never felt better in my life," Bud said finally.

And what was funny was that it was almost true.